GUARDIANS
OF
GLORY

ALSO PUBLISHED BY CHALK PATH BOOKS

THE LAST POST: An Original Anthology
Edited by Darren Everett and Peter Kendell

THE FAMILY WAY: An Original Anthology
Edited by Peter Kendell and Darren Everett

THE BOY and other stories
Peter Kendell

THE TIDES OF GLORY
Peter Kendell

GUIDING STAR OF GLORY
Peter Kendell

GUARDIANS
OF
GLORY

The Third Book of Glory

Peter Kendell

Illustrated by Jenna Vincent

chalk path books

CHALK PATH BOOKS

Published by Chalk Path Books
www.chalkpathbooks.com

First published 2017

ISBN: 978-0-9574711-9-1

10 9 8 7 6 5 4 3 2 1

CONTENTS

THE VIEW FROM THE SEA

G REETINGS, FRIEND, AND WELCOME TO THE WORLD OF SEA. LET ME introduce myself to you. My name is Deepdiver Farswimmer Brightwater Icecracker 'Downspeaker Anniefriend Gloryguardian Thrarn of the Gulf of Basrum. Quite a mouthful, you might say, so most humans call me Deep. Humans have such brief lives that it seems only fair to allow them to address me by a shortened name.

They can be funny about names. For example, the name of the world is Sea, as I have just said. What else could it be? And we know the star which shines above Sea during the day as the Greater Light and its dim night-time counterparts we term the Lesser Lights. Again, what else could they be called? However, the humans seem to feel the need to apply their own names to everything, so they call the world Glory. This was a word which made little sense to us when we first heard it, but when we were told that it connotes splendour and magnificence and beauty and has a spiritual dimension; and that a "glory" is an image cast upon a bank of mist by the Greater Light, we were happy to accept it. They do the same with the Greater Light, which they call Blessèd, and the Nearest Lesser Light which is known to them as Our Moon.

These names are honourable and we are glad when we hear them spoken. It is a pity that not all humans have a sense of honour. It is little more five hundred cycles of Sea around the Greater Light since they first came here, fleeing, they said, a terrible sickness on their home world, and settled on those parts of Sea that are not sea, where there is nothing but bare rock with no protecting cushion of water above it. It turned out that just as our world is called Sea, theirs was called Earth, which means ground-up rock, so naturally it was upon the rocky parts of this world that they made their home.

All should have been well. We should have been friends. We could have shared the world between us, each in our own part of it, but humans do not like to share. They used the power of their flying ship as a weapon to threaten us with death and great loss if we would not permit them to exploit the oceans as they wished. In return we had no choice but to banish them from our waters. I spoke for all my comrades when I told the invaders this, for I am one who is heard among his people.

After a short and brutal conflict we prevailed and our two races lived separate lives thereafter, each watchful of the other. The humans called us *Beasts* as if we were mindless creatures, devoid of souls, and mostly left us alone. If we communicated with them at all it was through their ship, the *Whistledown*. They had a shrunken name for her as well.

Hundreds of cycles passed and little changed in the world. The humans resented being deprived of access to our seas, so they threw their filth into our clean waters and did shameful things to the bodies of our deceased comrades. In turn, we slaughtered any human who dared to enter our domain with a reckless fury that horrified us nearly as much as it did them. For we are a peaceful race, as you should know, like the flying aeroforms who graze upon the surface of the sea.

And then, by accident, or perhaps by the intention of the 'Down, I met a human who was not like the others. Her love of the sea was as profound and as sincerely spoken as my own and, hoping that there might yet be a way to reconcile my people and hers, I, as a speaker for my people, granted her permission to sail her ship upon our oceans. With her consent, I added the name Anniefriend to my roll.

Strange and unexpected events – plots and politics and a near-disaster in the skies over Sea – followed the building of the *Guiding Star*; events which I could not understand until they were explained to me. Afterwards, many of the humans decided to return to their home world, led by Annie's brother Emmy. Annie was profoundly changed as a result of the loss of her ship.

We are at sea now, my friend Annie and I, in the place we both call home. Annie lies cradled in the arch of my neck with her tail dangling in the water and her body resting comfortably against mine. The sea was shaken by a storm earlier and we took shelter beneath the waves, but now the wind is light and the water is placid and we have risen to enjoy the warmth of the Greater Light. We are happy and content together, many hundreds of miles from the nearest solid land.

Between us, we are making a new world, one where humans and my people can live together in peace, and that is neither a quick nor an easy thing to do. But after the serious talking is done, there is time for storytelling, which is no less important than diplomacy. I have told her of the many feats of daring and exploration that my comrades and I have accomplished in the world of Sea and in her turn Annie has told me tales of the Lost Earth, as it is known. But there are other stories she knows, of human life on Glory, and these are the most important of all, for they tell of a history that was unknown to me; of the long years when humanity and my people lived apart.

Here are some of the tales she has told me.

ACROSS THE STRAITS OF MERCY

H E LIVED ON HORN, SHE ON BRIGHT. HE WAS THE SON OF A FULL professor at the School, she was but a farmer's daughter. Her name, though he didn't know it yet, was Imogen and they first met when... Oh, but wait a minute now. I'm being much too hasty. This is hardly news, is it? I'm telling you a long-ago tale from humanity's third century on Glory; it's old and fragile and rather sad, and it needs careful, delicate handling. Let's slow things down a little:

His name was Jack and he was the only son of two native Hornese. His mother had been a journalist, writing for the *New Star*, which was half a serious journal of record, half a chatty gossip rag. One day she – young, brunette and pretty – was sent by her editor to interview a scholar in his study-library high in the turrets and pinnacles of the Joyeuse and was surprised to discover that Doctor Robert Hallendorff was not the dried-up old fossil she had been expecting – despite his being a palaeontologist – but tall, lean and not in the least middle-aged. He in his turn was charmed into revealing rather more than he had intended about his research, publications, general interests, personal circumstances and plans for the coming weekend to Margaret Pullein, junior newshound.

Margaret and Robert were married less than a year later in the newly-built Museum of Humanity which was housed in the East Wing of the Joyeuse. Their many friends – although she had, perhaps, a few more than him – celebrated their nuptials with them in great style at the Waterfront, the best restaurant on Horn and, it was claimed, the whole of Glory. They moved into married quarters and for several years lived the kind of carefree life a couple can enjoy when they are still in their early fifties, well-paid and unencumbered by dependents. They toured the world: he to dig for the remains of long-departed native Glorian life to classify and catalogue, she to collect material for a successful series of travel books. They lived on many different lands and considered settling on all of them, but they always returned to Horn in the end. It was their birth-land after all, and Hornese society offered a level of culture and refinement that suited them well.

Glory's short, swift years passed and Robert's and Margaret's careers flourished. Margaret found herself working for the Board and Robert became a senior professor with life tenure and an ever-increasing involvement in the administration of the School. Their apartment filled up with furniture, books, clothes, rugs, paintings, recordings, relics and ethnic samples and although neither of them was a Monitor they each had their own screen, networked into the School's knowledge core.

They were happy in their work and happy with each other and, although it wasn't planned, happy when Margaret fell pregnant in the twelfth year of their marriage. Robert looked forward to passing on his learning and skills to his son and Margaret, watching her bump grow and feeling her child kick within her, thought of her future daughter's parties and dances and frocks, and a whole new area of experience to write about.

Jack Hallendorff was born in a private ward on a worldless night at the turn of the year. His parents took him home and raised him according to their instincts (as modified by their extensive reading on the subject of child-rearing) and the good advice that rained down upon them from their parents, relatives and friends. Margaret entered the society of mothers, making many useful contacts in the process, while Robert bought his colleagues cigars and showed them holos of the infant Jack with a proprietary satisfaction that they completely understood.

There were to be no brothers or sisters for Jack. One was plenty, his parents said, and creating a nursery in their apartment had upset the domestic order quite enough. He grew up quietly, went to school with the children of other professional couples and was content with his life. Although he showed no interest in fossils he was fascinated by dinosaurs, looking at films of them on his mother's screen for hours on end and bursting into stricken tears when she explained to him that there were no Apatosauruses on Glory and never had been. 'That was on Earth,' his mother said, 'where we used to live.'

'But haven't we always been here on Horn?' asked Jack and Margaret, sensing that her clever eight-year-old son was ready to be told about his heritage, sat him down by the drawing-room window and told him the story of how refugee humanity had been forced to leave the Earth, which had been desolated by the Ochre Plague, and flee to Glory. It was the moment every parent anticipates and dreads equally; when their son or daughter leaves the beginnings of their childhood behind them and takes the first steps towards becoming a grown-up citizen of the world.

Jack frowned for a moment and said, 'No dinosaurs?'

'No. I'm sorry.'

'But we've got the foys instead, haven't we? They're big too,

9

aren't they?'

'Yes, Jack, they are. They're very big and very dangerous.'

'That's all right, then. I still like dinosaurs, though.'

The Hallendorffs took a holiday every year. Because they were comfortably off they had, in the years before Jack's arrival, taken luxury tours on the Board's ships, enjoying the excitement of flying and the constant attendance of the crew as much as the places the ships visited; which tended to be the familiar tourist destinations of Glory, such as the Ringlands, the Poles and the mist-haunted forests and uplands of Edge. But after an ill-advised trip with a grouchy, teething Jack they abandoned their cruises and settled instead for regular weeks off on the nearby land of Bright.

Bright had over twenty times the land area of Horn and was chiefly turned over to farming. There were good reasons for this; the land already had the makings of a decent topsoil when the first landers surveyed it and, once it had been seeded by the biotechnicians of Gold, proved to be fertile. It was gently sloped, unlike its precipitate neighbour, and caught the wind, the rain and the light of the Blessèd sun equally well. It provided, in short, the perfect independent food supply for the land of Horn, with which it shared a Governorship. Anticipating what might happen one day, the first landers had ensured that the administrative and cultural centre of human life on Glory could never be starved out by any other land. Naming no names, of course, but the Edgeois, for example, despite their mineral wealth and rolling miles of productive acres, would never be able to place any undue pressure on the lawmakers of Horn.

Camping was popular on Bright, as were working holidays on its farms and plantations. Many people, too old for tents or disinclined to share their beds with the insects that helped maintain the land's ecology, stayed in hotels or guesthouses. For the quiet, solitary Jack it was a daily pleasure to slip away from his parents, who found it hard to let go of their work, and wander through the fields under clear skies, free of the towers, spires and minarets that cluttered the view on Horn. Robert and Margaret were not in the least concerned for his safety although he often left immediately after breakfast (with a packed lunch in his satchel) and rarely returned before suppertime. Bright was a safe and friendly place – it still is – and once she had warned her son to stay away from the cliff-edge and give a wide berth to any bulls (or Apatosauruses) he might meet, Margaret let him roam as he liked. Robert nodded and agreed with his wife.

One day Jack left the guesthouse where his family were staying and struck out across country with the idea of reaching a copse that he had spotted from his bedroom window that morning. This was Jack's tenth or eleventh visit to Bright and he was nearing his thirty-second birthday. He had grown tall and athletic over the past year and his legs had become capable of carrying him greater distances than ever before, and the area he could explore over a single day had grown correspondingly larger. Before long, his father said, he would be needing a tent so he could camp out overnight and Margaret added that soon he would no longer want to go on holiday with them: this with a twinge of sadness for the loss of the little boy he had so lately been.

Jack strode down a familiar lane, climbed a stile, and followed a hedge by the side of a recently-mown cornfield. The agriculture of Bright was mixed, so that in the course of a ten miles' ramble a walker might encounter all kinds of farming, from fruit orchards to greenhouses, from wheat prairies to hen-runs, from coffee plantations to cattle pens. The sky above his head was the open sky of Glory, marbled with clouds flying past under the influence of a high wind, which diminished to a gentle breeze at ground level. Perhaps it would rain later, perhaps not.

As he walked his mind freewheeled and he paid no more attention to his surroundings than was necessary to avoid tripping over fallen branches or getting caught in brambles. And so it was that he entered a field of sheep on a north-facing slope and was unprepared for the shout that greeted him.

'Hey, you!' It was a woman. She was standing by a hedge, dressed in rough brown clothes, carrying a shepherd's crook and wearing a scarlet headscarf.

'What?'

'You. Yes, you!' The woman waved her crook at him in emphasis.

'Me?'

'Are you stupid?' she asked.

'Yes, very.' Jack had always found this answer good at disarming the irritation of people who confused absent-mindedness with absence of mind. It didn't work this time.

'I thought so. That must be why you've left the gate open.'

'I have? Where?'

'Back there.' The crook pointed over his shoulder and Jack turned and looked behind him. There it was, the traitor gate, swinging in the gentle air.

'Oh heavens, I'm terribly sorry. I'll close it straight away.'

'See that you do, before all the animals escape.' And Jack ran back the way he had come and fastened the gate tight shut. Then he returned.

'There, I've done it. I must say, I'm most awfully sorry. Quite mortified. Not the right thing at all. Not like me. I'm sorry, I didn't quite catch your name.' Jack approached the woman, intending to shake hands with her to make up. It was the way disagreements were settled at his school.

'That's because I haven't told it you.'

'Oh, of course. Silly me. But, excuse me, could we shake on it? I'm sure it won't happen again.'

'It better hadn't. But, all right.'

'Thank you. I'm Jack Hallendorff, by the way.' He held out his hand.

'Imogen Blake.' They shook, and Jack noticed for the first time that despite her baggy, home-spun jerkin and trousers and the crook she carried, Imogen was actually a girl, no older than himself. Her face was burnt nearly as brown as her clothes and her eyes were blue and very direct.

'Do you live hereabouts?'

'That's for me to know.'

'I'm sorry. I should mind my own business. I'm too inquisitive for my own good. Well... Good day to you, Miss Blake.'

'Good day, sir. And don't leave any more gates open.'

'I won't.' And Jack turned and carried on downhill, while Imogen went back to her flock.

Jack reached his copse and enjoyed the novelty of standing completely enclosed by trees and the crunch of fallen leaves beneath his feet. He climbed as far as he could up an ash-tree and imagined that he was benighted under a frosty Siberian sky while slavering velociraptors circled the tree's feet and waited for him to slip and fall into their jaws; and then that his name was Mowgli and he lived raw and wild among the beasts of the Indian jungle.

But as he lay in his bed that night and waited for sleep to come – the swift sleep that is the just reward of hard physical exercise – it was not stories of the Lost Earth that kept him awake, but the memory of two unwavering blue eyes under a red headscarf.

If Robert and Margaret Hallendorff noticed that their son had become even less responsive than usual they said nothing about it, but put it down to his age and his hormones. They had read about the changes that Jack would be going through at this time and were expecting something of the kind. And Jack, who generally regarded his parents as rather a nuisance, ignored their questions. For the remaining days of his holiday he sought a north-facing slope and a field of sheep and a pair of blue eyes. Imogen was startled by his reappearance and acted a little warily at first, but Jack's obvious lack of guile quickly won her over and she let him join her in her work. He learned things from her: how to herd sheep and keep them from harm, how to distinguish a ram from a ewe (which is not as easy as you might think), how to spot the tell-tale signs of disease, when the animals were ready for shearing and which was the best pasture for them on any particular day. They filled drinking-troughs all morning and sat by the side of the field and shared his packed lunch at mid-day. And as the days passed they each greeted the other's appearance in the morning with greater pleasure and let them depart at dusk with greater reluctance.

The last day of the holidays came with horrifying speed. Jack and Imogen met at dawn and spent the whole day rambling across the dells and ridges of the land of Bright, fording its streams and climbing its hillsides, while Imogen's younger brother Craig minded the sheep, silenced by a bribe of chocolate. Once, Jack held out his hand to help Imogen across a ditch and for the rest of the day they made a game of seeing how long they could continue without letting go of one another.

And when night fell they did not separate, but found a hay-rick that was warm with heaped bales of straw. They climbed to the top, where they held each other tightly and shared their first kiss. Afterwards, they lay next to one another in enraptured silence, each watching the other breathe, while the stars wheeled around the pole and Our Moon arced across the sky.

The following morning the Hallendorffs packed their belongings and caught a tourist bus to the transporter bridge that linked the land of Bright to the land of Horn. They stood on the outbound platform and waited for the next passenger car to arrive. Margaret could not help but notice that Jack was very quiet – almost silent – and that he stood at the back of the car and gazed longingly back towards Bright as they rattled and swayed their way across the shifting sands of the Straits of Mercy to the landing stage on Horn. At low tide, Bright was joined to Horn by a sandbar, created by the tidal currents swirling around the lands and converging at the narrowest point between them. For an hour twice each day the bar was exposed to the air and the two lands became one.

The Straits were too shallow for the foys to pass through in safety except at high tide. The great sea-creatures avoided the area even then as it was too easy for them to go aground when the ebb-tide ran out. Instead, they patrolled the outer perimeter of the lands of Horn and Bright, maintaining their blockade of the open seas. Humanity would never be able to sail across the oceans while the foys forbade them to. That was an absolute proscription; it was the law, and it was rigidly enforced. The foys circled the lands and kept their vigilance. And they *listened*.

Jack and Imogen kept in touch. How? There is always a way, isn't there? Jack wrote letters on real paper and blew a week's allowance posting them to Bright. Imogen smuggled notes into bundles of wool which Jack intercepted at the despatch office. Ingeniously, Jack sent Imogen a copy of the Morse code and the young lovers stood for hours on the viewing platforms next to the bridge towers, flashing messages to each other with mirrors and praying that clouds would not interrupt the light of the Blessèd sun and ruin their improvised heliograph. Both of them were busy, he with school and she on the farm, so it was several weeks before they were able to meet again. Imogen pleaded with the cargo office to let her accompany a shipment – she claimed her father had told her it was very important that she see it loaded safely on board a goods vessel bound for the land of Falls – and eventually she got special permission to ride a freight car across the Straits. Jack greeted her joyfully at the Horn side of the bridge and, although they were awkward with each other at first and kept their distance for fear that things wouldn't be the same as they had been on Bright, it didn't take long until they were close once more. After that first reunion they met again as often as they could.

They were seen, walking arm in arm up and down the hilly streets of Horn or sitting engrossed in one another on the ramparts of the Joyeuse, and the people who saw them talked about them. Horn was not a large place, despite its standing as the capital of Glory, and rumours spread quickly. Margaret Hallendorff heard them and smiled and, once she was sure that the farm-girl was not trying to entrap her son into a shotgun wedding, gave the couple her secret blessing. She didn't bother to tell her husband. What did men know, after all? Her boy was happy in his first love, and that was all that mattered.

* * * *

Horn was a small, steep land and, even back then, heavily built up. There was very little flat ground anywhere and that was dedicated to the site of the First Landing. This would not have presented a problem except that Jack's school needed sporting facilities. It had taken a direct appeal to the 'Down before the case for clearing a games field had been agreed by the Board, but eventually permission was granted for land to be levelled and a sports centre built. It boasted a football field, a set of tennis courts, a swimming pool and, circling the whole area, a running track. Jack had always enjoyed running – to the annoyance of his downstairs neighbours and the frustration of his parents who knew that a four-room apartment in the Joyeuse was not the best place to raise a growing, active boy – and it was with delight that he found he had reached the stage where he was fast enough to run competitively. He had grown tall and good-looking and was beginning to come into his full strength.

The people of Horn had never seen any need to separate the sexes in sport and so Jack was just as likely to find himself running against girls as boys. One girl who regularly beat him – in the hundred yards, the two hundred yards and the quarter-mile – was Ursula Briggs. She was a year older than Jack, tall and wiry like him, and like him she was the child of academic parents. They had a lot in common, and so they often met out of school hours in clubs and at dances or while strolling in the shopping streets of the town, just like all the other students did.

Ursula was the first to notice that Jack was no longer mixing with his classmates as much as he once had and it didn't take her long to find out why. And, of course, as soon as she saw Jack in the company of a girl – a girl he clearly liked very much – she became jealous and wanted him for herself. We should not blame her too much for this. She had always liked Jack, and he had long been fond of her. Their shared interest in athletics would naturally have brought them together and it would have been odd if some kind of romantic interest hadn't developed between them. We should also add in Ursula's defence that she was not a snob. The fact that she might one day hold a significant position on the Board or at the School and that Imogen would probably never be anything more than a farmer's wife was not something that crossed her mind. In fact, when she first saw the girl from Bright, happy and smiling on Jack's arm, she was more inclined to like her than hate her, despite her incipient jealousy.

Had she been older and wiser... ah, how many stories turn on such a point? But she was not; she was young and inexperienced in the ways of love, and so she was impatient and felt that if she let Imogen continue to monopolise (as she saw it) Jack, she would lose him forever. And so she conspired to keep Jack always in sight. It soon became common for Jack to bump into Ursula on his way to school or for her to be on his table at lunchtime. He knew more of the history of the Lost Earth than she did so it was natural for him to help her with her homework. And, most telling, her running technique was more advanced than his, so they often spent extra time at the track, practicing starts and working on their lap times together. They were already taking part in events against junior teams from the other lands of Glory.

All this time Jack kept in touch with Imogen, seeing her at weekends and writing during the week and if his letters became shorter and his stays on Bright less frequent he hardly noticed it. He was leading a full, busy life and if someone had taken him to one side and asked him about his relationships with the two girls he would have been rather taken aback. As far as he was concerned there was no connection between his involvement with Imogen, who was sweet but no pushover, and Ursula, who was a school friend and a good training partner. And had that someone probed a little deeper Jack might have confessed that he quite enjoyed having two nice girls taking an interest in him. He was still less than forty years old and a male, after all. Many older men – old enough to know better – would have admitted the same, if pressed.

But Imogen noticed, and she feared that Jack was drifting away from her.

It was a Wednesday, but it would have made little difference if it had been a Monday or a Tuesday or any other day of the week. Imogen had arranged to come over to Horn for the evening to see Jack. She was tired after a hard day's work in the fields. The alignment of the worlds affected the weather and that day it was not at all favourable. She battled the wind and the rain morning and afternoon, went home for her tea, changed into her Horn clothes, caught the bus to the bridge, sneaked onto a freight car and arrived at the other side to find nobody waiting for her.

This had never happened before. Imogen stood on the blustery loading dock and looked around, momentarily confused. There was no sign of Jack. She was puzzled because up until now he had been completely reliable. Perhaps he was only late; he would be coming around the side of the stores shed any minute. If she went up there she could meet him on his way. She'd tell him off something rotten, and he'd have to make it up to her. Yes, that would be fun. But when Imogen looked around the corner of the building Jack was not there. Nor was he in the street beyond. That was it, then. He wasn't coming. A crushing weight descended on her heart and she turned and walked slowly back to the dock. It was coming on to rain again and her good clothes, the expensive things she'd bought in the fashionable shops of Horn, were going to be ruined.

Brushing the raindrops from her eyes, Imogen boarded a returning freight car. She held on tightly as it lurched to and fro in the rising wind and, although she hadn't meant to, looked back towards Horn. And through the veil of rain she saw him – Jack! – standing on the goods platform and looking out towards Bright. Immediately her spirits lifted once more. It was going to be all right. What a silly girl she had been to think that Jack had abandoned her. If only she'd been little more patient! He had been held up, no more than that. She lifted her right arm to wave to him and he waved back. Oh well, the evening wasn't going to be a complete washout after all. She had at least seen Jack even though she hadn't actually been able to hold him. Crossing the bridge took forty minutes each way, so by the time she'd got back to Bright, switched cars and returned to Horn it would be too late. She waved again and Jack waved back... and then she saw what she had not seen before. He was not alone. Ursula was standing next to him – standing very close – and her arm was on his shoulder.

Jack sent Imogen a note:

> *Darling Immy,*
> *Terribly sorry about last night. We were training in the*
> *gym – doing weights, actually – and I completely lost*
> *track of the time. A thousand apologies.*
> *Shall I see you Saturday morning as usual?*
> *Your loving,*
> *Jack*

Imogen read it and wept bitter tears. Her Jack had been with that Ursula and had lost track of the time. That put her thoroughly in her place, didn't it?

She spent the rest of the week unable to decide whether to send Jack a letter telling him not to bother any more or to turn up as usual and pretend that nothing was wrong. If she was extra nice to him, perhaps he would forget about that beanpole he'd been hanging around with. Should she ditch him, or give him another chance? There would be a certain satisfaction in telling Jack to get lost, but on the other hand she still found herself thinking about him constantly. In the end, she cornered her mother in the kitchen and told her what had happened. Her mother told Imogen that if she rolled over and let this Ursula push her aside she'd regret it for the rest of her life.

'If you want him, fight for him, girl,' she said, 'like I had to fight for your father.'

Imogen looked up and wiped the moisture from her cheeks. 'Really? Tell me more...'

Jack and Imogen met as usual the following Saturday. Imogen's mother had warned her to say nothing about Ursula in case she should appear jealous; advice that was sound but, Imogen thought, unfair. Hadn't she seen Jack first? And wasn't Ursula the interloper? Yes, but... So she followed her mother's advice to the letter. She was close but not clingy, attentive but not overbearing, lively but not unstoppable. She laughed at his jokes. She wore clothes that were attractive without being in the least bit inappropriate. And all this worked. Jack was relieved to discover that Imogen didn't hold Wednesday's *faux pas* against him. He still had no idea that she saw Ursula as a rival.

The day went well. It was clear and sunny and there were good things to eat and the excitement of watching the Board ships docking and setting sail from the pylons of Horn Port, as it was called then. Of course Imogen was used to seeing freighters overhead – Bright exported its coffee, corn and sheep-meat to the whole of Glory and imported machinery and parts from the lands of Edge and Scrape.

Imogen's parents would not let her stay on Horn overnight. She was still too young, they said. Jack had introduced her to his mother and father a month or two after they first met and there's no doubt that they would have been able to arrange somewhere for her to stay, either in their apartment or at a friend's. Everything would have been quite proper and above-board. But Imogen's father vetoed the idea – turned it down flat – and nothing her mother could say would change his mind. He was quite sure these Hallendorffs were perfectly respectable people, but Imogen had her reputation to consider. She could, after all, only lose it once. If she ended up marrying this Horn boy then it would do no harm if they were not tempted to commit improprieties before the wedding. And if she did not she would remain a suitable bride for a good man of Bright. This was a pity. Margaret Hallendorff rather liked the straightforwardness of her son's girlfriend and she had spoken to him about his responsibilities towards her, although that was really her husband's job. Nothing would have gone awry if only Imogen had been allowed to go home with Jack that Saturday night.

But that was impossible, and so Jack took Imogen down to the landing stage at eight o'clock and waited for the next car to arrive. They were standing hand in hand by the rail looking out over the Straits, happy to be together yet sad for their impending separation, when their farewells were cruelly interrupted.

'Jack! Hi! Oh, hello there, Imogen.' It was Ursula, kitted out in sports gear. Jack turned to greet her.

'Ursula! What are you doing here?'

'I came to find you. You remember? We were going to do some circuits this evening.'

'We were?'

'Yes, silly. The Falcons – the Falls under-forties? Yes? Here tomorrow? Hundred yards finals? Remember now? Come on!' Ursula turned back towards the land.

'Oh, Providence!' Jack turned to Imogen. 'Sorry, Immy. I'd completely forgotten. We've a meet tomorrow. I've got to scoot. You'll be all right, won't you?' He gave her a hasty peck on the cheek. 'I'll write and let you know the result. Love you!' And he set off after Ursula, whose smile was hidden from Imogen but as clear to her as if the girl had sauntered up and crowed in her face.

Imogen spoke to nobody about her humiliation. She wept in secret and she refused to give up. She would win Jack back somehow. And over the course of the following week she checked some all-important details on the public notice boards and forged a plan. She would beat Ursula; beat her on her home turf, so to speak. *Fight for him,* her mother had said, and fight she would.

The following Saturday it would usually have been Jack's turn to go to Bright, but Imogen wrote and told him she'd come over to Horn and see him there. She also hinted, without actually committing herself to anything, that she might be able to stop over, especially if Jack could find somewhere for them to stay. As before, they met on the loading dock under the five-hundred-foot tall support towers of the bridge. Jack took Imogen's hand as she stepped ashore, and she put her arms on his shoulders and kissed him passionately.

'Gosh!' was Jack's response. They stayed close, and held onto each other as they had in those first days on Bright. Ursula watched them from a distance and, as they ate their sandwiches on the top of the East Tower she joined them, hoping to interrupt their tryst. 'Hi Jack, hi Immy,' she said. 'Coming for a swim later?' She knew full well that Imogen couldn't swim. There were swimming pools on Bright, but they were mainly used by visitors.

'Sorry,' said Jack. 'We're rather busy today.' He smiled and clasped his girl's hand tightly.

It was time for Imogen to make her move. 'I need a little break,' she said. 'What about you?' she added, looking at Ursula. The other girl knew that Imogen would never leave her alone with Jack, so she nodded and the two of them went off to the convenience together. When they got there, Imogen cornered Ursula. She spoke plainly to her:

'I know what you're doing. I'm not blind.'

'I don't know what you're on about.'

'Yes, you do. Aren't there enough boys here on Horn that you have to steal mine?'

'Aren't there enough boys on Bright that you couldn't choose one of them?'

'I don't want them, I want Jack. And besides, we chose each other. We're meant to be together. Now – will you take your hands off him?'

'Why should I? You know you haven't got a chance. I'm here all the time, remember? You have to smuggle yourself across the Straits every time you want to see him.'

'Please,' said Imogen, 'I'm begging you...'

'You'd better accept it – you're losing him. Jack's moving on. He'll soon see it's me he wants to be with, not you. You'd better move on too.'

'I'll still come over here. He'll still want to see me, you wait.' Imogen could hear her Bright accent coming through. She'd been trying to suppress it. Nobody wanted to sound like a yokel; not on Horn.

'Perhaps he will. But he'll be mine, not yours.'

Imogen looked down despondently while Ursula grinned in triumph. She thought she'd won. It was time for Imogen to put her plan into action.

'I tell you what,' she said slowly. 'I'll leave him alone, though I don't think it'll do you any good, if...'

'If what?'

'If you agree to a contest. If I win, you stop pestering Jack. If you win, I'll not get in your way. You can try your luck with him.'

'A contest? What sort of a contest?'

'How about a race?'

'A race? On foot, you mean?''

'Yes, a running race. I win, you drop Jack. You win, I stay on Bright and get out of your hair. What do you say?'

Ursula was astounded. The Bright girl must be mad. She was at least five inches shorter than Ursula, she was far from athletically built, she'd probably not done any serious running in her life. The offer was far too good to refuse.

'You promise? Word of honour?'

'I promise.'

'All right, I agree. We'll race for him, though I'll tell you right now you'll lose. Shall we go down to the track then? Now?'

'Not now, tomorrow morning. And not on the track, either.'

'Where, then?

And Imogen told Ursula where they were going to race, and the Hornese girl gasped in astonishment. It was an utterly impossible and wildly stupid idea, and absurdly dangerous. She would have backed out if the stakes had been lower and she had not already given her agreement. But she could not admit how frightened she was; not to her rival.

'You're not scared, are you?' Imogen mocked. 'Do you want to give up now?'

'Never!'

'Then we're on. Tomorrow morning, four o'clock, by the Waterfront. Don't be late!'

They rejoined Jack, and Ursula found she had other things to do and went off and left them alone. And the most frequently told version of this story relates that Jack and Imogen wandered the streets and terraces of Horn hand in hand for the rest of the afternoon and went back to his parents' flat for tea and then, under the pretence that he was seeing her to the bridge and afterwards stopping over at a friend's, found a room with a soft bed where they could stay together all night long and truly become lovers.

Early the following morning, Imogen slipped from the bed where Jack lay snoring, put on her shoes and clothes and silently closed the bedroom door behind her. She tiptoed down the stairs, making as little noise as she could, and let herself out by the front door. It was only five minutes' walk through the deserted Sunday morning streets to the place where she'd agreed to meet Ursula.

The special attraction of the Waterfront, the restaurant where Jack's parents had held their wedding reception all those years before, was that it was built on a pontoon which rose and fell with the tide. Diners could enjoy the sight of the water sparkling only a few feet below them at any time of day or night irrespective of the disposition of the worlds, Our Moon and the Blessèd sun. An hydraulically-powered funicular lift ran parallel to the pontoon's guide rails. It allowed guests to reach the deck of the Waterfront – whatever the level of the sea – without having to climb five or six hundred laborious feet up and down the cliff-face. To eat at the Waterfront was expensive, but it was also an adventure. The ride in the glass-fronted lift was all part of the experience.

The two girls met at the top of the funicular, where a car was waiting for them. 'Ready?' said Imogen.

'Ready,' said Ursula. They entered the lift and started their descent.

Jack stirred in his sleep. He stretched out his hand to find Imogen, but she wasn't there.

The lift plunged a full six hundred and eighty giddy feet to the bottom of the cliff. To their left, in the dawning light, the girls could see the grounded pontoon of the Waterfront. Ahead of them, across a wide gap of wet, muddy sand with a river of seawater still flowing through its centre, stood the land of Bright.

'Are you ready?' Imogen asked.

'Of course.'

'Right. Look across the Straits. What can you see?'

'Not much. It's too dark.'

'Well, look up at the bridge. Follow it over to Bright. Yes?'

'Yes.'

'Now look down. There's a path goes down the side of the cliff, side to side in a zigzag. It stops about a hundred feet from the bottom. From there, there's a stair that leads all the way down to the sand. It's where the old chain ferry used to run before they built the bridge. Got that?'

'Er, yes.'

'Right, that's where we're heading. First to reach the bottom of that stair is the winner. Low tide is in...' Imogen looked at her watch, 'twenty-five minutes, but we won't wait until then. We'll start now. By the time we reach the middle, the sea will have gone all the way out and we'll be able to cross more or less dry-footed. Are you ready?'

'Yes.'

'Sure you're not scared? You can back out if you like. Nobody will ever know.'

'Of course I'm not scared.'

'Then what are you waiting for? Let's go!'

'Immy? Immy!' Jack threw back the sheets and looked around. She had vanished. He ran to the door and opened it. No sign. And none of her things either. What had happened? Where had she gone? He knew the answer to that – there was only one place she could have gone, and that was back home to Bright. He pulled on his clothes in a panic and dashed out of the door, onto the street and down the road that led to the bridge.

Not far into the race, and already Ursula was pulling comfortably ahead of Imogen. The sand nearest to the land was higher and it dried quicker. It made a smooth, flat, firm surface under her running spikes and she soon got well into her stride and made good speed. Imogen was wearing ordinary walking shoes and was struggling in comparison. After only five minutes she was lagging by a good hundred yards, even though both girls were running downhill.

Five miles from coast to coast at a typical long-distance running speed of eight miles per hour or so – the crossing should have taken no more than forty minutes. Low tide lasted an hour; longer if the worlds were directly aligned. It should have been an easy race, a safe race, but it was not. The winds, the currents, the condition of the ground; all were variable, all potentially hostile. Imogen and Ursula pounded across the sands, while the light grew around them and the morning breeze ruffled the surface of the sea.

Jack stood on the landing stage. There was no sign of Imogen. She couldn't have crossed over to Bright yet as the cables that pulled the cars were still motionless. They wouldn't start up until the first shift came on, which wouldn't be for another couple of hours. So, if she wasn't here, where was she? And why had she left him? What had he done wrong? They had never been as close as they had been last night. He could still feel the softness of her skin against his. He loved her, and she'd said that she loved him, so why had she abandoned him like this? And where on Glory was she now?

'Imogen!' he cried. 'Immy! Where are you?' But there was no answer.

The fast-drying sand was like a talking drum, collecting the sound of the girls' feet falling on its compacted surface, concentrating its energy, resonating with it, amplifying and broadcasting it. It spoke words that could not be mistaken by those who listened, in a voice that could not be ignored.

'Invasion!' said the voice. 'Invasion and threat!' This was a warning and it must be responded to, whatever the danger, whatever the potential cost. The drum-voice called loud and clear and it was heard, and the response followed; fast, powerful and deadly. The sea boiled and foamed in its wake.

Two miles covered, and the gap between the girls had stretched out by another hundred yards. Ursula looked behind her. There was Imogen, plodding gamely on. The girl had guts, that was for sure. She was not going to give up without a fight. Ahead the water continued to retreat. It would have gone completely by the time they reached the half-way mark. Good. Ursula pressed her advantage and upped her pace.

Behind her, Imogen kept going resolutely. She knew what Ursula had yet to realise – that the sand would grow ever softer and wetter as they neared the middle of the channel and that Ursula's narrow spiked shoes would soon start to lose their grip and sink into the mud. This would be Imogen's opportunity. She was not a trained runner like the Hornese girl, but she did spend every day out on the hills of Bright following her flock. She was more heavily made than Ursula, true, but she had strength and stamina on her side. She would overtake her by the four-mile mark at the latest and be well ahead when they reached the finish by the foot of the steps. And then Jack would be hers forever, won fair and square.

The sandbar narrowed ahead of the girls and the sea lapped against it impatiently.

The Blessèd sun was rising behind the land of Horn. The orange light of dawn streamed across the surface of the ocean and lit the coast of Bright so that it resembled a silhouette portrait of the smaller land projected against an umber background. The sandbar lay in partial darkness, one side shining golden in the new day's sun, the other holding on to the shadows of night.

Jack looked around, oblivious to the daybreak's beauty and the freshness of the morning air. Where should he go now? Back to his borrowed room? Perhaps he'd made some ghastly mistake and Imogen was there now, wondering miserably where he'd gone. Yes, that was probably it. He had been a fool to zoom off like that without checking twice. He'd go back. But as he turned to leave, his eyes caught a glint of light in the darkness below. He held a hand up to his forehead to shield his eyes and looked downwards. And there he saw them, two lines of footprints illuminated by the Blessèd sun as they had not been just a few minutes previously. He followed the lines towards Bright, and there! Two tiny figures moving across the sands. Even at two miles' distance he recognised them. His heart froze. He called out, knowing it was useless:

'Immy, Ursula, stop! Come back! Please stop!'

They didn't hear him, of course, so he did the only thing he could think of. He set off after them.

Sleektail Min of the Caverns of Grant was an adolescent foy, only two-thirds grown, and her name was still a short one. Like others of her age, her size meant that she was well suited to the coast watch and it was her task to listen out for the characteristic sounds of humans, especially humans who were invading the foys' domain. This morning, while patrolling a mile off the coast of Bright (which the foys call Rocksand) she had heard a set of steady, rhythmic pulses, picked up on the land and transmitted through the water. No, not one set, but two; and now three. This was no accident, no normal consequence of the tidal movement of the oceans. These were not rocks bumping against each other, pushed to and fro by the waves. No – this was intelligent life in action. These were humans, doing what humans always did; pushing their luck, going where they were not allowed. Did the stupid creatures never learn from their mistakes? Had they forgotten there were heavy penalties for leaving the lands? Apparently they had. Well… this was her call to duty and she would answer it whatever the danger to herself. She turned towards the land and followed the sounds of human footsteps into the Straits, keeping to the centre of the channel where the water was deepest, and tuning her ears carefully to guide her to the source of the sound.

It was a perilous journey for the young, inexperienced foy. The waters were shallow and constricting and she had to manoeuvre her flukes and fins with the greatest care. If the tide was going out even the lightest grounding could be fatal. She had heard terrible stories of the fate of comrades who had stuck on the sands. As the stricken foys had thrashed wildly trying to work their way off the mud, they'd only dug themselves deeper and deeper into it, and as the water withdrew it had supported less and less of their mass until eventually their bodies had collapsed under their own weight and they'd crushed themselves to death. That was a vile, shameful end for the creatures who regarded themselves as the natural rulers of the oceans of Glory.

Sleektail Min was afraid, but she was determined to overcome her fear. She had names to earn and she would do her very best to get them.

Ursula was overtaken by Imogen half a mile after she splashed through the wet sand left by the last of the ebbing tide. It was slack water now and soon the sea would return and chase the girls up the sloping sands to the coast of Bright. Both of them were deadly tired, but their race still had nearly two miles to run and they weren't only competing against each other now, but also against the tide. It would rise slowly at first and then gain speed rapidly, advancing across the sand faster than they could run. Their hearts pumped hard in their chests, their breath hammered in their lungs. The race was nearing its end and they were getting their second wind.

Jack was two miles behind them, fresh and running downhill. He made good speed in their pursuit and from time to time he stopped and called after them, 'Immy! Ursula! Come back! You'll get yourselves killed!' But nobody heard him and nobody replied. He pushed on, despite the stitch in his side and the sand rubbing his feet raw inside his shoes. He had to reach the girls and save them from drowning. It was all his fault; he knew that now. It had struck him like a thunderbolt as he rode the lift down the side of the seafront. He had been foolish and naïve and unfair. He should have realised what was going on with Ursula, he should have noticed that he was the only boy she did extra training sessions with, he should have made their position clear. And he shouldn't have treated Imogen so casually or taken her so much for granted. He hadn't taken proper care of either of the girls and now, unless he could reach them and save them, they were going to die, swept away by the rising tide. On and on he pelted, still stopping every few minutes to rest and call out, with desperation mounting in his heart. The tide was beginning to turn.

The cliff-face of Bright loomed ever higher in front of Imogen. The end of the race was in sight and she was going to be the winner. It had all worked out exactly as she had planned it. Straightforward people make the best deceivers, don't they? No one ever suspects them of chicanery until it's too late. She was already looking forward to the moment when she stood on the steps, looked down at Ursula and accepted her admission of defeat. She plugged on steadily.

Behind her, Ursula was in trouble. All her energy had been sapped by the clogging sand and her leg muscles were burning with pain. She knew she shouldn't stop to rest – it would only be harder when she had to start again and the tide would certainly have turned by now. But she couldn't help it, and she came to a halt and stood bent double, gasping for breath with her hands on her knees. For a minute she stood still, gathering her strength, and she was just about to set off in her hopeless pursuit of Imogen, whose victory was now certain, when she heard Jack's unmistakable voice behind her, faint but clear:

'Immy! Ursula! It's me!'

She turned, and to her horror saw Jack, less than half a mile away and nearing the narrowest point of the sandbar. The rising water was beginning to cover it.

'Jack, you idiot!' she cried. 'Go back! Go back now! Don't try to cross! It's too dangerous!'

He didn't hear her. The silly fool didn't hear her. So she turned and headed back in the direction of Horn, waving her arms to try to get his attention.

Meanwhile, Imogen, with the end of the race in sight, decided she could afford to look back and check on Ursula's progress. She stopped and turned and looked towards the west, shielding her eyes from the rays of the Blessèd sun. They half-blinded her but... yes! There she was. But, what was happening? Why was the daft girl running away from her, not towards her? Was she mad? Didn't she know how fast the tide was coming in? Was this some kind of trick? She held her hands up to her mouth to form a trumpet and shouted out, 'Ursula! What the hell are you up to?'

'Jack! Jack, it's Jack! He's on the sands!' And to her horror, Imogen saw her lover running towards Ursula. The two of them were only a couple of hundred yards apart and getting nearer to each other by the second. Had she lost Jack to her rival after all?

Sleektail Min came to the surface two hundred feet from the shallows. She dared go no further, not yet, not until the incoming tide had increased the water's depth by at least another fifty feet. Now, what was going on? Were the humans trying to launch a ship, or were they doing something really brainless, like sinking caissons in which to dig the foundations of another bridge? She extended her neck to its full length and raised her head a hundred feet above the water. Now she could no longer hear the tell-tale sounds of human activity, but she could see very well. And if she had been able to laugh, she would have done so. It was just too ridiculous. Three human children, running across the narrow strip that linked the two lands, that was all it was. As for why they were running towards each other, she had no idea. How could any foy understand what humans did, unless it was obviously motivated by greed? These newcomers to Glory, these interlopers, what use were they? Why did the foys tolerate them? Why, only because the humans lived on the lands which were useless – dangerous, even – to the foys. If they wanted the lands they could have them. The next Great Tide would wash them all away, and that would be good riddance to the lot of them.

Jack and Ursula met in the middle of the shallows. The water splashed nine inches up their ankles as they collided and held onto each other tightly for fear of falling. Imogen was two hundred yards away, but it was she who heard Sleektail Min break the surface and she who saw the foy lift her head to look at them.

'Foy! Foy!' she cried. 'Watch out, there's a foy!'

Jack and Ursula turned to look. The foy's spiny head towered above them. They stood paralysed with horror, knowing that their only chance was to stay absolutely still in the hope that it might ignore them. They had all heard stories about the foys and their hatred of humanity. They believed this foy would do everything it could to kill them and that their best hope lay in the shallowness of the water, while it lasted. The foy would surely not dare to swim any closer for fear of running aground. Not yet, anyway.

Imogen crashed to a halt a hundred yards off. She could see how near the foy was and she knew that as the water continued to rise it would be able to swim even nearer. Already it was so close that if it lowered its elongated neck it might be able to snap at them. They would soon have to run to higher ground but wouldn't that provoke the foy into action? Oh, why had she got them into this situation? For love? Was that it? What was love worth, if all it brought with it was death?

Sleektail Min blew an exasperated cloud of steam from her forward dorsal vent. Pshaw! This was no invasion and it wasn't worth getting upset about. It was only a children's game. She had been a child herself until only recently and she certainly wasn't going to spoil these young calves' fun. Nor did she want to add *Childkiller* to her list of names. She would report what she had seen to her comrades and they could decide what to do about it, which would probably be nothing at all. She should leave these silly humans alone and go back to more important matters.

The foy turned carefully and swam fifty yards out to sea. The tide was swelling nicely now, so she arched her back and dived. The sea heaved and swirled as her tail-flukes slid beneath the waves.

They watched Sleektail Min go, scarcely believing their good fortune. Imogen sighed with relief and she hardly minded it when she saw Jack and Ursula throw their arms around each other and exchange kisses. 'Did you hear that?' Jack said. 'It sounded like a dinosaur roaring! Roaring its head off!' They laughed deliriously, and Imogen laughed too. It was going to be all right. They were safe, and that was all that mattered. Ursula and she would sort out their differences later. 'Come on,' she cried. 'Tide's rising!'

'Yes,' said Jack to Ursula. 'Let's go. It's time we weren't here.'

And they ought to have made it to safety with no trouble at all. They really ought. It should have been so easy. There was time to spare before the tide began to come in so fast they couldn't beat it to the base of the cliff. But... a foy's body is huge, it displaces a great deal of water and a single beat of its tail can raise a fifty-foot wave on a sloping shore. The first surge from Sleektail Min's dive swept across the sea, knocked Jack and Ursula from their feet and threw them into the deep water on the far side of the sandbar. That was serious enough, but they were both good swimmers and they might have survived. But the wave's backwash excavated the ground beneath them into an enormous U and sucked them clear through sandy clouds of water, fighting for breath and straining helplessly towards the light, and into the foy's turbulent wake, where their bodies were spun and tumbled tens of yards below the surface of the sea, where their cries went unheard, where their flailing limbs could find no purchase, where there was no air to fill their burning lungs, where they drowned, and where, arm in arm and undivided, they died.

Afterwards Imogen wondered why she had not perished on the spot, struck down by horror and despair. And it is true that she stood shaking and crying for nearly twenty minutes and it was only when the incoming tide had flooded up to her thighs that the instinctive drive to preserve her life took over and she waded, and then walked, and then ran to the foot of the stair that was carved into the rock-face. Even then she could not afford to rest, but had to force her aching legs to climb the steps and then the zigzag path until, her face red and blotched with agony, she reached the lookout point by the old stone warehouse. There she fell back against the wall and sat, heaving with tears and blind with anguish, until her laboured breathing subsided and she felt able to get to her feet and walk.

Imogen trudged two miles up the road to the nearest town – which we now know as Care, but was then called Host – and found the Monitor's house. She knocked on the door, and the Monitor answered as he was bound to do, even though it was six o'clock on a Sunday morning. She asked to speak to the 'Down and the Monitor acceded to her request without demur, for he could see the desperation and pain written across her face. She sat in front of the screen and spoke directly to the ship and told her everything that had happened. The 'Down listened to her fractured tale with great patience and compassion and not a little distress, for she had observed the tragedy through her comsats but had been unable to do anything about it. She heard the girl's confession, but could not grant her absolution.

This story does not tell if Imogen ever found a way to assuage her guilt. It cannot take us to the room in which she met Jack's parents and where she explained her part in his death because it is not fit that we should go there, not even now. Ursula's parents and sisters also; they came together in a place that must forever remain private. Angry voices called for a war of retribution against the foys, but the

'Down refused to countenance it. She knew the whole truth, after all, and she recognised that Sleektail Min of the Caverns of Grant had not acted maliciously and could not be held to blame for behaving according to her nature. The ship remembered too well humanity's last attempt to conquer the foys and its dreadful outcome.

What we do know is that the name of the Straits became literally true; it was a mercy that the two lands were separated by a gap of five miles and that Imogen did not have to cross over to Horn unless her own need drove her. She took great care to avoid meeting any of Jack's or Ursula's relatives by accident, and they never again visited the land of Bright. Imogen grew up to be a strong woman and skilful farmer who became known for her ability to walk remarkable distances in a single day. She married late in life and prospered through hard work and determination, building one of the largest estates on Bright. Some said it was hardly fair that she who had been the cause of so much suffering and loss should go on to do so well for herself; but would it have been any fairer if Imogen's life had also been destroyed and no good had come of it? And had she not suffered and lost too? And did not her first words to the 'Down – *It should have been me! Why couldn't it have been me?* – re-echo in her mind for the rest of her days?

It was forbidden ever again to attempt to traverse the Straits on foot. This prohibition was not always observed, especially among the younger athletes of Horn and Bright. They relished the danger of the crossing and defied the authorities, who tried ineffectually to save them from themselves and their youthful folly. The elders shook their heads and sighed. Surely they had known better when they were young!

Imogen died at the fine old age of one hundred and ninety-six and was buried by her husband on the land she had farmed. But there was an exceptional clause in her will and her memorial was built elsewhere. A garden was made on the cliff's edge at the top of a zigzag path that led down to a stair, and in it was placed a stone tablet, inscribed with a short dedication, a date and two names, set into the wall. Above the stone stood the figure, moulded in the finest Edgeois bronze, of a young woman with her eyes cast down to the gulf below, her arms outstretched and her face gaunt with sorrow.

The garden was a shrine to the memory of the two who had died, and sportsmen and women soon began to gather there to celebrate the joy of speed and the honour due to those who run upon the lands of Glory. Over the years many of them chose to have their ashes scattered on its flowerbeds and lawns, and the sheer drop below Imogen's Garden came to be known as the Cliffs of Grieving. And that is their name to this very day, and the name they will ever be called among the peoples of Glory, until the greatest of all tides rises and our world is borne unto its final end.

THE CASTAWAY

I Am All At Sea

I RETURN TO THE SHIP ALMOST EVERY DAY. IF IT WERE NOT FOR THE precariousness of her position I think I would stay aboard all the time. However, that is a risk I must not take. It's very tempting, all the same. I could use the captain's cabin which, austere as it might seem to a landsman, is nevertheless well fitted-out with a comfortable cot, desk and basin. All the comforts of home – even a private head. Not that privacy is the issue now.

But no. Every time I come aboard the *El Dorado*, ducking my head and twisting my body to squeeze through the rent in the hull that is my only means of ingress, I can tell, by the steadily worsening complaints of strained metal and overstretched fabric and the ever-increasing list of the decks and companionways, that her end, while perhaps not immediate, is, all the same, inevitable, and that if I am not to go down with the ship I must not stay aboard her any longer than necessary. I must certainly not sleep in her.

So my task is primarily one of salvaging from the wreckage the things I will need if I am to survive. I have done what I can to stabilise the ship by paying out the remains of the forward mooring line (manually; there is no power to drive the windlasses) and looping it around the rocks. It took a day of hard labour, drawing out the heavy hemp cable one foot at a time and carrying the free end, also one foot at a time, away from the wreck and up to the outcrop where I have done the best I can, in my untutored way, to make it fast.

My efforts have been well rewarded. The rope, which was lying slackly on the ground when I first reeled it out, is now tautly suspended above it. The *El Dorado* has shifted downslope, and if I had not secured her when I did it is very likely that she would have been lost to me by now.

I am living in a cave. In this I am fortunate, I think. The vegetation here is sparse indeed and I would have been hard-pressed to find enough wood or foliage to build a shelter. And shelter is what I sorely need. With the ship's accommodation out of bounds I must take refuge here, on the cold bare land.

I was fortunate also in my discovery of this cave. It has a narrow entrance that opens up as it goes back into the hill. It proved relatively easy to make a kind of door from the materials I have brought from the ship, which helps to keeps out the cold. I have no fire, as there is no wood to burn, but I have brought two cabin heaters, a cooking stove and a supply of paraffin, and that, together with the bedding I have recovered, have proved sufficient.

By the way, I once asked the ship's chief engineer why the cabins needed individual heaters when there was so much waste energy given off by the *El Dorado*'s engines. Could there not be hot-water pipes? He smiled tolerantly and pointed out that every gram of weight expended in the provision of pipe-work for the heating of cabins that might or might not be occupied was a gram of paying cargo that the *El Dorado* would not be able to carry. Individual portable heaters were employed by all the Board's vessels, he said. Revenue, he added, tapping the side of his nose with his right index finger, and he returned to his turbines and tanks leaving me wondering if I were not, despite my small stature and slim build, also an item of unprofitable excess mass.

I have decided to write this account as a form of self-defence. The court of Posterity is a place of stern judgement and if my body, and perhaps also the corpse of the *El Dorado*, are found at some future date and there is no word of explanation or excuse to justify the fate of either of us, it is possible that an incorrect judgement could be arrived at, and a sentence handed down that would represent, at the very least, a miscarriage of justice.

And so I have appropriated this book, the ship's log, from the captain's cabin and it is here that I shall set out my version of events.

To start off with the most salient point; none of this is any fault of mine. I am the innocent, not to say injured, party in the case. I cannot overstate this fact.

So far as I can tell, everything that Captain Thomas wrote in the log, up to his very last entry, is complete and correct. I would not like anyone to think that I would defame my colleagues in order to enhance my own reputation. Such tactics tend to backfire, I believe. So my account of events must naturally follow on from his. I shall tell it in my own words and eschew Service jargon.

To commence, then; I was left as the sole officer in charge on the night of the twenty-first of February. The officers and crew had gone to the land variously to spend their pay and report back to the owners. We had just completed a triangular voyage, and each leg of our journey had been fully laden and propitious. The Board already knew this, of course, as the *El Dorado* was fully equipped with apparatus for wireless communication as well as a Monitor's screen. Nevertheless, there were way-papers to be signed and portside officials to be dealt with.

It was not unusual for me to find myself in this position. Each of the navigating officers had his own duties to attend to on the land – purchasing stores, negotiating contracts, refuelling, recruiting – and the hands, their tasks completed on board, had a full round of drinking and wenching ahead of them. It would be my job as the *El Dorado*'s doctor to sort out the sore heads and minor injuries that the crew would be sure to bring back on board with them the following morning.

A ship's surgeon is a strange creature, neither fish nor fowl. By virtue of his education and presumed family background he is considered a gentleman, and therefore an officer. He is assigned a rank – usually that of lieutenant commander – and messes in the wardroom. He has a private cabin and shares a steward with his brother officers. But while the vessel on which he serves is under way he has no practical function. He is there in a purely reserve position. If an officer or man is taken ill or is hurt then the surgeon's duty is to restore him to active service as quickly as possible. At such moments the very survival of the ship may depend upon his skill and efficiency. But at all other times he is a superfluity, taking up space that could be used for cargo and consuming food and drink that could otherwise be left on the dock. But... the Service is ruled by the Board, and the Board has decreed that for humanitarian reasons if nothing else any vessel with a crew exceeding ten officers and men or a rating of more than two hundred tons must carry a certified doctor.

I should mention here that there is one rule that all landsmen – and the ship's doctor, despite his notional rank, is regarded as a landsman – disobey at their peril. It is this – that at no time must they take any part in the operation of his ship. The surgeon is to regard himself as a civilian and keep well out of the way of the crew as they perform their duties. In addition, he may not question the action of any crew member – not even the most junior cadet officer or greenest recruit – nor may he make any inquiry about the principles or practice of navigation. Any infraction of this absolute law may result in his instant expulsion from the ship – whether she be in port or not. The Service is very jealous of its mysteries. Nobody who is not appropriately qualified may touch any control, wire, handle, valve or spar. It is a simple matter of safety, which is ever paramount. It is important that you understand this point fully before you go on to read the main part of my account.

As stated above, I was alone on board the *El Dorado* that night. My assigned duties were easy and few. At two-hour intervals I was to check the readings of certain dials and gauges. A walk around the ship and a visual inspection of the fore and aft mooring ropes, and my tasks were done.

Incidentally, you may have formed the impression that ships such as the *El Dorado* are routinely moored by the nose only. This is often true at minor and improvised ports where there is little traffic and enough room for a ship to swing around in the wind. However, at busy depots such as the one where the *El Dorado* was berthed at this time, ships are tied up alongside an elevated loading dock.

I had been provided with a check-list of items to sign off on inspection. It was simple enough even for a landsman like myself to fill in. So simple that, once midnight had passed, and I being tired, and having taken a few glasses, and the night being calm, I turned in, resolving to rise before the crew returned and tick the appropriate boxes retrospectively.

Do you see how honest and straightforward this account of mine is? How freely I admit that I neglected my duties? The awful outcome of my dereliction will quickly become apparent and you will find that I freely accept the blame for it. One small action (or inaction) over a short space of time and everything changes, does it not?

To resume; I awoke at 06:00 hours. I can always wake at a time of my own choosing; a result of my hospital training, I believe. Immediately, landsman though I am, I realised that something was wrong. At all times a ship has her native sounds and rhythms, but they are overlaid by circumstances. A docked vessel sounds, moves and feels different from one that is free, and a free vessel is herself transformed when she is under way. So, even before I raised my scuttle blind I knew that the *El Dorado* was no longer tied up at her moorings. The view from the window confirmed it.

I threw open my cabin door and dashed, half-dressed as I was, along the passageway and down the spiral companionway to the bridge. What I saw there only reinforced what I already knew. The ship was floating freely, completely surrounded by sparkling ocean. There was no sign of land in any direction, either viewed directly or via the navigator's magnifying periscope. The diffuse lines of foam riding on the caps of the waves suggested a wind of approximately twenty knots although, of course, it could not be felt, even though an open port.

My first thought was that I should run up the turbines and attempt to make my way back to port. I knew that I must have drifted westwards driven by the prevailing winds and that, so long as I kept the Blessèd sun on the starboard side of the vessel (taking chronometer readings into account) I should be able to make landfall with no great difficulty. Once in sight of land, I would find civilisation and a place to dock. There was only one problem with this scheme. Even if I had known how to start the engines and steer the ship I would not have been able to. The captain and engineer both held keys to the engines, and both keys were required to start them.

No go with the turbines, then. I would have to drift wherever the winds sent me and I should have to hope that I would not be forced south to the dreaded regions of ice.

What about the screen or the wireless? Surely I would be able to call for help? There was a Monitor's screen on the bridge and the radio shack was situated next door, as one might expect, and although there was no power available from the generators, there would be batteries, I knew. They were always kept freshly charged against just such an emergency as this. But first, the screen. I stood in front of it, clapped my hands twice and cried 'Help!' six times, as I had been taught. There was no reply. That was puzzling. I tried again. Still no reply. The screen remained dark and its speaker silent. I noticed that a pilot light was flashing amber. Did this mean it was faulty, or merely in standby mode? I tried a third time. Still nothing.

There would be another screen in the Monitor's cabin, but that was strictly private and I was not yet ready to defy the rules of the Service – and common decency – and break down its door. Instead I resolved to try a call on the wireless, although I had no idea how to operate the transmitter. Sitting in front of the set, I turned knobs and flicked switches until the dials lit up and a crackling hiss came from the headset. I picked up the microphone, pressed the button mounted on the side and spoke, 'Hello, do you hear me? This is

Doctor Powell on the LAV *El Dorado*. Help, I am cast off and adrift without motive power. I am unable to make progress. Please reply.' I released the button and listened, but I heard nothing but noise. I called again, many times, without success. After a while it seemed that the lights on the wireless panel were glowing less brightly than before and I guessed that its batteries were becoming exhausted. I sat back with a sigh and turned off the set. Something was wrong. Either nobody was listening to me or – unlikely as it may sound – I was no longer in the world of men but had somehow been transported overnight to a place where I was the only living human being. That idea frightened and excited me equally.

I left the bridge and returned to my cabin to take stock of the situation. In one respect it was extremely serious. I was all alone and far from land, adrift in a vessel that I could neither steer nor control and of whose working principles I was largely, by the custom of the Service, ignorant. If anyone was aware of my predicament they were apparently doing nothing about it.

On the other hand, I was in no immediate danger. The ship was in ballast, having discharged her cargo, and so there was no shortage of fresh water for me to drink (salt water is not used for ballast as it causes corrosion). In addition there was plenty of food to eat – the galley stores were well stocked and I was the only person on board.

The *El Dorado* was riding smoothly, travelling vanes-first under the pressure of a gentle easterly wind. She felt very stable (the effect of the ballast) and her mechanisms were humming and clicking and whirring and buzzing in their normal manner. After all, her engineer was a highly capable man who kept all the machinery in as near a state of perfection as he could. In fact she was a very well-found ship, with a competent crew and conscientious officers. It was probably my fault that the wireless had not responded to my attempt to communicate with the land and no doubt a search party was already setting forth to find me. In brief, all was as well as might reasonably be expected and the patient would surely soon be returning to normal everyday life. How was that for a diagnosis, Doctor?

Pretty encouraging, I told myself, and I left the confines of my cabin and proceeded down catwalks and ladders to the stern observation port, where I picked up the binoculars that were chained there and looked out, expecting to see aircraft already within sight. Nothing yet, but what of that? The ocean was broad and the skies were wide and there was lots of time for my rescuers to find me. Meanwhile, I would enjoy my isolation.

Lots of time…

I Tangle With The Force Of Gravity

L OTS OF TIME… SO I MADE THE MOST OF IT. There was nothing to be done operationally. Not by me, anyway. What I had to do – my duty – was to keep the *El Dorado* as safe as I could. I had to look after myself as well. I had to make it as easy as possible for the search and rescue teams which, I was sure, would be out looking for us to find us. To that end I entered, without permission, Captain Thomas's cabin and tried to find the emergency orders that I thought were likely to be kept in his desk. They were not, and although I hesitated to ransack though his personal possessions I made as thorough a search as I could. However, it looked as if someone had got there before me. There were unmistakable signs of tampering. The captain, like all Service officers, was scrupulously tidy in his ways, but there were places where things had not been properly replaced, where cabinets had not been fully secured.

For the first time, I began to suspect that I was not the victim of an accident, but of deliberate sabotage. A visit to the mooring nacelles hardened my suspicions. I should have noticed immediately I left my cabin and went to the bridge, but in the initial shock of finding that the ship was adrift, I had missed an obvious clue. Both fore and aft lines had been cut. A further thought struck me and I hastened to the radio shack. A quick inspection was all it took to establish that the wireless aerial's connection had been detached from the back of the set and thrown into the sea. I could see its far end trailing above the water, hanging down from the *El Dorado*'s nose and inaccessible to me. I wondered if the Monitor's dish was in a similar state.

I took further stock of the situation. From one point of view it made little difference whether the vessel had been cast adrift deliberately or not. She was still floating out of control out of sight of land. However... the lines had been cut from *aboard* the ship, as evidenced by the fact that the trailing ropes were only a few feet long as viewed from the bridge. Unless the presumed saboteur had leapt to the dock after cutting the lines (a dangerous thing to do) he might well still be on board the *El Dorado*. I would have to make a search.

I took a kitchen knife from the galley and a pair of soft-soled slippers from the slop chest. To scour the one thousand foot length of the *El Dorado* from vanes to prow, single-handed, for a putative stowaway who would be doing his best to avoid detection or ambush me was a tall order indeed.

All the same, it had to be done. I worked methodically, starting at the top and proceeding downwards. On the upper surface of the hull, positioned centrally, was the glass cupola of the conning tower. It was used by the navigating officer to take sightings of the worlds and the stars and struck me as a likely hiding place, due to its isolation. I climbed the access ladder into the dome, as stealthily as I could, but it was empty. The view of the sky was superb, but the burning rays of the Blessèd sun, which was very nearly directly overhead and focussed by the curvature of the glass, made the viewing chamber as hot as an oven. I left hurriedly.

The upper three quarters of the hull were packed tight with the ship's lift tanks. If someone had hidden in the narrow gaps between them, he posed little threat to me. He would be Ray-frozen by now and unable to move. In fact, he would be dead.

Below the tanks lay the cabin and cargo hold. Much of this space was occupied by the rubber membrane which, multi-compartmented and filled with fresh water, constituted our ballast. I saw nobody there. That only left the crew accommodation.

Many of the cabin doors were locked and I had to force them with my shoulder. All revealed neatly laid-out unoccupied spaces. So did the communal cabin, still known as the forecastle, where the hands and ratings lived and messed. I returned to the hold, which, apart from the ballast, contained nothing but a few crates piled on one side. I was curious as to their contents so I crossed over to them. To my horror, the deck suddenly gave way beneath my feet and I found myself falling into open space!

My memory blurs curiously here, but by some great fortune, my flailing arms caught hold of an iron handle and arrested my fall. Either someone was looking after me or (more likely) my instincts for self-preservation were still in full operation. When I once more became aware of what was going on I found that I was hanging by one hand, suspended over the open sea 300 feet below, the upper half of my body pressed against one of the *El Dorado's* cargo hatches. I raised my feet until they were resting against the flange at the edge of the hatch and, my safety assured for the present, tried to work out what to do next. First, I waited until my heart stopped thudding in my chest. I was breathing deeply as my body, flooded with adrenaline, prepared itself for violent physical exertion. Very well, I would exert myself. Grabbing hold of the handle with both hands, I let my legs hang free and commenced swinging my body from side to side, in the hope of getting my legs up to a level where they could take a purchase on the edge of the hatch. I tried this for several minutes, left and right but could not succeed in raising them any higher than my chest. To make things worse my hands were getting slippery with sweat and I ran the risk of losing my hold and plunging to my death.

I stopped and recovered my composure, as best I could, for I was feeling sick with fear. Very well, I would have to take another approach. My feet were once more resting on the lower edge of the hatch and I had a secure grip on the handle. The hatch was about ten feet deep and the handle was halfway up it. I am quite tall, at almost six feet. If I could somehow get my feet onto the handle I would be able to stretch up to the edge of the hatch and pull myself up and over it. Easy; or so I thought.

But I was wrong. It was impossible to exert enough leverage to get my feet up as far as the handle. I tried walking them up the inner surface of the hatch, but the strain on my hands became intolerable. The hatch bounced on the backstop of its hinges as I moved, trying to throw me off like a bucking horse. I very nearly gave up at that point. The situation seemed quite hopeless and for a few moments despair took hold of me and whispered false counsel in my ear. Why not give up the struggle and let go? I might survive the drop to the sea and, who knew, a passing ship might spot me.

No, that was ridiculous. I should be dead the moment I hit the water and, if I were somehow to survive the fall, killed very soon thereafter. So I rested. And then it struck me. The hinges. Suppose I… Yes, I would have to try. Wedging my feet firmly against the lip of the hatch I gingerly turned myself around so my back rested against its surface. I held on to the handle as best I could with one hand behind my back. Then I leaned forward a little and jerked backwards, striking the hatch hard with my posterior. The hinges above my head creaked, and the hatch door moved slightly up and in, as if it were trying to close. I hit it again, and it moved again. Good. Now, if I could only catch its inherent rhythm, every time I threw my weight against the hatch door it would swing a little higher and eventually I would be able to grab hold of the opposite edge of its aperture and swing myself up.

I leaned forward and back again and again, and as I found its natural tempo the door swung higher and higher each time. Perhaps a few more times... The hinges behind me were under a terrible strain, I knew, with my weight and the weight of the door being forced hard against them on every pendulum-like swing. I would have to be quick now. I thrust back against the door as hard as I could. A cracking sound came from the hinges and in desperation I lunged forwards and upwards. Behind me the tormented metal of the hatch cover screeched in its distress. I echoed its cry.

My left hand did catch the opposite lip. Just, by my very fingertips. I got my right hand over the edge as well and, knowing I could hang on for only a few seconds more, made one last effort and lifted myself bodily up and over the edge. I lay panting on the floor. Perhaps I blacked out. After a few minutes I staggered to my feet and made my way, with infinite care, to the side of the hold where I rested, still short of breath, with my back against the wall. It was then I saw two things that chilled me to my soul. First; while I had lain semi-conscious by the edge of the gap the door had come completely off its hinges and disappeared into the void. The other was that the as-I'd-thought solid floor to which I had leapt was not solid at all – it was the other half of the hatchway. It had had a double door all along and if it had not been properly fastened (as the lost door had not) I should have fallen to my doom just when I believed I had reached safety.

I had access to medicinal supplies of spirits and felt badly in need of a stimulant. Keeping to the wall of the hold I worked my way carefully around to the door, keeping as much distance as possible between myself and the hole in the deck. I shut the door behind myself with a bang, and twisted the locking dogs home as tightly as I could. The keys to the medical chest were, as always, in my pocket and I lost no time in opening it, taking out the bottle of brandy that I kept there, and pouring myself a good five fluid ounces. I took the glass down to the bridge, sat in the captain's chair, swirled the brandy around a couple of times and tossed a sizable swig straight down my throat. After a while, and two more hefty doses of liquor, I felt on more of an even keel. I returned to the medicine chest for a top-up.

At this point I feel I must deal with a possible misapprehension you may have acquired about my character. There's a common stereotype about doctors who join the Service. They are presumed to be in some kind of disgrace; for, after all, why should a member of a well-regarded profession, who is in a position to make a very comfortable living on the land, take instead to the sea or the air, for a Service stipend? Surely such a man must be on the run, from his family, or his wife, or some woman's husband. Or he has made some clinical error and been told – quietly, in a private session in an office at a discreet address – that he should abandon medicine or, if he does not wish to give it up, pursue it somewhere else. Again, perhaps he has an unfortunate personal habit – drug addiction, sexual perversion or an undue liking for drink or drugs – that makes him unsuitable. These stereotypes do not hold up – certainly not in my case. For a start, I am unmarried and not romantically attached in any way. For another, the Service vets its officers very carefully indeed. No person with dubious morals would ever be allowed to serve on one of its ships. Again; its vessels are – and have always been – completely dry. No drunkard or addict would last more than one short trip before being found out and peremptorily dismissed. And lastly, it must be obvious that the Service expects the very highest standards of competence from all its members, including doctors. That is sufficiently clear, I think.

As I sat in comfort, with my drink by my side and a panoramic view of Glory's sea and sky in front of me, the shock of my narrow escape from death wore off and some measure of the excitement I had previously felt began to return to me. For, after all, I was in no great danger. I was still confident that in a few hours I would be found and rescued. There was, of course, no question of my being held to blame – I had performed my duties to the letter, as certified by the entries I had made in the ship's log. I resolved to continue updating the log, which I did right up until the time of the wreck.

I will not burden this account with large amounts of minute hour-by-hour detail. That may be found in the log, as I intimated just now. But what the log does not record is my state of mind, as the involuntary cruise of the *El Dorado* progressed. My mild elation persisted after the effects of the brandy wore off, even as the Blessèd sun faded into the east. I knew that the night-time air, being cooler, was denser than in daytime and that the ship might be expected to gain altitude as the hours passed towards dawn and lose it again after sunrise. However, at no time during the day had we come anywhere near sea level and I was confident that, so long as the tanks remained intact and the Fleury Ray continued to function correctly, there was no risk of the *El Dorado* ditching while I slept.

The operating principles of the Ray are, naturally, the most closely guarded secret, or Mystery, of the Service. Paradoxically, while the skills of its ignition and maintenance were once only acquired after many years' intensive training and experience, the capabilities of self-management apparatus have by now advanced to the point where the engineer has only to check a gauge every hour or so to reassure himself that it is shunting lift (or nullifying mass, whichever you prefer) correctly. 'And where's the bloody Mystery in that?' the ship's second engineer once said to me in an unguarded moment, going on to tell me tales of hapless colleagues who had lost their Rays and been unable to build them back up; and of the disasters that had been consequent on their failures.

So the ship, although un-powered and un-steerable, was not about to sink into the deadly waters below. Its altitude was, however, well below the norm for operating aircraft, which was in my favour. Surely, any pilot or captain who saw us riding below him would suspect something was wrong and either contact the Board or come to our aid himself? But the hours and the days passed, and nobody came.

I Consider Motives

IN THE EARLY DAYS OF MY AERIAL SOJOURN I SPENT MOST OF THE daylight hours on the bridge, except that when the weather was dull I would sometimes ascend to the conning tower. On my third visit there I discovered that next to the access ladder there was a door which led directly out onto the upper surface of the *El Dorado'*s hull. Gingerly at first – for there are many cautionary tales told of hapless airmen who have been swept into the void and I was still recovering from my narrow escape with the hatch – I walked out onto the silvered metal. Of course I need not have worried about the force of any steady wind as the ship was drifting with it at the same speed. It would have taken a sudden violent gust to blow me away.

The view from the top was quite breathtaking. To either side of me the hull fell away like a miniature planet or the top of a rounded hill but to the front and the rear it stretched largely level until dipping down to the prow at the nose of the ship and the vanes at her stern. Light blazed all around me, blue and white, reflected from the sky which arched overhead, like the painted ceilings of the Joyeuse on my home land of Horn. The sea itself was only visible where it met the horizon. It was obstructed by the swell of the hull to port and starboard and the bulk of the ship – five hundred feet to the prow and another five hundred to the stern – completely blocked the view to fore and aft.

An aluminium catwalk with low rails to either side led away from the conning tower, so I was able to walk most of the way to the bow, where it stopped. Lying down on my stomach and peering forward I could look backwards along our course although there was never anything to see but ocean and sky, however often I looked. No land; but that was not so very curious, was it? The same catwalk also led to the stern, but the great eighty-foot-high vertical cliff of the upper tail vane blocked my view. I did not dare to try to climb down onto either of the horizontal stabilisers, even though there were metal access ladders fixed to the hull's surface and each of them was the size of a pair of tennis courts. I have no head for heights and, before you ask, my vertigo only applies in cases where I am exposed to the open air. I can look out of a tower window and feel perfectly safe, but put me on top of that tower and I will feel dizzy the moment I approach within a few feet of its parapet.

(I discovered later that there were safety ropes, with slotted rings attached, which airmen fixed to the catwalk rails if it were necessary to go topside while the vessel was under way, perhaps at a speed of 100 knots or more. My respect for my erstwhile comrades was doubled when I realised this fact.)

The feeling of space I experienced on the topside of the *El Dorado* was so fresh, so intoxicating even when compared with the all-round view commanded by her underslung bridge, that I broke into the ship's stores and appropriated spars, ropes and a tarpaulin and rigged – clumsily, I'm sure – a shelter next to the conning tower. Thereafter, I spent much of my time there, sitting on a folding chair and reading or lying on a mattress I had purloined from the sick bay. After all, it was effectively my property, as ship's surgeon, was it not? With a drink by my side and a good book in my hands and a gentle subtropical breeze wafting over my face I was as happy and contented as I have ever been. The stocks of food were holding up well, there was plenty of drinking water in the ballast tanks and my situation was still surely only a temporary one.

Every time a shadow passed overhead I leapt to my feet and rushed out from underneath my canopy and scanned the skies for the rescuers I was still sure were quartering the charts for me. But no; it was never anything but a high-flying aeroform, or a narrow wisp of cloud, or Hally entering his transit across the face of the Blessèd sun.

I am a creature of conventional habits, and they include fixed and relatively early bedtimes. As I am not a watch-keeping officer I have never had to work night shifts, as it were; not since my training days, as I have already mentioned. This was perhaps another reason for the estrangement between the flying officers and myself; that they stood watches and I did not. However that may be, I was accustomed to spend the time from Captain Thomas's post-prandial address until the sounding of the breakfast gong in my cabin, reading quietly or catching up on my notes, or asleep. I am, and have always been, an excellent sleeper.

As the days passed – pleasantly on the whole – and my solitude continued uninterrupted, a feeling of unease grew in my mind. It was beginning to look as if my trust in a swift and timely recovery were misplaced. But how could this be? Why had no stratospheric lighter-than-air vessel or orbiting comsat detected the outline of the *El Dorado*'s hull, skylit against the azure sea below? There was no immediate answer to these questions and had it not been for my sighting of the Board's navigation beam I should truly have come to believe that my ship and I had been cast adrift from the world I knew and now sailed the skies of a distant world in a remote star-system; perhaps even the lost skies of Old Earth herself.

To consider – item: the *El Dorado* had been deliberately cut loose from her moorings. Item: the cargo hatch had been improperly secured. Item: the screens (I had broken down the door of the Monitor's stateroom a few days earlier, only to find his screen was also out of order.) and the wireless apparatus had been disabled.

Item: the engines were inoperable. Item: the only person on board – myself – was not an airman.

Some person or persons unknown wanted rid of the *El Dorado*. Or rid of me. But why? I had not, so far as I knew, offended any member of the crew. My service record was unblemished. On every occasion that my skills had been required I had acquitted myself with distinction. At least fifteen airmen owed their lives to me, as was freely acknowledged by all concerned (and entered in the ship's log).

So if my life were not the object of the *El Dorado*'s sabotage, what of the poorly-secured hatch? Was it a trap intentionally laid for me, or merely the saboteur's means of egress from the ship? It was impossible for me to tell and, given that I was alone, irrelevant now.

But if not me, what about the ship? The *El Dorado* was not a new vessel, but she was well-designed, well-built and well-maintained. A valuable asset, in other words. Why would anyone wish to destroy such a fine investment? It made very little sense. Matters of commerce have always been something of a mystery to me. The ailments and injuries of men and women are my business, not the movements of cash and capital. But I had seen no other ships since I had woken on that first morning of my involuntary odyssey. Had all trade in the world come to a full stop? And why? Surely, surely, there was not war? Surely, surely we had left war behind us? There has never been a war in all the history of Glory.

These thoughts circulated in my mind – round and around – as I sat in the night-time cupola of the conning tower, wrapped in a woollen blanket against the cold, and watched the stars flicker in and out of visibility as the southern aurora flashed in sheets of ghostly flame from horizon to zenith and Our Moon stood teetering on the edge of the horizon. I came to no conclusion and eventually made my way stiffly back down the ladder and returned to the close darkness of my cabin, and my bunk, and my locked door.

For, as I have said, I had finally seen some evidence of the continued existence of the world I knew. I had seen the vertical light of one of the Board's navigation beams. I know I should have mentioned that a few paragraphs earlier and kept everything in strict chronological order, but my obsession with discovering the reasons for my abandonment seems to have overridden the requirements of coherent storytelling. I will try to make up for that lapse now.

I am sure you will understand my desire to tell nothing but the absolute truth.

I Am Illuminated

B ORN ON HORN, FULL OF SCORN," THEY SAY. NOT WE HORNESE ourselves, of course, although we like to think we have as good a sense of humour as the next man. But the fact – the simple fact – remains; that Horn was the land that was chosen as refugee humanity's first settlement on Glory. We know this and so does everyone else. Other lands are larger, or more fertile, or are centres of trade, or specialise in important industries such as shipbuilding or the extraction of metals. Every land has its share of Glory.

But Horn was first – first of them all. It was on Horn that we first came to realise how truly fortunate we were and it was on Horn that the first deeds of Glory were done. So we who were born on Horn are not scornful of those who grew up elsewhere; on Gold, or Edge, or Falls or Bright or even the far-distant archipelago of Grain, for in the end we are all children of the Lost Earth. We know that everything is chance, as it is called, and that we are all equally Blessèd, wherever our home lands may be.

Still; there is a separation, although it is not of our making, and it lies behind the second line of the verse, "All apart and all forlorn." The Hornese are expected to excel in all that they do, and any failing is seized upon by the rest of the world as an example of our unjustifiably high opinion of ourselves. It is grossly unfair, of course, but what of that? We are who we are.

I intended to give a short account of my life here, but I seem to have got sidetracked by other matters. All the same, it is important to me that you be familiar with the place of my birth and my upbringing.

My childhood was happy, but solitary, as I have no brother or sister. This was not so unusual on Horn, where small families are the norm. My parents were both in public service and very busy people. I do not think that I was deprived of their attention, but it was shared with the inflexible requirements of their jobs, which were to do with resource allocation and administration and were rather too abstract in their nature to interest me. I was a boy who liked doing things with his hands. Had I come from a humbler home I might have turned into a gardener or a builder of houses or a maker of instruments. As it was my family was comfortably off and, as I was bright and showed little aptitude for management, it was – as they told me later – down to the throw of a token whether I became a doctor or a Monitor. Fortunately, they chose me a career in medicine. I would have been a hopeless cleric.

Is that all I need to say? Perhaps it is enough for now, for I wish to return once more to the accidental voyage of the *El Dorado*.

It was a warm night, perhaps nine or ten days into my journey. Too warm – my cabin was much too hot to sleep in – so I took a book and the syrinx I had borrowed from the first mate's locker and climbed up to my shelter by the conning tower. I moved the seat from underneath the canopy so as to catch the light. There was easily enough of it to read by as the sky was crowded with celestial bodies catching and reflecting the rays of the Blessèd sun. Hally swelled above the north-east horizon, illuminated in quarter-phase and casting his orange-yellow glow over the tranquil ocean. Above me, but in opposite hemispheres of the sky, were Our Moon and Sally, both full and brightly lit and shining down on my ship like floodlights in a busy port. The atmosphere was clear, except for some high cloud and the usual haze hanging over the surface of the sea.

I read a little from my book – it was an ancient work by Currer Bell – and picked up the syrinx to strum a few chords. I had taken a fancy to the instrument as it was so ridiculously easy to play, or at any rate to make attractive sounds with. Several times I had heard its soothing tones echoing down to me along the corridor that led to the non-commissioned officers' quarters and wished I could gather the courage to ask to try it for myself.

G major, A minor, D seventh, G major, C major, D seventh, G major... I let my fingers roll around the chords. They made a pleasant sequence – one that I was sure I had heard in many of the songs the airmen like to sing. As I sat and allowed the gentle sounds of the instrument's vibrating strings to evaporate into the night air while I bathed in the radiance from above, I slowly fell into a trance, or at any rate began to hover on the edge of sleep. I let the syrinx slip slowly down to the hull-metal by my chair. My breathing became stertorous (I have been told that I snore).

Had my head not been tilted over to one side I would not have seen it. Just on the fringes of my vision, out of the corner of my right eye, somewhere far to the north, there came a short blink – no more than a fleeting speck – of green light, followed a second later by one of red. Green, red, green, red, green, red... and then nothing. There had been just six flashes, like a coded message.

I was fully awake now. What had I seen? I was not sure, but it seemed to me that the spot of light had moved slightly between each flash. The object – whatever it was – must surely have been some kind of aerial vehicle, as anything at ground level would have been invisible behind the horizon. This seemed possible, as the El Dorado's running lights were also red and green, although they shone steadily, without blinking. Or, perhaps, the light could have come from the top of some high mountain. To work out how high such a peak would have to be was well beyond my trigonometrical abilities. But why had the light stopped so suddenly? Had there been a crash or breakdown of some kind? I stood with my hand resting for support against the back of the chair and stared in the direction the light had come from, hoping to see it again.

I gazed northwards for seeming hours, becoming cramped despite the warmth of the night air. 'Give up,' I told myself, 'it was nothing. You were half-asleep anyway.'

'But no,' I replied. 'Suppose it is what I've been hoping for; an aircraft out searching for me?'

'So what if it is? It can't see you.' That was true enough, and I deeply regretted that in my ransacking of the ship for books and musical instruments I'd omitted to take the obvious step of looking for signal flares. I could have lit one now and run to the prow with it. I could have held it up; focused it northwards with a piece of metal like a mirror or a tin lid. It was no comfort to me that the odds were very long against such a light being seen. Long odds were better than no odds at all.

I slumped down into the chair, knocking against the syrinx whose strings – all thirty-two of them – sounded simultaneously, playing a strange discordant accompaniment to my despairing thoughts. Why had I been so stupid? I was hardly fit to be let out on my own. Why could I not pay more attention to everything that was going on? I must at least learn how to look after myself, otherwise how could I look after anyone else? These and other pieces of scorn from my childhood revolved bitterly in my mind. I stood up, gathered together *Jane Eyre* and the syrinx, and prepared to go below decks. I took one last glance to the north... and there it was! Green... pause... red... pause... green... The aerial beacon had returned! The quality of its light had changed, however. Instead of being a sharply defined moving dot, it was now a diffuse blur, and it was stationary. Why should this be? I stood with my chin in my hand and thought... And finally it came to me. If I had been a navigating officer and used to standing night-time watches I would have understood immediately, I am sure.

I had seen the 'Down herself, beautifully lit by one of one of the Board's vertical navigation beams. Light is only visible when it strikes something and the beam had been shining brightly but unseen by me until it found, first the 'Down, and later some high cloud. If the night sky is clear a ship's navigator has no need of artificial guidance as the positions of the stars and worlds provide all the information he needs. It is only when cloud obscures the heavens that he needs assistance and it is then that the beams provide it by lighting up the very obstruction that cloaks his sightings.

The 'Down! Never before had I had such a clear, first-hand, direct connection with the foundations of our world, extraordinary though that may seem. I went to bed both inspired and depressed. Inspired, because who can touch history and not be overwhelmed and brought to tears by the achievements of his ancestors and aspire to live up to them and transcend them if he can? But also dejected, because my isolation, which up until that point had mostly been an enjoyable holiday from business, and people, and their insoluble problems, had become a most unwelcome loneliness. I was filled with a sharp desire to find people again, to converse with my fellows and to feel solid ground beneath my feet once more.

But there was no foreseeable end to my travelling. I might drift alone and undiscovered for years, like the Nederlander of legend, for there was no reason why I should ever come to land, unless the El Dorado were to sail all the way around this world of Glory and bring me once more to the port from which I had first been cast away.

I Suffer A Restless Night

T HERE WAS A SOUND IN THE NIGHT, A ROARING, CRUMBLING NOISE like thunder or rock falling from the peak above my cave. It was loud enough to wake me and, fearing that I might be trapped in the cave I rose from my bed, wrapped a blanket around my shoulders and groped my way through the darkness towards its narrow entrance. I cursed myself for my foolishness in leaving my only lamp by the entryway to my shelter.

I had now, so far I could tell, been living on the deserted land where the *El Dorado* had come to rest for eight days. Long enough, as I described at the beginning of what must seem like an interminable and poorly organised tale, to gather around me the essentials of survival. Not long enough, however, to be certain of the sustainability of my continued existence. My resources were finite and strictly limited. This land was small and precipitous and possessed neither a spring nor any significant vegetation. Once my supplies of water and food ran out I would be in desperate straits indeed. But now it looked as if I faced a more immediate problem than starvation.

After stubbing my toes twice and hitting my head against the roof of the cave three times I found the piece of cloth that I had hung across the entrance. Now all I had to do was crouch down to the right and find the place where I had left the lantern. I groped around and, after what seemed like an age, my hand brushed against it and – damn! – knocked it to the ground. I heard it roll away into the back of the cave.

Continuing to swear immoderately, I considered what to do next. Should I go after the lantern, or continue down the passage to the open air? No, leave the lamp. It would take a further age to find in the pitch dark, and it might have been broken by its fall and be useless anyway. I got on my hands and knees and crawled forward, every moment expecting to hit my head against the stones which, I was rapidly convincing myself, had fallen across the mouth of the cave, sealing me inside.

Inch by inch, like a dog returning unwillingly to its master for chastisement, I made my way over the rough ground until a release of pressure on my ears and a chill breeze against my face told me that I was outside and in the open air. I stood up carefully and blinked. I looked around me. Yes, there were the stars, and there was the peak above me, silhouetted against the golden light of Hally.

So my first fear had proved groundless, but... the grinding sound had not been an imagining or a dream. I have, I am told, a weak imagination and I never dream. But if the noise had not been made by crashing rock or thunder – for there was no rain and the ground was perfectly dry – what could it have been?

The answer to that question was suddenly terribly obvious. The *El Dorado*! Had she broken from her temporary moorings? Had I heard her scraping over the ground as she drifted free of the land? Was she lost to me? I was stricken by a shock of panic. The ship had become a constant in my mind; but if a gust of wind had torn her loose and swept her away... I am, as you will have ascertained, not a man of action, but I ran like a mad berserker from a history book down the hill and around to the place where I had last seen the *El Dorado*, not minding how often I fell or how much skin I abraded from my knees and elbows. Why did it have to be this particular night that the light of the worlds was hidden from me and the land cloaked in darkness?

Back and forth, back and forth, blundering into rocks, tripping over boulders, waving my hands in front of my face to prove to myself that I could still see... I said only a moment ago that I do not dream, but I suffered terrible nightmares in my desperate search for the *El Dorado*. And then, just as I realized that I had become hopelessly lost and that I should have to wait until daybreak brought the light of the Blessèd sun if I were to find my way back to the cave, I tripped over a different kind of obstruction and, even as I fell flat on my face, cried out in triumph. The mooring rope! I had found the line by which I had secured the ship to the land! I got to my feet and, letting the rope run through my fingers, worked my way carefully downhill until I could see the bulk of the *El Dorado*'s hull obscuring the stars. Breaking my own rule about going on board at night time, I climbed through the hole that I had cut in the fabric of the vessel and, more certain of myself now that I was inside and in relatively familiar surroundings, felt my way to the main corridor and thence to the captain's quarters, when I lay down on the bunk, still wrapped in the blanket I had brought from the cave and, exhausted by shock and fear, fell fast asleep.

You must not suppose that I had, now that I was safe on land, ceased wondering about the circumstances which lay behind my unexpectedly setting out to sea. I still did not know who had cut the ropes which had held the ship securely in her dock and once I had settled on board it seemed that the question had become unimportant. I knew I was alone then, as I was now. And yet, it would not go away, that insistent nagging in my mind; the desire to know for certain what had happened, and why.

And... when I listed the suspects in my mind – a prankster, an anarchist, a thief (but a failed one), a stowaway (but where was he now?) – I realised that there was one further suspect I must add to the list.

Myself.

I am sure that you, my reader, have already thought of this; that I, having found myself on board this ship in unexplained circumstances, might be the one who was responsible for my own predicament. We are a cynical race, we humans, always ready to distrust the motivations of one another; and even ourselves. It would be quite plausible, would it not, that I, having made off with a valuable airship, would concoct a story to explain the disappearance of the *El Dorado*, while at the same time exonerating myself from any possible blame?

So I do not necessarily expect that you will believe the account I have written here, or take it at face value, even though I know, and would readily affirm to any authority you might bring me up before, that I did not cut the ropes that secured the *El Dorado* in dock five of the Aeroport of Phyle, on the land of Scrape.

There. That is straightforward, is it not?

Ah, you say, but... Just suppose... Suppose I did it unknowingly? The ways – the self-deluding ways – of humankind are manifold. I might truly believe in my heart that I had not sabotaged the ship, and yet speak an untruth notwithstanding. My unconscious, hidden self might have deceived my conscious awareness. I might have a long-concealed leaning towards self-destruction and be looking for a significance in death that I did not possess in life. For I am, as you will have gathered, not an especially social creature. I am reticent and easily ignored. Perhaps, then, I seek notoriety through dishonest means, as it is clearly apparent that I am quite incapable of achieving a great reputation by using honest ones.

To these sneering, pseudo-psychologically-based accusations I can make little answer, except to shrug my shoulders, and say little, except to ask, 'If all this is so, why was I neither followed nor found? Why have I not been found yet? Had my ship and I become invisible somehow?' Surely that is answer enough.

I Come To Land

T HE NOCTURNAL DISTURBANCES HAVE BECOME MORE COMMON AND it is an unusual night when I am not woken at least once by sounds of movement – rumbling, tapping, scraping. During the day these sounds seem to abate, but it may only be that I am out and about more at that time and naturally less sensitive to them.

Every day, as I say, I am out and about. Now that my subterranean home – for so I think of it – is becoming ever more well stocked with tins of food and other items salvaged from the *El Dorado*, and my future survival is at least a little more secure, I have more time for exploration. After I have done my essential morning duties – checking the mooring rope, filling a demijohn of water from the ballast tanks, checking the ship for signs of further damage – I have a modicum of leisure for other things, such as writing up the log or trying to learn more about this land where I have come aground.

It is clearly one of the places that was rejected by the first landers. It is steep and bare, rising to a rocky peak two thousand or more feet above high tide level, with little horizontal ground to be found anywhere, and it supports only a small amount of scrubby vegetation of an older kind than may be found on the settled lands. The *El Dorado* came to rest on one of the few level parts of this land; a U-shaped valley on the northern side. It was fortuitous indeed that the winds carried her there for otherwise I should have had to climb all the way up the land from tide level.

Perhaps this is the right place for me to record how it was that my aerial idyll came to an end and I found myself once more standing on solid ground.

* * * *

According to the ship's log I had been airborne for fourteen days. Although I may have intimated previously that my standards of log-keeping had occasionally been more nominal than fastidiously precise, I did my duty to the best of my abilities once I realised that my record might be the only formal document relating to the loss of the *El Dorado* and than any discrepancy or internal inconsistency in its contents would be certain to show up under a forensic semantics examination. Do you not see how careful I have been?

On the afternoon of the day before my coming to land, I had just taken lunch in the wardroom – a modest meal of biscuit and tinned meat – and, as was my habit by then, returned to the conning tower and my jury-rigged shelter for a snooze. The weather, as had been the case during the greater part of my voyage, was clear and sunny. I believe the ship have been propelled by one of the high-speed winds of the upper atmosphere which caused our forefathers such trouble when they first came to Glory and that these winds had been scouring the sky clean of clouds, for the weather had been uniformly bright.

I walked around the conning tower scanning the horizon over the prow and to port and starboard. The view in our direction of travel was, as usual, blocked by the upper vane but I had discovered that the best way to see around it was to go as near to the front of the ship as I could, then turn about and look behind me. Incidentally, I believe that the airmen must have used some kind of television apparatus to see astern, for naturally the lower vane hid the view from the bridge as effectively as the upper one obstructed the tower. I used my hand to shade the left side of my face from the sun and gazed at the junction between sea and sky. Nothing special... but... hmmm. Was that a cloud? I was not sure, but I made a mental note to take another look later on after I had read a few more pages of my book and taken a short nap.

This is a chronicle of factual events, not a work of fiction, and it is not my intention to try to engender an artificial tension and excitement in the reader by teasing him. I can safely leave that kind of thing to the likes of Mr Currer Bell of Earth, who was capable of drawing out the grand revelation of the plot of his novel over the space of many hundreds of pages. I could, I suppose, describe how it was that when I woke three or four hours later and looked astern the cloud had vanished, and how the following morning it had reappeared, and the puzzlement it caused me, but I am a man without imagination and, although I have the work of a master in front of me as I write, I have no mad wife hidden in the attic, nor any concealed and unlikely love to confess, nor yet the skill to describe such a discovery in an effective manner. So let me tell the story briefly and plainly.

When I ascended to the conning tower that following morning and discovered that the cloud was once more ahead (which is to say, astern) of the *El Dorado* it took me a while to understand its significance. It was only when it registered in my mind that the cloud was stationary – a fixture in the heavens – that I realised the implications. A fixed cloud in the sky must reflect a fixed land in the sea. Any practical airman can tell you that. The moisture-laden air from sea level is forced upwards when it encounters a land and the water-vapour it carries condenses out to form clouds. So far as I could ascertain this cloud, and the land it both indicated and concealed, was between five and ten miles off. I would pass very close by it. Of course, I did not expect to make landfall; I knew that the wind which carried the ship would fork when it struck the land and that the *El Dorado* would go to one or the other side of it.

Hour by hour, minute by minute, we drew closer. The form of this land became clear – a single mountain of two or three thousand feet with its peak wrapped in cloud. I regarded it with mixed feelings. One the one hand my trip had to come to an end eventually, so why not here? On the other, this land looked inhospitable, bare and, crucially, uninhabited. Anyway, it was out of my hands. The ship went where it would, whatever my wishes.

Soon, as I stood by the aft side of the conning tower with my back resting against its metal skin, both sides of the mountain came into view, split down the middle by the upper vane. Closer and yet closer and my ship and I were still headed directly towards the land. Surely our path would diverge soon. Surely. But now we were less than a mile away and the peak filled the sky, dominating it, eclipsing its azure beauty with an ugly jutting rampart of grey-brown rock. I stood transfixed as if held in a hypnotic trance; overwhelmed by terror and incapable of movement. Why did the *El Dorado* not veer to one side or another? The wind – did it blow straight *through* this land? Providence! It was too late! We were going to crash!

'Stop! Stop!' I shrieked, as disaster rushed towards me. I held up my impotent hand. 'Stop!'

And then, with a terrible grating, tearing roar the lower vane hit the side of the mountain. The ship screamed in pain as her weight crushed the vane against the rock of the land like a ruined limb, and her whole body convulsed in agony. The tail bucked, forced upwards by our forward momentum against the slope of the land, and I believe that I was tossed ten feet into the air by the shock of the impact. I fell hard on the other side of the conning tower and was thrown sideways across the ship's upper hull. All this time we continued to slide across the face of the land. The *El Dorado* slewed sideways, the ghastly metallic howls from below growing ever louder as the vane crumpled into the hull and the rear control station was torn off and tossed away like an unwanted toy. Somehow I clambered up the side of the hull and caught hold of the upper catwalk rail. I did not have the harness and slotted ring of the airmen to secure me, but I had desperation and a determination to survive. I held on to the rail with both hands, while the ship yawed and rolled and did her best to sling me to my death.

We had been flying at a height of about eight hundred feet above the ocean when we struck the land, moving at, I would estimate, a steady fifteen knots. That was a lot of height and a considerable speed and as we scraped over and around the mountain, with me holding on for dear life lest I fall and be crushed between the hull and the fast-moving, stony ground, I began to wonder if we would in fact merely skid over the face of this land and, pushed onwards by the wind, drop off its far side. Although I could hear that appalling damage was being caused to the ship's underside, her upper portions where the lift tanks were housed were not at any risk and we remained buoyant, even as the ship's spine was bent up by the onward rush of our mad career.

It may seem as strange to you as it does to me, but my primary emotion as the ship ploughed across the land was one of terrible, grievous sorrow. She was too beautiful, my El Dorado, to be treated this way; wrenched apart, scarred and spoiled. Her lovely smooth lines distorted, her flawless skin ripped and torn, this joyous creature of the air pulled down and raped by the brutal earth. Even stronger than the fear of imminent death was that sorrow; and wasn't that strange? I find it hard to explain; how I could have so come to love this ship – this inanimate assemblage of fabric, metal and wire – that I felt her agony as keenly as if knives were slicing my flesh and flaying me alive.

Our mutual torture went on, and on, and on, forever, although I am sure that a stopwatch would have recorded that it lasted no more than half a minute. But eventually it ended, as even the most dreadful pain must end; in relief, sleep or death. Our motion ceased and I pulled myself up onto the catwalk, hardly noticing that my hands were bleeding and my body badly bruised. I looked around me, hanging on to the conning tower in a vain attempt to still my trembling arms and legs and saw that the *El Dorado* had come to rest in a valley cut by some long-gone glacier into the side of the mountain, with her stern jammed into a rising col at one end and her hull cradled by the valley sides, much as she might have lain in dock. I did not know how stable her position was, so I descended into the hull and attempted to make my escape from her.

I knew that the bridge must have been destroyed just as the rear station had been, but I was astonished as I climbed down the ladders and companionways that led past the lift tanks to the lower part of the hull to see how much of the vessel was still intact. I had thought that her frame would have been bent by the force of the impact but in fact all her internal lines were as straight or elegantly curved as they had ever been. This meant only one thing, as even such a non-airman as I must appreciate. The *El Dorado*'s Ray was still in full working order and her tanks were still supporting her. Only a fraction of her real mass had struck the land. She might fly again! She might yet live!

I will not drag out this already overlong story with the details of how I abandoned the ship and found the cave which has become my shelter. You will appreciate, I am sure, that the ship's continued lift made her a dangerous place to stay in as a strong wind might at any time have picked her up and taken her out to sea once more.

Although I had enjoyed – despite its underlying peril – my time on board the *El Dorado* when she was intact and undamaged, to set out once more in a crippled vessel was madness. So like Robinson Crusoe or Ben Gunn of fable I set up my home on the land and made of it the best I could; and like them I lived with no hope of rescue. I did not know how long I would last before starvation or thirst killed me, but I had learned one very important fact about myself; that I loved life and would do everything in my power to hold on to it. That was something well worth knowing, would you not say?

I Conclude My Log

T HIS IS THE STORY OF A DEAD MAN. I BELIEVE I HAVE KNOWN THAT all along, but have denied it to myself as I – as everyone – denies it. We are all going to die, of course, but death is something we prefer to stay unseen and remote. Even I, who have seen many deaths in the course of my life, have always regarded my own death as no more than a distant possibility. It has been a matter to put aside for now, while I get on with the important business of living. And why not? To live our lives only in preparation for their end would be to repudiate their significance – to throw the gift back into the giver's face as something unwanted and of little worth. Like you, I have wrapped my death up in its cerement, and put it in an old suitcase, and stored it in the attic, as an article that may be useful some day but is only getting in the way at the present.

I have said previously that I am determined to hang on to life by every means available to me. That remains true, despite what I have just written. It is a question of self-awareness, no more.

Some mornings I awoke full of optimism and plans for the day ahead. Others were a windowless wall of despair and best written off, except for fulfilling the basic obligations of survival. This day – the sixteenth since my landing – started well. The interior of the cave became light enough to open my eyes and I rose and went outside to perform the necessary and see what kind of day it was. The Blessèd sun had already ascended halfway to the zenith so the hour was clearly well advanced. It was warm; the sky was clear to the west and cloud-mottled to the east, promising a certain coolness later. So, I should make the best of the sunshine while it lasted. I had been finding the transition between the open air of the mountainside and the closeness of the cave rather too abrupt for my liking and it had struck me that I could recover the tarpaulin and spars that had comprised my shelter next to the *El Dorado*'s conning tower and make a kind of portico in front of the cave's entrance. It would be pleasant, I thought, to sit out there on sunny evenings and read one of the books from the small library I had salvaged from the ship. In addition, the cave's interior was becoming cramped with stores, not all of which needed to be kept indoors.

As usual, then, my first objective was to visit the *El Dorado*. The valley where she lay was located about three hundred feet below the level of the cave and a few hundred yards eastwards around the land. As I scrambled down the slope towards her I could not help but notice that my feet had already begun to wear a recognisable path in the ground. That started off a train of thought in my mind that ended with a determination to search the cabins and common rooms for boots and shoes. Sooner or later I would be needing replacement footwear. I was still compiling additions to my mental list of items to take from the ship as I rounded the pinnacle of rock where I had attached the mooring rope.

What came as such a terrible shock to me as I reached for the rope to grip and help me around the outcrop is, I am sure, no surprise to you, my sophisticated reader. But if you have any trace of empathy in your heart you will get a slight hint of my feelings when I found that the rope was no longer where I had left it. You will understand that I was so stunned that I stood still for a moment and held my hand against my chest. You will maybe have experienced that sensation of the land dropping away beneath your feet, the darkening behind the eyes, the harbingers of despair; like the first pain of a wound before your body comprehends how badly it has been hurt. And you will understand too that hope – the blessing and curse of us all – warred with conviction in my mind; the conviction, unfounded yet on concrete evidence, that the ship had gone. I knew that I would have to step out onto the ledge next to the valley and discover the truth.

So I did step out onto the ledge and I did look across to the *El Dorado*'s resting place and I did see that she was gone and it was a different kind of shock; as the sight of the body of a loved one lying on the mortician's table is different from hearing the news, brought by a grave-faced proctor or tired surgeon, that she has died. I sat down on the bare ground and let darkness swoop over me and then – needing to know everything – I jumped up again and stumbled up to the saddle of the col and shaded my eyes and gazed downwind. And perhaps I saw a shining silver disc, illuminated by the Blessèd sun, far distant and receding before the trade-wind. I stood and watched for a very long time until it had completely disappeared from my view.

I had not been able to carry every item that I had removed from the *El Dorado* directly up to the cave, so there was a cache of stores lying by the foot of the valley. Moving those articles – especially the heavy ones, such as pieces of furniture and machinery – kept me busy for two or three days after the ship's departure. It also kept me from brooding on my loss; except that I could not help doing so in the darkness of my cave when sleep would not come. I alternated between blaming myself and absolving myself from blame. Yes, I could perhaps have secured the ship better, but no, I had done what I could under the circumstances. Yes, I should have spent more time taking everything possible from the wreck – for now that the *El Dorado* was gone I could call her that as I would not have done to her face, as it were – but no, I had had to establish myself in my new home, and that had taken time.

I am where I am and I must live with it – yes that was sane, that was right, that was the correct and constructive way to deal with my predicament; but I kept picturing myself in the time before, when we were still together. Does this sound maudlin? Carrying on in this way over a mere ship? Then I am sorry; for irritating you, for wallowing in my grief, for not facing facts. But I am sorry for you too, for it must be that you have yet to lose someone or something dear to you; and you do not yet know how it feels, and when it does happen to you – as it must – you will be left lost, rudderless, and in need of someone to show you the way you must go.

It is now fourteen days since I lost the ship. Most of those days are missing from the log, not just because they were blank to me, but also because they were full of labour and weariness and I fell into bed at the end of each one unable to do anything but sleep. But every night my slumbers were disturbed by sounds of movement and I sat up despite my tiredness, startled by some clatter or rumble or creak transmitted through the stone. During the day, as before, I had to concentrate on my immediate needs. Water was the first. I arranged all the containers I possessed in such a way that they would collect and store rainwater. I used the tarpaulin that would have furnished me with an outdoors shelter to line a natural declivity in the mountainside and make a cistern; which reservoir would, I hoped, serve to tide me over dry spells. It was out of the question to attempt to bring sea-water up from tide level and distil fresh drinking water from it. I could not carry such a weight of water the thousand or more feet up to the level of the cave; not on a regular basis. And besides, apart from a limited supply of spirit which was all I had to cook with, I had no fuel to boil a condenser.

The water situation was manageable, I thought; the rain fell most nights and often during the day. Food was another matter entirely. I estimated that the preserved supplies, such as tinned meat, vegetables and milk, that I had rescued from the ship would last me no more than thirty days. Thirty days! And then, starvation. That was a grim outlook.

There were only two possible sources of food available to me. Firstly, the sea. There might be sea-kelp, or any number of other kinds of vegetation that I could collect from the rocks when the tides were out. There would doubtless be molluscs to pry from the crevices. From time to time the body of one of the greater or lesser beasts might be washed up, but it would be unlikely to remain there for long; the land fell away too steeply, and I would not be the only hungry creature competing for its flesh. That thought made me shudder, as I need hardly tell you.

And secondly, the air. Those of you who are land-dwellers will wonder what I mean, but that is only because you do not know the skies as the airmen do. You have not seen the aeroforms as they have.

History tells us that the first landers observed that the aeroforms flew unconcernedly over land and sea, taking no especial notice of the land except to gain enough elevation to avoid damage to themselves as they flew over its solid surface. But since man's introduction of trees, with their snagging branches, and birds, with their sharp beaks, Glory's native fliers have become shy of the lands and their coasts, and they either avoid them altogether or fill their sacs as they approach the shores and raise themselves high above them. Landlubbers usually only see the aeroforms as black dots against the open sky, but for we airmen it is a different matter.

If only I were able to wield my pen with the skill of a writer like

Currer Bell! He was able to evoke the landscapes of Earth so vividly that, even at this distance of space and time, the reader feels he knows the moors, fields, houses and schools of Bell's England as well as he does his own land on this, our world of Glory. But I do not have his talents, alas, and a simple bald description will have to do.

I have seen the aeroforms in their home seas and from their native altitudes. I can tell you about their different shapes, and why some are orange, some blue, some pink and some a livid white. I understand their cycles of life and death – how important their dependent streamers are to their stability and survival. And, most importantly at this present time, I understand how they find and ingest their food, for I have seen it many times from the bridge of the *El Dorado*. We often see the aeroforms flying in squadrons great and small, in their constant search for food. All scan the ocean, but one creature will be the first – floating higher than its fellows with its sac fully inflated. It can see furthest, and it is its duty to seek out the stain – green against blue – that betokens a layer of plankton near the surface. It sees a likely patch; and in a fraction of a second it has vented its gas and fallen rapidly to the tide level. The others follow; they have seen it, or heard the characteristic flutter of escaping methane, or caught its reek. There is a downwards rush, and soon a whole flotilla of aeroforms is hovering a few feet above the sea, with their hungry streamers trailing in the water, sucking and filtering the plankton up into their stomachs.

What a sight it is! Like a multicoloured hive of bubbles hugging the ocean, the creatures cluster together; feeding, mating and, I believe, talking to one another. It has been said that a really big plankton-field can attract a crowd of three or more thousand aeroforms at a time. I have never seen as many, nor perhaps will I, for when the outliers of the herd sense the approach of an oncoming vessel they signal to their peers, and suddenly gas reinflates their flaccid sacs and they make a dash skywards, safe from we humans in our clumsy craft. And that is the best moment of all; this instant of flight, this soaring heavenwards, streamers flying beneath them like pennants. No other world under the Blèssed sun can show such a sight as this. I have known a watch of hard-bitten veteran airmen break into spontaneous applause for the sheer uplifting joy of it.

It is a foul atrocity; that I now have to try to hunt and kill these beautiful creatures for food, but my need drives me on to do things that I would not do otherwise. I have taken to watching the skies for them and haunting the leeward shore of the land. It seems to me that from time to time plankton or algae must drift against the land and attract the aeroforms to it. If and when that happens I will be ready, with a lance that I have made from one of the *El Dorado*'s spars. The mere thought of killing, even for food, fills me with revulsion, but I know that when the time comes my empty belly will not permit me to refrain from doing what I must do if I am to stay alive.

I have wondered in the past why good men sometimes commit dreadful acts. Now I know, though I am very far from being a good man.

The strangest thing has happened. Beyond belief, if I had not seen it, but now that I have had some time to think about it I am full of foreboding.

It had been seven days since I made my spear. My stores had been running down inexorably, although it had rained several times and my improvised reservoir had several gallons of fresh water in it. I had been practicing throwing the spear and found that I could achieve a range of fifteen yards or more and an elevation of several feet. Every morning I used the glass I had rescued from Captain Thomas's cabin to look into the east, hoping to spy some oncoming aeroforms illuminated by the dawn light, and today I saw a flock of maybe a dozen at a range of no more than a mile or two. My hopes rose, and I ran down to the tide line, which was high this morning. So much the better, I thought, if I had to carry the body of an aeroform up to my cave.

I reached the tide line at more or less the same time as the fliers. They were bunched together near to a small inlet, their streamers dipping into the lapping waters. Immediately I got there I realised that the best way of killing one of them was also the worst, Ideally, I would stand up the slope a bit and throw my spear downwards onto the upper hemisphere of the creature's gas-bag. But that, I recognized now, would be madness. If I succeeded in holing its sac, the aeroform would fall into the sea, where I would not be able to reach it. If I missed it, I would lose my spear. I would have to go right down to the shoreline and wait until they took off. Then, if I hit one, it would fall on the land and my weapon would be safe.

I picked my way carefully down to the tide line. The water was slowly receding, which was a relief – I would not get caught by an incoming tide, slowly though it would move on this steep mountainside. Then, moving inchwise so as not to alarm the creatures while they fed, I crept around the inlet until I was almost at right angles to the shore. Good, this was the perfect position. I squatted down and waited while the aeroforms sucked up the nutrient laden water, filtering it and spilling the waste fluid from the collar where their streamers joined the lower part of the sac. It would not be long now…

And it was not – only a few minutes. One of the aeroforms,

glistening a brilliant green in the morning sunlight, lifted its trailing streamers free from the water and began to drift slowly onshore and uphill. This was my moment! I leapt to my feet, pulled back my arm and pitched the spar with all my strength, straight at its bulging gas-bag. I stepped back with the force of my throw and nearly fell into the water. But had I hit it? I hardly expected success with my first attempt at spear-throwing.

Yes... There was a shriek from above and a powerful whiff of gas. The aeroform's sac rippled and heaved. I had injured it; mortally, I hoped (but still my shame and horror welled up in my throat and threatened to choke me). I ran uphill after it as it lurched and fell towards the rocky ground, reaching it just as the first of its damply clinging streamers began to snag against the boulders. I think I intended to jump on top of it and force the rest of the gas out of it before slashing it open with my knife and grounding it forever. But just as I was about to make my leap I was struck forcibly in the back of the head and knocked face-forward to the ground. I rolled over and looked up.

It was another aeroform – a blue one this time. I covered my face with my arm, afraid that it was going to attack me, but no, it had another aim in view. It floated over me, rolled up the hillside beyond and, to my utter amazement, wrapped its streamers around the body of its fallen comrade, now almost completely deflated, and pulled itself down onto it. Then with a tremendous whoosh of gas it blew its own sac up to an extraordinary size and shot up vertically, with its companion held tightly to itself. I rose to my feet and looked on, completely astonished. I had never seen such a thing; never heard of such a thing. I watched the pair through the glass as they gained height and sailed up the side of the mountain, awed and, I have to admit, almost brought to tears by what I had seen. It was such a contrast – I, the human, intelligent and civilised and murderous, and this, the beast, faithful, and ready without hesitation to risk its life for another. I would like to be able to finish by saying that the two linked aeroforms disappeared into the sky and that I resolved never to try to harm any of them again. But I cannot, not because of any epiphany I may have experienced within myself, but because of the vile, horrible thing that was to happen next.

Up they flew, never straying far from the rising side of the mountain, until it became clear that they were going to pass directly over the crest of the peak. I had not felt the need to climb so high, and to take the risk of falling and hurting myself merely for the sake of reaching the top had not seemed worthwhile. But I watched closely as they soared and I was not surprised when as they passed the last ridge, they suddenly raced upwards at a terrific speed, caught as I supposed in an updraft such as the *El Dorado* had sometimes experienced when passing over the more mountainous lands. My glass followed them as they rocketed skywards so I clearly saw what took place then; the sudden change in the aeroforms as first their streamers and then their bodies started to blacken and give off sharp jets of smoke. Some hidden fire was pouring heat into their bodies and cooking them alive. They suffered the most appalling agonies, I know, for my ears were skewered by their combined screams of pain. Those cries did not last long, for with a shockingly loud concussion the straining sac of the leading aeroform exploded in a bright red flare of light and the pair fell from the sky and disappeared behind the peak, trailing blue-orange fire after them.

The remaining aeroforms flew low overhead and brushed by the northerly side of the land, preferring to risk piercing their gas-bags against the rocks and thorns of the hill-side rather than pass over the deadly peak above. I sat and rocked back on my heels, stunned and not ready to weep just yet.

The theory – or hypothesis, if you prefer – that I have formed is one that I must test. It will be at great hazard to myself, I know, but my life becomes more and more worthless each day as my food runs out. It is this – that the land on which I am stranded is *volcanic* and becoming increasingly active. The roaring noise that woke me all those nights ago was the sound, I am convinced, of magma finding a new way to the surface and the rumbling, rattling and scraping that I have heard since are pieces of loose material falling back onto the molten rock or being ejected from the volcano's cone. I think it was the hot air rising from the crater that caused the sudden headlong flight of the aeroforms and a spark or flaming cinder that ignited their gas-bags and killed them. True, I have smelled no sulphurous gases, but the wind blows towards me from the open sea and away from the land and I think it not so very improbable that I have not noticed them.

I am going to climb to the summit of this land and find out the truth for myself. There is enough food remaining in my reserves to last me for a three-day ascent and, although I have no expertise in scaling the rocks, I shall take it slowly and use the materials – spikes and cords, mostly – that I saved from the ship to help me.

I shall leave this book here by the side of my bed, in the hope that I will be able to continue with it on my return from the heights. If, as may well turn out, I do not return, it will serve as my memoriam. To you my reader, I say: be kind and do not judge me too harshly, for we are human, you and I, with human failings, and though we fully deserve the sternest justice for our misdeeds, still we may hope for mercy.

And now farewell! I shall depart in a few minutes, once I have secured my home and read one last chapter of Mister Bell's book. I feel we are linked, Currer Bell and I, across the centuries and the light-years, for even though we leave nothing more than words – those fleeting things – behind us, yet we may both someday, though we know it not, be remembered.

Cameron Alexander Powell BSc MD, of the LAV El Dorado, *in this 534th Year of Glory.*

JOHANNA AND THE GLEANERS

The Spine

JOHANNA CHEN RIDES HER PRECIOUS BICYCLE DOWN THE SPINE OF Edge, this early Hally-morning. Soon the Blessèd sun will rise, but the inner world is already giving enough light to steer by and she does not want to be late. She is on her way to Stilt Town, pedalling briskly against the sea-breeze with her head down and her long hair flying behind her like a black banner.

She is wearing kelp-fibre trousers and a short woollen jacket, both in a neutral shade of ecru. It is a popular colour this year among the young people of Edge, who have never gone in for ostentation in their dress. One item only stands out in the orange-yellow Hally-light – Johanna has tied a brilliant red rayon scarf around her neck; the fabric flutters and tangles in her hair, making of it something almost heraldic.

Of course she does not actually live in Stilt Town. One only has to look at her to see that, although she fondly imagines that she has dressed appropriately for her expedition. Johanna's family comes from the city of Maybe, twenty miles upslope from the tide line and to all intents and purposes the capital of Edge. They are important people there.

The road is wet under her tyres. It has rained heavily overnight and she must take care not to skid on a damp patch of paving and come off her bicycle. She might hurt herself or – worse – damage the machine. The light is improving by the minute, however, and the likelihood of Johanna having an accident steadily recedes. She can enjoy the ride and the view. And what a view it is!

To her right the ground rises twenty feet or so to the top of the Spine. The ridge is gently undulating, with an occasional outcrop of bare rock poking through the ferns and lichen. Unseen on the far side is the narrow-gauge railway which carries material from Stilt Town or, to give it its full Board designation, Resource Extraction Point Three (Edge), to the industrial centre of Shore. The wagons are not designed for the use of passengers; they must either travel with the taciturn brakeman at the rear of the train or, if they are lucky, share the footplate with the driver and fireman. A well-appointed passenger car is kept in the depot at Shore for the use of important travellers such as Monitors, Governors and, of course, representatives of the Board. Johanna would spurn this carriage even if it were offered to her. She has her bicycle.

The Spine falls away steeply to the left of the road as it descends to an infinity of sand and above it, as the Blessèd sun rises over the Spine, is displayed the superlative blue and white sky of Glory. If Johanna were to pay more attention to the view than the needs of safety dictate she would be able to see the black dots of aeroforms silhouetted against the wide expanse of the morning sky, side-lit in gold by the reflected light of Hally and, if she looked downwards to the sands, small groups of scavenging humans, already hard at work digging for treasure.

But Johanna has more important things to look out for. The main part of the Spine is nearing its end. The railway and the road converge at this point and take a two thousand foot leap across the void to the first and greatest of the Stilts; those slowly crumbling pinnacles of rock which continue the track of the Spine into the endless sea, like the dots and dashes of Morse code.

The bridge, built of concrete and reinforced with monomolecular fibre, springs across the gap between solid land and ephemeral spire in a single shallow arch. It is one of the wonders of Glory. As Johanna and her bicycle begin their crossing the observing eye ignores the structure of the bridge beneath her wheels and grants her the benison of flight.

Flight... If the winds are favourable it is a five-day journey from Edge to Horn and Johanna had anticipated the trip with a mixture of joy and trepidation. To soar weightless above the endless seas of Glory on a top-line Board vessel... What a rare delight! What a privilege! Or so her mother had told her, as she hugged her goodbye at the departure gate. Her father had stood stiffly by his wife's side, afraid to reveal his overwhelming pride in his daughter's achievements by shedding public tears over their farewell. A brisk handshake and he had vanished, back to his official car and his official business, while Johanna's mother bombarded her with advice, most of which turned out to be comically uninformed. After all, what could she be expected to know about the life of a female undergraduate at the School on Horn?

Johanna hadn't minded her mother's fussing. She knew love when she saw it and although she hated to leave her family behind she was so looking forward to her new life she could have put up with much, much more and not lost her smile.

And now... Six years of hard work and study had passed,

crowned with success, and Johanna was forty-four years old, flying home to an uncertain future. She had, she suspected, irritated the passengers and crew of the LAV *Midland Counties* almost beyond endurance by her constant pacing up and down the ship's catwalks. Some days she walked, some days she kept to her cabin and some days she, in complete defiance of Board regulations, donned an airsuit and safety line and climbed the ladders to the airship's upper hull, to follow the walkway all the way to the prow where she lay on her front and gazed forward for hours on end, thinking, thinking. She so wanted to be home, she told a young lieutenant one evening, sharing a late cocktail in the ship's tiny bar.

'And what will you do when you get home, Miss Chen?' he asked.

She had her answer ready. 'Oh, my father wants me to take a position with the Board,' she said. 'He's a Monitor, you know.'

Lieutenant Corbishley, who knew perfectly well that Johanna was the daughter and only child of Monitor Chen of the city of Maybe on the land of Edge, nodded and moved the conversation onto less weighty matters. He was a socially adroit young man and, like Johanna, of good family.

'Beautiful, intelligent, *and* rich!' his cabin-mate said later as they changed watches. 'You're in luck there!' George Corbishley merely smiled.

Telegraph poles punctuate the bridge across which Johanna now flies. Beyond its landing point crouch the railway terminus and its associated depots, service points, warehouses and workers' huts. The road runs straight past these buildings and heads out back to sea. This first Stilt is by far the largest, at nearly half a mile in width, and it is the place where the raw materials which have been recovered from the beach are packaged up for processing on the land. It is not, however, Johanna's destination today. She lets the line of poles guide her to the bridge which leads to the next Stilt. This does not need to carry the railway and so it is much lighter; a spider's web of tracery carrying a suspended roadway made of cartilage and bone.

'And what will you do now you are home, Johanna?'

This was the question she had been waiting for. That nice young lieutenant who'd wangled her a suit and a line; he must have thought her so homesick she was desperate for a first sight of the Precipice of Edge which, at five miles in height, can be seen more than a day before a ship makes landfall. If only he had known how much she feared it! Well, not *feared*, exactly but...

Johanna looked around the table. In recognition of her triumphant return she had been given the place of honour at its head. Her grandfather sat at the far end, with her father on his right and her mother on his left. Aunt Lian and her sister Aunt Mai faced each other on Johanna's end of the table. Two servants stood discreetly by the door, ready to take away the plates when Johanna's mother gave them the signal. The walls of the dining room were covered in wood panelling – the table was also made of wood – and softly hissing gas lamps provided a gentle illumination. In the middle of the table was a large metal dish, on which rested the remains of a joint of beef. Johanna let her eyes roam over this assemblage of extraordinary comfort and wealth. All these riches were hers to enjoy, would be hers to own one day. With her degree in law – from the School on Horn, no less – she had earned her entrée into the ruling class of Edge. And not just of Edge, but the whole of Glory, if she wished it. All this by her own efforts, by her innate qualities of diligence and intelligence. But more than this; her family had money and influence. A quiet word in the right ear from her grandfather, and no door would be closed to her. A junior stewardship this year, a regional sub-governor's post in ten, promotion to the Board to follow in due course. Her father had been appointed a Monitor before his ninetieth birthday; Johanna could easily surpass his achievement through simple hard work and dedication. The path to success stretched from her feet into a happy and fulfilled future. All she had to do was take her father's advice regarding her first steps on that path. All she had to do was ask.

Johanna looked straight into her father's eyes and told him what she would do now she was home.

Pappy

T HIS SECOND STILT DOES NOT HAVE A SMOOTH, FLATTENED TOP LIKE the one where the railway terminates; so the road is built on top of an elevated causeway that runs past spoil heaps, ruined workshops and other industrial detritus. Johanna hurries on to the next bridge, dismounts and pushes her bicycle over its slick and slippery surface. Two men – road-menders leaning on their shovels – watch as she crosses. 'Nice funnies!' one of them shouts. The other whistles his appreciation.

Johanna does her best to keep a straight face, although she is sorely tempted to giggle. The workman's crude words do not bother her; in fact she welcomes their honesty. On Horn, where the use of roundabout, subtle, diplomatic language is preferred, even mandatory, such an outburst would be the cause of great offence, as indeed it would in the social circles of Maybe. Here, it is part of the everyday way of life. She rather enjoys the men's admiration – and there is something else. Her enjoyment gives her a comfortable feeling of superiority over the other members of her family, whom she regards as being overly interested in the keeping up of appearances. They are petty bourgeoisies, she feels, rigidly constrained by their upper-class status and cut off from the rest of the world; unable to experience the whole gamut of what real life has to offer. Her mother, her aunts; they would have a fit of the vapours if men such as those even dared to speak to them, let alone use such coarse expressions. She can rise above that and she is *better* than them.

School has turned Johanna into an egalitarian, and she is out to do good works in Society. She wants to make changes. She wants to make a difference.

* * * *

'But I want to make a *difference*, don't you see?' Her words fell into a pit of appalled silence. Johanna looked around the dining table and saw nothing but horrified faces. Her mother waved her hand in a jerky motion and the servants hurriedly left the room, closing the door quietly behind them. Her father turned in his seat and faced Johanna directly.

He spoke calmly at first, warning his daughter of the likely personal consequences of her rash decision. When she refused to change her mind, he extended his arguments beyond the cost to herself – her reputation, her future career, her place in society – and began to accuse her of selfishness. It was all very well for her to destroy her own future, but what of the debt – of gratitude, not to mention the expenses incurred in a six-year residence at the School – and what of her family? What of the work her ancestors had put into building up the family's status on Edge, and indeed throughout the entire world of Glory? Did she, the child of comfortably-off parents, despise their hard work, their sacrifices? Did she have any idea of the extent of their struggles? Their suffering? At this point her mother took out a handkerchief and began to sob quietly into it.

When Johanna still insisted that she had decided what she was going to do and that she would do it whatever anybody said, her father's voice rose in pitch and volume. He moved beyond emotional blackmail and began to threaten her. He would *force* her to take the position he had obtained – by calling in a number of costly favours – on the Board's staff. He would assign one of the servants to be her bodyguard; to keep her from harm, so he said. Johanna still refused to change her mind. Then, damn her! If she would not do as she was told voluntarily then she would not do anything. He would lock her away in her room. She could bloody well stay there until she had come to her senses and she could live on bread, water and scuttlers for all he cared.

'Make me!' Johanna shouted, rising furiously to her feet. 'Go on, make me, you, you—'

Her grandfather, who had sat impassively through the last ten minutes while tempers flared and first Johanna's aunts and then her mother, still weeping copiously, left the room, slowly raised his left hand.

'Be quiet, Johanna, and sit down.' His voice was soft, mild and perfectly clear. She obeyed instantly. Her father sat back in his chair, thinking himself vindicated and looking quite unbearably smug. 'And you, Eric, compose yourself. We will get nowhere by bellowing at each other like pregnant foys. Will we?'

At last, Johanna has reached the final Stilt. Or, rather, group of Stilts, for the last column of rock is riven by two vertical fissures running at right angles, dividing it into four quadrants. It is as if a giant – a god of ancient Earth, say – had taken a mighty hammer and chisel and split the Stilt like firewood. The chasm, wide at the top and narrowing as it falls a thousand feet to the tide line, dizzies the eye.

Stilt Town has thrived and grown around the four legs of the last tower. The dwellings of the people who live and work there cling to the rock faces like an accretion of barnacles on a pier. Crazily hanging from the narrowest of ledges or wedged into crevices and suspended by cords woven from the discarded intestines of the greater beasts, the platforms known as *flats* jut out into the void, unevenly spaced one above another. Between them run hand-winched platforms which, counterbalanced by bags of water made from the sacs of snared aeroforms, are the only means of ascending and descending the sides of the rocky columns. The wind eddies and gusts around and through the gaps, seeking out holes in the sides of the huts and sheds which, made of the same membranes as the suspension bridges which link the Stilts, constitute the homes, shops, offices and warehouses of Stilt Town. The structures constantly flex and bow in the never-ending gale. Over all hangs the characteristic smell of *Foialensis Gloriana Magnor*, the greater beast whose hide, meat, bones, hair, tongue, glands, organs and fins are the principal exports of Stilt Town.

Johanna dismounts once more and pushes her bicycle to the nearest elevator. Someone is waiting for her – a small child of ten or eleven. He waves Johanna and her bicycle onto the platform and shouts down the shaft, oblivious to the vertigo which has Johanna standing squarely in the centres of the queasily swaying lift.

'One to come down!' he cries, and 'Morning, Miss,' he says to the young woman from the big city many miles up the tilted land of Edge. He releases the restraining ratchet and the lift begins its unsteady descent.

When she was a little girl, Johanna liked nothing more than to slip out of the side door of her house and go round to the back, where her grandfather lived in a private three-room annex. Although he had retired from official business before Johanna was born he was still accustomed to receiving important visitors, and after an episode when she had burst in on a close discussion between him and the Governor of Horn and Bright they had set up a kind of coded signal. If a certain vase was standing on the windowsill of Pappy's kitchen then the coast was clear and she could come in. But if the vase was not there, or a Board car was standing outside, she would have to turn around and keep whatever it was she wanted to talk about until later.

Johanna approached the back door with some trepidation. She had an apology to make, and she was carrying a bunch of freesias with her as a peace-offering. Today, thankfully, the vase was in its usual place and Johanna was able to let herself in quietly and put the flowers in it. She filled it with water from the kitchen tap and carried it through to the sitting room. As she had expected, her grandfather was dozing by the empty fireside. She stepped up to his chair, touched him lightly on the shoulder, and spoke softly in his right ear.

'Pappy? Pappy? It's me.'

He sat up, instantly alert. 'Jo? Ah – there you are. Make us some tea, would you?'

'Yes, Pappy.' Johanna had long known where everything was kept in the kitchen and shortly the old man and the young woman were sitting facing one another across the hearth, cradling their cups in their hands. There was one thing Johanna knew she had to say straight away.

'Pappy, I'm sorry. For all the fuss – upsetting Mum and Dad and Aunt Lian and Aunt Mai like that.'

'You could have chosen your moment better.'

'Yes, I'm sorry. But Daddy asked… and what else could I have said?'

'You could have been kinder.'

'So could he!'

'And you didn't need to shout. You should have known that. What did they teach you on Horn? About the right way to conduct an argument?'

Johanna sighed. 'Yes, I know. But…'

'Yes?'

'I know what I want to do.'

'And you've not changed your mind?'

'Pappy!'

He smiled ruefully. 'Sorry. I should know better than that.' Johanna flushed. 'But listen. I want you – now we have settled down a bit – to tell me again what you intend to do. There's nothing like having to explain an idea to another person to make you aware of its flaws.'

I've just come back from six years of studying law! What does he take me for?

Pappy Chen, reading her mind, smiled to himself. Firstly, because he could interpret her inner thoughts so readily. And secondly, to see her exercise the self-discipline she would need if she were to make her way among the ruling class of Glory. She was still young – only forty-four. She was bright and determined. All she needed was a little support.

'This school you want to set up. Who is it for?'

'The Stilt Towers. Their children, I mean.'

'Why?'

'Why?'

'Several whys,' said Pappy. 'For a start, why Stilt Town?'

'Because there's no school there. Because they need a school.'

'Why do they need a school?'

Johanna sat up and leaned forward. 'Isn't it obvious? Wait a minute, I see what you're getting at. You think they don't need arithmetic and they don't need to write anything down and because they get washed away by the tides half the time they don't need to learn anything. It'd just be wasted on them – right? You think they're just... *machines*. Machines to work and make money for us. That might be good enough for you, but it's not good enough for me. It's not fair!'

'You say that's what I think. But do you *know* it? What do you mean by "not fair"?'

'I mean that I want to put something back. I've got everything and they've got nothing. I want to give them something.'

'Do they want to have it?'

'I... I... don't know. But they deserve a chance. It's their hard work and everyday danger that's made us comfortable and well-off. There'd have been no chance of me going to the Board, or to the School on Horn for all that, if we'd come from Stilt Town. "Stinking of foys," that's what I used to say about them. I know better than that now. I want to make up for it.'

She's going to be quite somebody one day, said Pappy Chen's long-dead wife, still alive in his memories. *I should know. She's just like you.*

'I see,' he said. 'At least I think I do. But what do you want me to do about it? I'm not the Governor any more, you know. I've no budget, no staff, no real power.'

Johanna threw back her head and laughed. 'Oh Pappy! You *are* silly!'

As befitted the capital city of the land of Edge, Maybe boasted a high street, built of solid respectable stone. It ran along the side of Jade Park from the railway station at its lower end to the Bureau at its upper, and it was lined with specialist food shops, clothes boutiques and kiosks selling everything from sweets to shoelaces. Johanna walked slowly up the road, looking at the window displays and ignoring the other passers-by, and stopped to buy an astonishingly expensive cup of coffee from a street-vendor's barrow. She carried it into the park where she sat on a bench under a lime tree and sipped it slowly, while watching the shadows the tree's swaying limbs cast move rhythmically over the grass. And while she drank her coffee she remembered another bench, on another land. She was happy to be home, of course she was, but she missed Horn, and the School, and the friends she had made there. They had often met up after classes to talk about... well, everything; their studies, the state of the world, what clothes or music were in or out of fashion this year, who fancied whom. They'd sat and talked for hours in Horn Town Gardens or the School cloisters. And they'd drunk coffee, the fierce dark kaffe of Bright, Horn's twin land across the treacherous Straits of Mercy.

This was only Edgeois coffee – bland, milky and sweet – but its aroma still had the power to transport Johanna back to Horn and those intense all-night conversations where she had first conceived the idea of a School for Stilt Town. Not a School in the Hornese sense, of course, but a place where the students could catch at least a glimpse of the world of learning; something beyond the everyday grind of working, eating, sleeping and dying. *Can I really do it?* She had asked herself that question often enough. Now she had to prove that she could. It was time to get moving. She emptied the dregs from her cup onto the grass, disregarding the twenty-five tokens it had cost, and returned it to the seller. There was business for her to do.

The manager of the Central Board Store had been tipped off by his floor staff and he was ready to greet Governor Chen's granddaughter when she opened the door. He scarcely blinked when she presented him with a letter of requisition signed by the old man himself and paused only for as long as it took to find her a chair on which to sit and a cup of watery tea to drink before first validating her order with the Bureau and then handing it to one of his deputies to be fulfilled. Johanna took a sip for politeness's sake, put the tea down, and followed the underling closely around the store, checking every article, counting the goods as they piled up on the pallet and making sure that the delivery arrangements – to the Board depot in Shore, and as soon as possible – were perfectly understood. Then she left abruptly and strolled back down the high street to the Monitor's house, stopping only to buy a nice red scarf from one of the better shops.

The Herb Garden

J OHANNA PUSHED THE DOOR OPEN, PARKED HER BICYCLE NEXT TO IT and took her place behind the table at the front of the classroom. This was it; the culmination of two month's work, of organising, supervising, arguing and even – despite Pappy's advice – shouting. This was the first day of the first term of the first academic year of Stilt Town School.

She had chosen that name herself – or rather selected it on the advice of the Town Council. Johanna might have preferred something grander, but the Council had decisively voted her down. 'We're not going to have a Marine College, we're not going to have a Faculty of Edge and we're certainly not going to have a bloody Symposium!' So the leader of the Council – a grizzled, sunburned gleaner-woman of eighty or ninety – had told her with an air of complete finality. 'This is Stilt Town and you're setting up a School here. Stilt Town School it is. Or nothing.' So Stilt Town School it was.

They built it a hundred feet above the tide line, on the north-west column of the Last Stilt, facing inwards. In contrast with its ramshackle neighbours to the left, right, up and down, it was a substantial piece of construction. The flat platform was made of solid wood and the struts which supported it, cantilevered out from the living rock, were constructed from the same fibre-reinforced concrete as the bridge which connected the Stilts to the mainland of Edge. The walls and roof of the schoolroom, however, were made of traditional foyskin and ribs. There was no point in making the learning environment any more strange or off-putting than it was already.

Three rows of desks. Five desks to a row. Fifteen places and, for this first morning at least, they were all occupied. Anywhere else, there would have been a crowd of parents, brothers and sisters around the door, curious to see what was going on, but not in Stilt Town. In Stilt Town you worked. You worked hard and you worked all the hours you could. You had no time or energy to waste on trivialities like education.

'But Pappy!'

'No, I insist. You must not live in the Resource Extraction Point itself. It is too dangerous. I have spoken to your father and mother about this and they are in complete agreement with me. In fact, it is a condition of your being allowed to go ahead with this project.'

'But where will I live? I can't travel down from Maybe every day! It's nearly thirty miles!' Johanna strode restlessly around the room. Her grandfather sat motionless in his chair and waited for her to stop.

'That is very true,' he said when she eventually sat down. 'That is why I have arranged for you to live with your Aunt Lian in Shore. We own a small house there, not far from the railway station. You will find it quite convenient, I think.'

'Convenient!' Johanna exploded, leaping to her feet again. 'Living with Aunt Lian? Convenient?'

'Yes, very convenient. She is an excellent housekeeper and you will have very little time yourself for the everyday essentials of life, like washing, cooking and cleaning. Think about it.'

Johanna thought about it. Aunt Lian... she was old and boring and dull, but... her house was neatly kept and she could cook pretty well. Her bread... yes, that was always good to eat, and her casseroles were thick, meaty and delicious. But...

'Yes,' said Pappy, anticipating her as usual. 'You're quite right.

It's ten miles from Shore to Stilt Town. Come with me.' Johanna helped her grandfather to stand and together they left the sitting-room of his annex and went outside through the kitchen door into the small herb garden that Granny had planted there, up against the wall. Pappy took a small brass key out of his jacket pocket and gave it to Johanna. 'Over there. Do you see?' He pointed to the corner of the garden where a lean-to shed nestled among the moss, nettles and thyme. 'Just pop in there for me, would you?' Johanna took the key from the old man and walked carefully around the outside of the herb beds, keeping to the gravel path. The key slipped easily into the lock of the shed door and turned smoothly. Johanna pulled back the door – it grated on the path – and peered into the darkness.

Governor Chen said later that you could have heard Johanna's shriek of delight in Scarp, a hundred miles north of Maybe. She came charging backwards out of the shed, tugging at the bicycle she had found inside and trampling all over the basil and rosemary that grew nearby. Their fragrance rose around her in a heady cloud. 'It's only an old one, I'm afraid,' Pappy said, 'but I've kept it in good order.'

'Did it use to be Granny's?'

Yes, my love, breathed a silent voice.

'Good morning, class.'

'Good morning, Miss Chen.'

And so the first day began; with a mutual greeting, followed by a serious getting down to work. Johanna had constructed a careful syllabus for her school, assuming that all the children, whatever their age, would be at the same low level of educational attainment. She had also assumed that they would be willing students for, after all, what else could she do? So the end result was that by midday, with the Blessèd sun standing at the zenith and Hally beginning to set, both Johanna and her students were thoroughly worn out. They sat on the veranda in front of the schoolroom and ate their lunch with their feet dangling over the edge of the flat. The six-hundred-foot drop to the rocks below was a matter of no concern to the children so, of course, Johanna had to ignore it as well. What she found it harder to ignore was the fact that she had a well-filled lunch box, with a meat pasty, some of Aunt Lian's home-made onion chutney, and a pear in it, while most of her companions had no more than a few small pieces of dried pollock and some gritty black biscuit to chew on. Perhaps she would bring some extra food with here tomorrow. Aunt Lian would be happy to oblige.

An instinct told Johanna that it would be unwise to send the children home directly after lunch, however tired they were, and so she had them gather around her at the front of the class and listen while she told them about life in the greater world of Glory; of Shore and Maybe and Scarp and Precipice and the other towns on Edge. She described the fields of wheat that grew on the plains to the north of Maybe and the lives of the villagers and farmers who lived among them. There were forests there, she said, where the trees had been planted by the first landers; where some of them were more than three hundred years old. She introduced new words to them; oak, and beech, and ash. And *sacred*.

And when, at the end of that first day, she took the lift to the top of the Stilt and rode her bicycle across the suspension bridges to the railhead, there was a goods train waiting there, just in time for her to throw her mount into the brake van and run to the front where she stood on the footplate and swayed in time with the sideways rocking motion of the locomotive. First over the great arch and then along the side of the Spine and finally, after running through fields of rice by the side of the river Ease, to the steam-hissing, smoke-blackened depot in Shore, where Aunt Lian was waiting for her with a flask of tea and a piece of walnut cake.

How We Came To Glory

JOHANNA STEPS FROM THE LIFT PLATFORM AND PUSHES HER BICYCLE along the ledge-path which, clinging limpet-like to the side of the Stilt, connects all the flats on its level. As part of the works that Johanna, with her grandfather's covert assistance, put in place when her school was built, this path is fitted with solid railings on its open side; an extravagance by Stilt Town standards.

Luis is waiting for Johanna at the entrance to the school-house, ready to take her bicycle and wheel it to its customary place against the rock wall. He is a beautiful child; twelve years old with huge brown eyes under a bushy fringe of dark hair, and he has an enormous crush on his teacher.

Over the past six weeks that have passed since that very first lesson, Miss Chen and her class have got to know one another pretty well. Their ages range from eight to twenty-two, there are six boys and nine girls and their homes are scattered across all four of the Outer Stilts. Some live on the upper levels, safe from the fluctuating tides of Glory's oceans, and some have perilous homes just above the tide level, where the direction of the wind or the disposition of the worlds can make all the difference between a comfortably dry night and a hurried flight upwards to safety.

'Why do your family live down there where it's so dangerous?' Johanna asked fourteen-year-old Marie, a week or two after she had started her new career in Stilt Town. The girl looked at her teacher as if she were demented, stupid, or both.

'If you live high up it takes forever to get down to the beach when the tide goes out. If you're already at the tide level you're first in line for the beach and you get the first gleanings.' *Isn't that obvious?*

'But why don't the people from the upper levels come down to the lower ones when the tide starts to go out? Then everyone would get an equal chance.'

'Because we don't let the bastards do that.'

That told me.

Johanna has learned more from the children in her class than she had expected. She had thought when she first conceived the idea of the school that she would spend most of the time lecturing to her students and the rest of it in tutorials, just as if she were still at the School on Horn. Fortunately she researched the basics of elementary education before the first day or Providence only knows what might have happened.

Especially, she believes she has learned a little patience.

The schoolroom walls are covered with posters and charts, printed on beaten kelp fibre. There is a map of Edge, showing its roads, cities, rivers and mines, and next to it a satellite photo from the Monitor's bureau for comparison. There is a history tree, showing how humanity spread over Glory after the first landings and built its governing institutions. Next to that is a pyramidal hierarchy diagram illustrating how those institutions work in practice, with the Governors of the Board at the top, Monitors a little lower, professionals below them, then employers, technicals, artisans and, at the bottom, plain citizens. Some versions of this diagram show all the different members of society as parts of a circle, with responsibility, wealth and power flowing around and between the peoples of Glory and emphasising their interdependence. Johanna prefers the honesty of the pyramid. It clearly shows who is on top and who is not.

Geography is also represented in Johanna's school. There are both a globe and a Mercator map of the world of Glory, together with images of the companion worlds of Hally, Sally and Our Moon. By convention, the lands of Glory (except Edge) are magnified by a factor of five to make them easier to see. Only the charts used by the navigators of the Board's airships are printed to true scale.

Next to the maps is a handwriting exemplar with sample letters and words for the children to copy onto their slates. Then Johanna's blackboard, and next to that is a big sheet of kelp-fibre on which every child has drawn a picture of him or herself – stick-figures with sun-ray hair, mostly. Johanna has written their names and the names of their parents next to the pictures, as a record and a reference in case a student goes missing. This has not happened yet (although two children have been withdrawn from the school, to be replaced by others), but Johanna dreads the day – which must surely come – when a student is absent, not because they are unwell, or helping with harvesting, but because one of the many perils of Stilt Town has claimed their life.

Johanna calls the roll, although as every seat in the classroom is filled today it seems hardly necessary, except for the purposes of record-keeping. Still, she feels a familiar surge of relief that all her student are well. Then she launches into the morning's work, starting with a song. She taps out the tune on a small keyboard and writes the words on the blackboard. The class recites those words line by line until everyone knows them by heart. It is a very old song from another, far-off world:

And did those feet in ancient time,
Walk upon England's mountains green...

Only one or two of the older students are able to read the words on the blackboard. This, Johanna feels, does not matter at present. It is enough that the class is singing together, however uncertain their command of tune and lyrics. As for her choice of material, she could not say; only that *Jerusalem* appeals to her and she had a feeling that her students would enjoy singing it, as they do.

Then she tells her class to fetch their slates from the rack and they settle down to their counting exercises. Johanna is by no means a born teacher, but she is intelligent and has learned as a part of her legal training how to extract the essential core of an argument and present it with clarity and concision in a form which anyone can assimilate. She's even learned to modify her speech so that the Stilt Towners can understand her Horn-Maybe accent.

Their arithmetic work concentrates on the practicalities of life in Stilt Town – how many fifty-pound jawbones will a one-ton lift carry, how much fish will feed a family of five, how many years older than Haiyra is Semila, how fast does an Our Moon tide run on a Sally-afternoon when Hally is three-quarters behind the Blessèd sun? This last question is moot, for Glory's tides are notoriously unpredictable. Even the oldest, most experienced gleaner knows their experience is worth nothing without information to work from, and the daily bulletins that come down the line from the Monitor's bureau in Maybe are of crucial importance to the people who live and work in Stilt Town.

After a solid morning's work Johanna and her students have lunch as usual on the vertiginous indoors-outdoors of the veranda. The air today is cold and foggy, hiding the opposite Stilt from view and covering everything and everyone with a clammy layer of moisture. They soon go back indoors where it is more comfortable and slightly warmer.

It's story time. Sometimes Johanna talks, as she did on the first day, sometimes she manages to persuade one of the more outgoing students like Tanith or Yolande to tell their own stories to the class.

Today, however, Johanna has brought something very special with her.

It is a picture book; a treasure. It was given to Johanna on the occasion of her twenty-sixth birthday as a joint present from her father and mother, aunts and grandfather. Beautifully printed in full colour on real paper and bound in embossed calfskin, it is by far the most costly thing she has ever owned and if her parents ever got to hear that she had taken it with her to Stilt Town they would probably disinherit her on the spot.

The title of the book, printed in gold lettering on its cover, is *How We Came To Glory*.

Johanna calls the children forward and they sit on the floor in a semicircle. 'Today,' says Johanna, 'I am going to read to you from a very special book.' She holds up *How We Came To Glory* so everyone can see it. 'It tells the wonderful story of our ancestors who left Earth and travelled to this world and settled here. Will you all promise to be very quiet so I can read it to you?'

The students nod. Johanna opens the book to the first page of the story. Each pair of facing pages has a titled paragraph of text on the left and a full-page illustration on the right. The text is printed in a large bold jet-black font and the pictures are rendered in textured acrylics with sharp, clear lines and bright, vivid colours. None of the children have ever seen anything like it and there is a gasp of amazement when Johanna holds it up for them to see. She reads the first paragraph:

The Dying Earth

"The Earth had been infected by a terrible disease which killed all the people and all the animals that lived there. Only a few people escaped it because they lived in space."

This picture gave Johanna nightmares when she first saw it. The Infected Earth, its blue seas and green lands blotched with an ugly brown stain floats in space like a canker cell under a microscope. In the foreground a man and a woman, wearing white spacesuits, observe the death of their home planet through the window of an orbital habitat. Tears flood their eyes.

The next page is worse:

The Moon Dies

"Even the people who had made their homes on Earth's Moon did not escape. The disease came to them from Earth. It hid in the bodies of visitors from Earth."

Under a wide glass dome, with the dying Earth visible in the meridian, men and women, boys and girls lie on the ground. One girl holds up her hand and you can see that it is coloured the same vile orange as the Earth. Johanna's class holds its breath in horror.

The Only Ones Left

"Only one place was immune to the cursed infection. One space-home had left Earth and flown away before the infection could strike."

A long cylinder floats in space. The sun looks smaller than it does when it is seen from Earth.

The *Whistledown*

"The people who lived in the space-home made it into a ship that could sail between the stars. They decided to fly to a new world."

The cylinder is dwarfed by a set of sails, each many thousands of miles from side to side, connected to the space habitat by invisible threads of monomolecular fibre. The sails billow under the pressure of the sun's rays.

The Sleepers

"There was not enough food on board the *Whistledown* to last for the journey, so everybody slept while the machine navigators looked after the ship."

The Whistledown *leaves her orbit, propelled by the solar wind and the livid green light of launching lasers mounted on the moons of the giant planet Jupiter. We see the people from the first page of the book asleep in two capsules fixed in an array of more than a thousand.*

'Did they dream?' asks Marie.

'Yes, of course they did,' says Johanna.

The Blessèd Sun

"After thousands of years, the people of Earth reached the system of the Blessèd sun. The machines woke some of them."

The Whistledown *falls into the gravity field of the Blessèd sun like a man parachuting to the ground. The man and woman look up at the star, their faces full of gladness. Its rays light up the long-dark interior of the habitat.*

The Worlds

"The people found four worlds orbiting the Blessèd sun. They gave them joyful names: Hallelujah, Salvation, Glory and Amen."

A planetary diagram of the worlds of the Blessèd sun. Golden Hallelujah is a close-orbiting gas giant, three times the size of Jupiter. Brown Salvation is a Mars-like world, as is Amen, small and airless. However, while Salvation is an independent world, Amen rotates around the jewel of the system:

Glory

"Hallelujah was too big and too hot, and Salvation was too small and too cold. So was Amen. But the most beautiful world of the Blessèd sun was just right."

Glory could be the Lost Earth's twin − a sea-blue world marbled with spiralled clouds. The only difference is that, while the continents of Earth were immediately visible from space, there appears to be nowhere to live on this world. There is no land to be seen anywhere.

'That's where we live!' cries out Luis.
'Yes, it is,' says Johanna, smiling.

We Come to Glory

"The people woke up. They boarded the lifeboats and descended through the air to the land of Horn."

A white shuttlecraft perches on the crest of the hill that is now the site of the Joyeuse of Horn. Smiling people file from it, carrying their children in their arms. The sky is a brilliant blue, dotted with clouds. The land is covered with a green sward of grass and lichen.

'That's nearly the last page,' says Johanna. The class sighs collectively.

We Live in Peace

"There has never been a war in all the history of Glory. Everyone lives in peace and contentment on our beautiful world, sharing its treasures and delights equally. Truly, we live under a Blessèd sun."

A montage: the happy citizens of Glory are seen at work and play, sowing, reaping, flying airships, building windmills and sea-turbines, tilling their gardens, getting together for evenings of song and merrymaking, holding their grandchildren on their laps.

'That's it. The End,' says Johanna closing the book. Did you like it?'
'Yes!' says the class, speaking as one.
'And would you like to hear some more?'
'Yes!' says the class again, only twice as loudly as before.
And then, meaning nothing but good, she tells them the whole truth.

What They Had To Learn

T HE FOLLOWING DAY, JOHANNA CYCLES TO HER SCHOOL AS USUAL and conducts her class as usual, although the children seem a little quieter than they were. The day after...

At first Johanna thinks she must have made some mistake on her way to the school. Perhaps she took the wrong lift (but it looked right) or descended to the wrong level (but the fence was in its usual place by the side of the ledge-path). She looks around. Yes; the opposite Stilt is in its expected place and at its expected distance. She leans over the edge of the platform (something she would not have dared to do only a week or two earlier) and looks down. Yes, it is the correct distance from this flat to the rocks below. The acoustic – the way the sounds of the wind and the distant ocean are absorbed and reflected by the spaces around her – is familiar. This is the right place, then, or at least it seems so. But where is the school? Where has it gone?

The flat is totally bare – a simple wooden platform. There are no walls and no roof, no desks, no chairs and no table. They have all gone. Johanna looks around her in bewilderment, still not completely sure that she has not made some foolish mistake. She pushes her bicycle to the rock wall and leans it up against it just as, only a day earlier, Luis had done. Faithful Luis; Johanna smiles to think of him. But wait – this is silly. She has come to the wrong place, of course she has, and even now her class is probably running riot and she will be in trouble for not supervising them properly. Johanna takes hold of her bicycle. She will go back up to the top of the Stilt and try again. Up there, everything will be clearer and she will be able to laugh at herself for being such a dope as to come down the wrong Stilt, as she is rapidly convincing herself she must have done. *Come on now, Johanna. Let's get moving.*

She gets as far as the path, but can proceed no further. There is someone blocking the way – the gleaner-woman who heads the Council of Stilt Town. She is a person with no formal powers. The land of Edge, with its ultimate authority derived from the Board, owns, and has responsibility for, the operation and management of Resource Extraction Point Three. The Council is merely an administrative convenience. It saves the Governor the trouble and expense of policing Stilt Town. So long as shipments of raw materials reach the processing plants in Shore regularly and to quota, it little matters to the Board how the Stilt Towners run their ramshackle neighbourhood.

'Please,' says Johanna, 'I need to get to my school. I seem to have come to the wrong level or something. Can you tell me the right way to go?'

The woman says nothing, but continues to obstruct the path. Johanna is more puzzled than angry. 'Please?' she says. 'I'm terribly late – the children will be missing me.'

'The children will not be missing you,' the gleaner-woman replies at last. 'They are not coming to your school anymore.'

'Sorry? I don't understand? Not coming?'

'Your school is closed. The children will not be attending your school, or any other school for that matter.'

'What? Not attending my school?'

'That is what I have just told you. Are you stupid, girl, that you do not understand me? Do they train dunces on Horn?'

Is she trying to provoke me? Johanna's hard-won patience is starting to wear thin. *Who is this woman, anyway?* She takes a deep breath and composes herself.

'No, I am not a dunce and I am not stupid. But my school, which was here, I'm sure, yesterday, has gone. Will you not tell me why?'

The woman is six inches shorter than Johanna and she is of the humblest imaginable birth. Despite these differences, there can be no doubt who is in command of this situation. Still, she recognises that this silly high-born girl, who has done something so serious that she cannot be allowed to continue working with the community's children, has at least shown the good sense and courtesy not to try to browbeat or threaten her. She deserves an answer, maybe even an explanation, and she shall have one, like it or not. With the greatest ease and naturalness the woman sits on the floor of the flat, pulling her knees up in front of her. Johanna follows her example. The woman speaks:

'Two days ago, you read to your class.'

'Yes.'

'You read from a book, did you not? *How We Came To Glory*?'

'Yes. I've brought it with me. It's in one of my saddlebags.' Johanna points to her bicycle. 'Would you like to see it?'

'Not just now, thank you. Did you enjoy reading the book to your class?'

'Yes, very much.'

'Did your class enjoy having it read to them?'

'Yes. I'm sure they did.' *Where is all this leading to?*

'Tell me, Miss Chen, do you like teaching?'

'Yes. Yes, I do.'

'Are you a good teacher?'

Johanna pauses for a moment. 'I try my best. I'm sure I've got plenty of room for improvement.'

Johanna's lame joke passes the gleaner-woman by; or she chooses to ignore it. 'You have no training, though.'

'No.'

'A shame. Had you been trained properly we might not have been having this conversation today. May I see the book, please?'

Johanna fetches *How We Came To Glory* and gives it to the woman. 'Do not worry,' she says. 'I have washed my hands this morning. I will not soil your book.' Johanna had genuinely not considered that the gleaner might accidentally mark the pages, but she is nevertheless abashed. If the woman notices Johanna's reaction she makes no sign of it. Instead, she carefully leafs through the book, studying each page in turn. Johanna cannot help but notice that her lips move as she reads.

'This is a lovely thing,' the gleaner says eventually, letting the book fall shut with a last soft rustle. 'A very lovely thing. Thank you for letting me see it.'

Johanna, who has waited as patiently as she can for the woman to finish, takes the book from her and replaces it in her saddlebag. 'Please,' she says, returning to her position on the floor, 'are you saying that it was wrong for me to show the children my book? Are you saying it's too good for them?'

'No!' The gleaner-woman's face flushes briefly. 'Nothing is too good for our children.'

'You don't think I was giving them ideas above their station? Showing them something they could never hope to own themselves? Sowing discontent? Fomenting discord among the future workers?'

'They work now! Everybody works!'

Johanna presses her point. 'But if they see that there's a better life outside Stilt Town, they might not want to carry on working here. They might want to better themselves. They might leave.' *And then where would be your authority, Council Leader?*

'And do what? Move to the north? Work in the mines? Live in

Scarp or Shaft or Scree or Precipice? Never see the Blessèd sun for fumes and mist? Die of choke-lung?'

'Is that all you think they're good for? Mining? Or scraping a living off the beach? Running away from the tides day and night?'

'No!' The woman stands up. 'Do not speak of things you do not understand!'

Johanna also rises to her feet. 'Don't tell me what I understand and what I don't understand! I was born on Edge, just like you. I know perfectly well how fast the tide runs. I know all about the risks you take every day; the quicksands, the Beasts, the winds. I know how hard you work to extract the materials we all need.'

'You do not!'

'I do. I have seen it in the eyes of the children.' Johanna puts her hands on her hips. She lowers her voice. 'And so have you.'

The gleaner-woman's shoulders slump a little. 'I have. Let us sit down again and calm ourselves.'

When they are comfortable once more, Johanna says, 'You told me just now that nothing was too good for the children.'

'Yes.'

'And you told me that I was not wrong to show them my book.'

'Yes.'

'But what if I said that the book was full of lies? Do the children deserve to be told lies?'

'I have read no lies in your book.'

Johanna hesitates. 'Do you know what we mean by falsity in exception? There is a phrase for it in old Latin. It's a legal term and it means to lie while telling the truth, usually by the omission of material facts.'

'I have not heard the expression, but I understand what you mean.'

'Then what I am asserting is this: although *How We Came To Glory* contains no direct lies, it nevertheless omits material facts in such a way as to deny the truth.'

'And the truth is what you told the class after you had finished reading from the book?'

'Yes it is. My conscience would not allow me to leave the children with the impression that the book told, as we put it, the truth, the whole truth and nothing but the truth. Is the reason you want to shut down my school that I told my class the whole truth? Would you have me lie to them?'

'No, I would not.'

'Then you must agree with me that I did what I had to do and that my school must be allowed to continue.'

'I'm sorry, but that cannot be.'

'But why not, in the name of Glory?'

'You are young, Miss Chen, and you are fierce and ambitious —'

'Don't patronise me!'

'Peace.' The woman smiles, just a little. 'The young make one kind of mistake, the old make another. That is our nature. But the old have already made the mistakes the young make and, if they are wise, they remember them. You wanted to help the youngsters in your class; now let me help you.

'When you read from your book, with its lovely bright pictures and its exciting story of humanity fleeing the dying Earth and reaching the safety of Glory after a long and arduous voyage, you gave them something good. You gave them inspiration, you gave them a message of hope. But when you went on to talk about all the things that are bad and wrong about this world, you took hope and inspiration away from them again. Don't you think they know how unfair life is? Don't you think they know how hard it is, how treacherous? Of course they do. They took that knowledge in with their mothers' milk. There is not one of those children who has not lost a loved one or a friend; in a fall, or drowned in the sea, or lost in the sands, or crushed between the jaws of a Beast.'

'But—'

'Let me finish. Even so, if you had stopped there, the damage would have been serious but not fatal. But when you went on to tell them that their lives – all our lives – are meaningless, that was the cut to the throat.'

'But the Great Tide—'

The gleaner-woman holds up her hand. 'We do not speak of it. It is like Death. We are all going to die someday, but it is useless to spend all our time talking or thinking about our deaths, for to do so is to make our lives meaningless. What is the point of telling the children about an arbitrary fate that may strike at any time, whose effects are terrible, *and about which they can do nothing at all?* The people of Earth did that. Everybody could talk to everybody else at once and everyone knew what was happening anywhere in the world at any time, all the time. Fears and threats and horrors sped from land to land in moments. But it didn't make them any happier, and when the Ochre Plague struck it came out of nowhere, or so it seemed.'

'You would rather live in ignorance, then.'

'We are not ignorant. Am I ignorant?'

Obviously the Leader of Stilt Town Council is not.

'We had to tell the children that you had told them some dreadful lies and that you were so wicked we had to send you away. I am sorry for that. It was a terrible thing to do, but it was the thing I *had* to do. That is what it means to be a leader. They tell me that one day you will be high in the offices of the Governorship – perhaps be a

Monitor or even a member of the Board. I think that when that day comes you will understand.'

'So you will continue to be stunted in your ambitions? You never want to be anything more than you are now?'

'Better that, than to have our children walk in needless fear. Please go now, Miss Chen. Despite what I have had to say in Council, I do not think you are a bad person. Far from it – you are honourable, decent and honest.'

'Too honest?'

The gleaner shrugs her shoulders. 'This flat is solid and well-built. It will make an excellent weighing station or loading dock for our materials, or we might build ourselves a gathering-place here. We like to play and sing the old songs to one another. Did you know that?'

'No.'

'One day you must come and hear us. I am told I do a memorable rendition of *Blue Suede Shoes*. Goodbye, Miss Chen.'

Both women stand and take each other's hands. They bow to one another. Then Johanna pushes her bicycle to the path and wheels it to the lift. Invisible hands operate its mechanism and she rises to the top of the Stilt. From there she rides furiously to the Spine, watched closely by concealed eyes, and thence to her home in Maybe – an uphill journey of thirty miles in all. She arrives at her father's house tired, hot and thirsty, but she does not stop to drink or take a bath. All the way home a suspicion, planted in her mind by the Council Leader's words, has been growing like a weed and she must root it out as soon as possible. So instead of pausing to refresh herself, Johanna goes directly to the back of the house, to the herb garden, and bursts into her grandfather's apartment, dumping her bicycle outside and paying no attention to the presence or otherwise of the tell-tale vase on the kitchen windowsill. She storms into the sitting-room.

'You knew! You knew all along!' She thumps the back of the old man's chair.

'Sit down, Jo.'

'No I will not! You set me up! You've been talking to that woman.'

'Which woman do you mean?'

'You know who I mean. That *dwarf* who thinks she runs the place. You're in it together, the pair of you. You set out to humiliate me, from day one. Teach young Jo a lesson, you thought. Put her in her place. Just because she's been to Horn doesn't mean she doesn't need taking down a peg or two. You and Dad… It was revenge, because I made him look stupid at dinner. Don't bother trying to deny it.'

Pappy knows better than to try interrupting Johanna when she is as angry as this. But later, when she has talked – or shouted – herself out, and they have both shed a tear or two and he has finally persuaded her to accept a cup of tea and a piece of apple strudel, they both find that they cannot fight one another for very long. They kiss and Johanna leaves, to go to her room and arrange to meet some of her old, neglected friends, and Pappy sits back in his chair and sighs. Presently he falls asleep.

You are a rascal!

Yes, I admit it.

Did you really know Jo's school would fail?

I thought it was likely. Actually, it lasted longer than I thought it would. That's our granddaughter for you.

She's very upset.

She'll get over it. And, you know, she was never really suited to be a teacher. She's much too combative. She stood up to Patience Latimer—

Your Council Leader friend—

She stood up to her much better than I could have done at her age. She's got guts, our Jo.

And...

And we've done some good, I think. First, to Jo. She's never failed in any of her projects; not until now. I think she'll learn something useful from this little setback of hers.

And...

Well, we've persuaded the Stilt Towners to let us build them a good, strong, solid new flat. Either they'll use it as a meeting-place, which'll help bind them together—

I'm not sure those idiots on the Board would appreciate that. Or—

Or it'll become a safe place for storing materials and it'll help reduce their losses and boost their output.

And our profits.

That's true.

Like I said, you're a rascal.

I never denied it.

Goodnight, Pappy.

Goodnight, Granny. Goodnight.

INTERPLANETARY

Pole

THE DAYS UP HERE ARE COLD AS HELL AND THE NIGHTS ARE COLDER than that, with ice-black skies and a dry frost on the fenders of my 'mobile that sticks there until well after the Blessèd sun has come around. But what the heck. It's home; at least that's how I've come to think of it.

I chose to be here, so I shouldn't complain. It's not so bad if you're down on the equator. Life is much harder – and colder – here at the polar bases and you can wait as long as you like for daybreak. All day long, all year round, the Blessèd sun hovers on the horizon, never rising or setting, and the only change is the direction of the shadows. They are long and dark and they swoop and dive over the low hills that surround the base. They can drive a man mad; that is known, that is a fact.

Why do men come here, then? Why are there not remote sensors at the poles communicating directly with the equatorial settlements via the comsats, the groundnet or even the *Sweetheart* herself? It is this, I think; that for some of us madness has a charm, a glamour, a seductive lilting voice that calls and cannot be resisted. Perhaps that's why the 'Down summoned us. Perhaps that's why we responded to her summons. Perhaps that's why I went north.

There were three of us madmen living at the North Polar Survey Establishment, as it was officially known. We called it the nuthatch. There were Jeremy, Janey and me, Jonathan. The Three Jays, and each of us daft as a jay, each of us with his or her tic, twitch or annoyance:

Jeremy – infrastructure: 'Jeremy, for heaven's sake would you just sit down for a moment? Stop pacing up and down like that. It's driving me round the twist!'

Janey – computation: 'Tapping, tapping, tapping. Fingers on glass, fingers on tabletops, fingers on teeth. If you don't stop it soon I'll cut your nails off all the way up to your wrists!'

Jonathan – sensors: 'If I see you pick one more bogey out of your nose, sniff it, crunch it and eat it, so help me I'll walk out the door without a suit!'

Each of us finds a way to escape from the others when it all gets too much. The people who designed the base knew there'd be "personal interaction issues", as the official manual puts it, from time to time – or even all the time – so they made sure we got our own private spaces. Apart from our cabins, which are basically insulated boxes hanging off the sides of the main structure and contain little more than a bed, a screen – yes, we're all Monitors here – a wardrobe, a head and a suit locker, we each have our own individual working areas. Jeremy is mostly to be found among the pipes and wiring of the fusor, the air plant or the ponic garden downstairs. Janey sits with a pair of phones on, murmuring into a mike or tapping (tapping!) on a board and staring at a screen. She's most definitely on another planet when she's in coding mode and her withdrawal is better than Jeremy's chattiness ('Hey, look at this interesting blockage I've just cleared!') but much spookier. Half the time you don't know who she's talking to, or which dimension she's inhabiting.

We've made it a rule that, no matter what needs doing (barring absolute emergencies), we always get together for a meal at the same time each day. We've chosen eighteen hundred hours, Horn time, as the baseline. The food isn't great – how could it be? – but there's usually something fresh from the ponics, like carrots, cress or lettuce, to go with the synthetic this, artificial that and man-made the other.

We talk about the day's work, the next day's work, the next week's work, the probability of a supervisor's visit, anything that's worrying us. We laugh and chat, Jeremy stays in one place, Janey doesn't tap her nails too much and I keep my fingers out of my nose. Then, once we've had some coffee – real kaffe, freshly roasted and ground – we say goodnight and retire to our rooms. What we do there is strictly private. I don't know what Jeremy or Janey get up to, and I don't want to know. Likewise there's no reason why I should tell anyone what I do in the privacy of my cabin. But we all have screens and we can access the nets, view what we like, talk to whoever we like, without worrying about paying for bandwidth (which is quite limited here, so we're careful) or being watched. We're Monitors, with Monitor's rights and privileges, and we're grownups. We're trusted.

Like the others, my escape is part of my job. Sensors are, by their nature, remote so out of the three of us I have the most regularly used exosuit. After breakfast it's my routine to zip up and go outdoors more or less straight away. That way if there are any problems I'll discover them sooner rather than later and I'll have the rest of the day to sort them out. Just as I said at the start, it's cold – dangerously cold – outside and so I have to take precautions. My feet, for example. They have to be kept warm, or I'll get frostbite. But if the soles of my boots are too warm – more than minus ten, say – they'll melt the ice underneath them and make it slippery, increasing the likelihood that I'll lose my footing and fall. So I have to keep the boots in the lock, put them on cold, turn on my heated socks and cycle out onto the surface as quickly as I can before they heat up too much.

That's the kind of survival trick you learn, and learn fast, up here.

There are literally hundreds of sensors for me to look after. Not all of them every day, of course and, apart from a quick once-over visual inspection and snow-clearing, I probably spend no more than a couple of seconds on each one. It's only when Janey's programs find something anomalous in her data that she asks me to go out and run a specific set of tests. Like, for example, if a thermometer returns unexpectedly high or low figures or one of the scopes apparently discovers a new star or planet. I'll check, and more than likely, I'll find a slightly loose or corroded connector or a speck of dust in an optical system. Of course, sometimes I don't and Janey does some more analysis and correlation on the results and perhaps she finds something new and significant. More often than not, though, it's a malfunction of some kind. After all, if the sensors were infallible there'd be no need for me to be here and I'd never have left home to go and work in Sally's Frozen North.

This morning I was making one of my regular tours of the perimeter; those low hills I mentioned before. Out of the shadows and up to the sunlit heights. That's an exaggeration by the way; the hills rise to no more than one or two hundred feet above ground level, but because the base is in a dip the climb to the top of the first one is higher than that. Once you've reached the top you can walk around the outside of the ridge. If it weren't so improbable given the way the celestial mechanics work around here, you'd think we were sitting in the middle of an ancient meteorite impact crater, like one of Glory's Ringlands.

At the top of each hill is a collection of instruments, housed in an environmental container. An absolute thermometer, a differential mass sensor, a radar pipe, a ranging laser, a 5D strain gauge, a wideband EM listener, bundled together with netcomms gear and a power pack. It's a pretty standard rig and it's replicated all around the base, not just on the hills, to form a sensor grid. Janey's computers can assemble the information from the sensors to build a wide-ranging picture of our environment.

One of the hills is special. It's special because its summit is more or less exactly at the North Pole. The obvious advantage of being situated here at the top of the world is that we get a tremendous view up and out of the orbital plane. The equally obvious disadvantage is that we get a rotten view parallel to it. So because it's so useful to be able to look in any direction you like at any time, both north and south bases are equipped with a powerful optical telescope and because it needs to be able to see over the horizon, it's mounted at the top of a tall mast. Yes, there's a pole at the Pole and if my distant ancestors had come from Eastern Europe (on Old Earth, of course) you'd have been able to say there was a Pole on the pole at the Pole.

As it was, it was only me, and I wasn't going to go up there today, only Janey called to say the scope's PTZ rack had got itself stuck again and could I just pop up the mast and free it, pretty please? Just pop up the mast? Right. The thing is, the mast is a kilometre tall; that's well over three thousand feet. It needs to be that high for the scope to get a decent view. There's a ladder – a set of handholds really – attached to the side, just in case someone might feel like taking a bit of exercise climbing up it. Hmmm. Fortunately, there are also three sets of bracing wires, one at three hundred metres, one at six hundred and fifty and one – thank heavens – attached to the instrument platform at the top. So, rather than getting all sweaty in my suit making that climb it's much easier for me to clip a shackle round a bracing wire, step back, and fire one of my suit's thrusters while I count to three. And zip! The world falls away at a very satisfying fifty feet a second, and if I time it right – and I generally do – my velocity has fallen to zero just as I reach the platform. It takes around three minutes and the view is terrific, especially if you're fond of looking down at low brown hills lightly dusted with solidified CO_2.

This time I got to the top with a metre per second of excess speed and stopped with a bit of a jerk. Not serious, no damage done. Because I'm careful I clipped a fresh shackle to the equipment platform's rail before unclipping the first one from the wire. Why take needless risks? Then I took a look at the scope. There was nothing obviously wrong – the dome was unmarked and the optical access hatch was open, just as it would have been when Janey's systems started making observations a few hours earlier. I'd have to take a closer look, then.

It didn't take long to find the problem. There was nothing wrong with the rack, but the stepper motor that drove it had slipped out of alignment. It's a common fault. I rejigged it, spun the mount a couple of times and checked it for binding. That was fine, so I replaced the dome and the hatch and fastened them back down. I could have left it there, but I've learned that it's always worth looking for incipient faults while you're on the scene. You never know what you might find that'll save you a lot of hassle later on. So I set down next to the scope mount, jacked my AE-35 diagnostic box into it and routed the optical I/F to my face-ups.

Now then... Let's try something straightforward first. Demeter, say. I punched the name of Hally's second moon into the AE-35 and waited a moment while it did a couple of sums. Yes, it decided that Hally was visible, but not in transit. Now, where was Demeter? Sunside of Hally? Yes, so what were the necessary pan and tilt settings? Got that. Right, let's go; and with a dizzying swoop – perhaps I should have delayed turning on the face-ups – the scope swung silently around on its bearings and pointed itself towards the heart of the system. Once locked on, it zoomed in on the little world like a man diving to his death. And there it was – a half-moon, airless, speckled with craters, clear and sharp in the adaptive optics. I smiled. Demeter was a dull place and far too hot to live on, but a good preliminary test of the scope all the same.

Good. What next? Oh yes – let's try the atmosphere penetrators. Give me... give me a land near Glory's terminator. What's visible? Right, okay, Bright's the word. Oh, and turn the video feed off this time until you're there. Again the soundless rotation of the scope on its mount and suddenly my eyes were filled with blue. Dark blue below, pale blue above and a fuzzy area in between. That was Glory all right, but where was Bright? Damn, what about the adaptives and the penetrators? Would I have to strip the scope right down after all?

And then as the secondary integrators kicked in the picture on the inside of my helmet suddenly leapt into detailed focus. I gasped. There were the Cliffs of Grieving, tall and dark-sided in a low tide, capped with green and shimmering in a slight haze that faded as the

AE-35 got the measure of Glory's air currents. Zoom in... there were settlements at the top of the cliffs, weren't there? Closer, closer, until it felt as if I, from my seat at the top of the mast, could read the inscriptions on the memorials in Imogen's Garden and look straight into the windows of the cliff-top houses. I could pan over the fields, watch the birds singing silently in the trees, see the fish surfacing in the lakes.

I locked the scope and the picture stabilised still further. The AE-35 continued tracking the motions of the planets; Glory's rotation and this world's orbital path and spin, giving me a perfectly steady view. I was sitting on top of one world gazing into the heart of a land on another. I sat as one hypnotised, entranced, ensorcelled; transfixed by beauty. I never noticed when the Blessèd sun's terminator passed over the land of Bright, casting it into darkness, nor did I pay much attention or feel any fear when my suit's O_2 alarm went off. I had passed on to another world, you might say, and there seemed to be no particular reason why I should ever return.

Skimmer

THERE WAS A TERRIFIC FUSS ABOUT IT, OF COURSE. JANEY SHOUTED IN my phones to get the hell out of there and get my sorry arse back indoors as soon as, while Jeremy suited up, cycled himself through the airlock and bounded across Sally's dusty ground up the hills towards the Pole. Meanwhile I tore myself away from the scope, shook my head to clear it, attached a line to the bracing wire and jumped off the instrument platform with gay abandon. I was in a hurry.

'Jon, you idiot!' shouted Janey. 'Fire your thrusters! You'll crash!'

That was a good idea, so I fired my thrusters. It would have been better if I'd been pointing upwards when I did it. I hit the ground at ten metres a second. It hurt. It would have hurt a lot more if my suit hadn't noticed how fast the surface was approaching and inflated its airbags, but it still jarred me pretty badly. I lay there stunned while the bags deflated around me with an inaudible hiss and waited for Jeremy to reach me.

'What the hell did you think you were doing?' he said as he helped me to my feet and put my arm around his shoulder.

'Watching. Observing.'

'For four hours?'

'How long?'

'Four hours. You ran your suit out of O_2, you were there so long.'

'Oh. Ah.'

Back in the base I desuited. 'Let me look at that,' Jeremy said, taking the suit away from me. 'I'll need to check it over and replace the bags.'

'Thanks. Can you get me a spare from the stores? I'll need to get out again. Finish my inspection.'

'Not just yet.' Janey appeared in my doorway. 'You've had a shock. Take a rest. Have something to eat. Watch a film.'

'No... there's stuff I need to do. I've not finished checking the sensors.'

'It can wait. Now, lie down.' And, without my having a chance to do anything about it, she shot a hypo into my left arm and I folded up.

I must have slept the clock around. That's Glory time, of course. We try to stick to it here on Sally, even though it has nothing to do with the rising and setting of the Blessèd sun on this little world. Glory's day is a bit longer than the Lost Earth's, and her twenty-five hour cycle has been hardwired into our DNA, so we stick to it. I woke with a buzzy head, but a shower and a brisk air-dry dealt with that. Coffee and a muffin were what I wanted; that and an apple, so I put on jeans, socks and tee and wandered into the galley. I got them all right – our stores were always full – but I got something else as well.

Jeremy and Janey were waiting for me at the table. 'Hi,' I said. 'Fancy some coffee? I'll get it for you.'

'Sit down, Jonathan.'

Janey looked stern. There's not supposed to be a hierarchy here – we don't have ranks and all that and there's no commander as such; but all the same Janey was in charge. I had no idea how it had happened, but it had. By whatever means, her willingness to take on responsibility, our willingness to let her, laziness, fate, her access to the nets, she had somehow become the senior member of our crew. So I sat down.

'You're feeling better.' It was a statement, not a question, but I answered it just the same.

'Yes, thanks.'

'You had us pretty worried back there.'

I nodded. 'It was a close call.'

'Too close.'

'It won't happen again.'

'What were you doing?'

'I was... I was... looking at Glory. The land of Bright, to be precise.'

'I know.' Of course she did. She had screens. Jeremy anticipated my next question.

'There was nothing wrong with your suit, Jonathan. You just stayed out too long.'

'I'm not blaming you, Jeremy.'

'Nobody's blaming anyone.'

Silence fell. I knew there was a word hanging in the air. The gravity on Sally is so light that words can float for ages, suspended like dust.

'But.'

'But this isn't the first time, is it?'

'Er...'

It wasn't. I hadn't actually put my life at risk before, or anyone else's, but I had been late on duty quite a few times and I had clocked up a lot of screen time staring at images of my home world. Surely that was only natural? And what was Janey doing monitoring me?

'I've had a chat with the equator and they think you could do with a change.'

'No, no. I'm fine.'

'You will be, Jon.' I turned to the entrance. There was a new face in the room.

'Jorge! How... nice... to see you.'

The skimmer that had brought Jorge Cavanaugh to the base was waiting for me outside. Personal possessions aren't something we go in for in a big way up here so it took me, oh, all of five minutes to pack all my stuff and transfer through the access pipe to its cabin. It set off and, hey, less than thirty minutes had passed since I'd woken up. I was still eating my apple.

Skimmer travel is fun for the first hour or two; then it gets monotonous. There's no human pilot, just a local brain with the *Sweetheart* as backup. You really don't want to have to rely on that as the average flying height of a skimmer is less than a couple of hundred feet from ground level, rising and falling with the underlying terrain. That's what makes it fun – the feeling of sticking to the bones of the land, the slight sense of danger, the rush of adrenaline. Earthers would have called it a rollercoaster ride. I've seen them in old films.

If the *Sweetheart* took over control of the skimmer it would have to slow right down to allow for comms lag and the transfer would take forever. I trusted the brain – after all it belonged to the same family as the intelligence in my suit and that had done a pretty good job of saving my neck at the pole. I sat back, gnawed my apple and enjoyed the ride as Sally's rusty landscape sped by at a couple of thousand kay pee aitch.

It was becoming obvious I had seriously screwed up and I wondered if Jeremy and Janey had had secret conversations about me over a private link:

I'm worried about Jonathan.

Me too.

I think he's losing touch.

Me too.

It was too late to worry about it now. I had enough nous to realise that however good a case I put to the authorities at the equator and however indispensible my skills I wouldn't be going to either pole again. Not in the next year or two, anyway. So I sat back and enjoyed the ride.

Skimmers are constructed the way most things are up here. Spartan, in other words, with exposed metal and plastic where it doesn't matter and soft cushioning where it does. So although the cabin lacked decorative refinement, it did feature four seriously comfortable reclining seats, a compact but fully functional head, a respectable stock of food, a media library and a minibar. The trip from the pole to the equator would take eight hours and I had already slept for twenty four hours. I had the choice between watching eight hours of vintage TV or getting plastered.

So I chose both, and somewhere between episodes four and five of *Hot Reach* and my fifth or sixth rum punch I reached the stage where I stopped worrying about what I would do next. The horizon rose and fell in front of me, the skimmer banked left, then right as it sought the passes that led the way south through the ranges of the temperate belt, the seat moulded itself to my body and enfolded me in its comfortable embrace. Behind us rose a trail of plasma, ejected from the drive motor at near lightspeed, below us the bones of the billion-year dead creatures that had once roamed Sally's long-gone seas and rivers were briefly disturbed by the skimmer's lifters.

They practically had to carry me off the vehicle when it finally docked at the equator.

Choice

N OBODY DOUBTS YOUR COMMITMENT, JONATHAN. NOBODY AT ALL. More coffee?' Heather Smythe pointed to the side-table, where a small dispenser steamed quietly. As head of human resources she got privileges – a private office with two chairs, an outside view and her very own coffee machine.

'Thank you, no. Would you excuse me a moment?'

'Of course. Take as long as you like.'

I stood up and walked over to the window. The pockmarked surface of equatorial Sally, brilliantly lit by the midday Blessèd sun, met the deep black of the sky at the horizon. The land or the sky? It seemed I had to make a choice – one as abrupt as that distant division between light and darkness.

But not yet. I turned around and leaned over the front of Heather's desk. 'Can I come back and talk to you again tomorrow?'

'It's just as I said. Take as long as you like.'

I probably wasn't meant to go outside on my own any more, but I did anyway. It was not as if I had much to do, whereas it seemed that everyone else at the equator was fully occupied. So nobody paid much attention when I put on my suit, exited the air lock and picked up a mobile. I was half-expecting it to be blocked to me, but the board lit up normally when I slid in my key and the brain asked me where I wanted to go the same way it usually did. Nor did it argue when I asked it for manual control.

There's a road that leads from the surface egress ports and circles the base, and from it some rough tracks go to the commonly used places that are positioned a ways off from it, like the launcher, the mine, the antenna complex and the landing strip. The wheels on a mobile are so big and its brain is so clever that the ride is much smoother than you might expect, even when you take the controls yourself. I circled the base twice and then chose, almost at random, the road that led to the launcher.

The mobile bounced and swerved across the flaky surface, but I didn't mind that. It felt more real than yesterday's smooth, nausea-inducing swooping flight across Sally's undulating latitudes. More grounded. Sally's mobiles are ballasted and carefully sprung to assist traction and reduce discomfort in the low gravity of Glory's sister world and the brain does what it can to help. Even so, I'd had enough bouncing and jouncing by the time I reached the first ring of the launcher's accelerator. I got out of the vehicle and looked around me.

The view of Sally's surface varies little, wherever you are. The same uniform dusty brown of the ground, the same near-black of the sky. The main differences between the bases at the equator and the pole are the light of the Blessèd sun which rides high in the sky at midday and rises and sets at the beginning and end of Sally's short day, and the high silver arch of the launcher's primary loop. I stood at its foot and looked around.

There was the mobile, still venting heat, there was the launcher's power stand, there was the road back to the base with a slight haze of dust still hanging over it, and there was the base – or rather its top levels – with its antennas and dishes fixed to its roof. Of course, most of the base was underground. Everything was lightly tinted with the predominant red-brown colour of Sally, either by reflection or because a film had built up on it over time. I looked up. Yes, even the launcher was ever-so-slightly discoloured.

I looked up... and there, to the right of the Blessèd sun, was

Glory, blue and white, a beautiful streaked sapphire hovering in the sky, huge against the surrounding darkness. And there, on the other side of the sky, amber-gold Hally, glowing with lambent energy. Both worlds alive and full of thrilling possibilities. And... Sally. Dead, except for the human presence, her seas long ago stolen from her by Glory's gravitation, robbed of her future. Important still; not only historically for her role in the coming of humanity to the system of the Blessèd sun but also for her continuing significance as the primary safe haven of the Guardians of Glory.

I was a Guardian too, but I was not a native of Sally. Only a very few were. I scanned the horizon again and saw desolation. I looked skywards and saw life. And then my decision was not a decision at all, but a foregone conclusion.

Acceleration

I SPENT MY LAST EVENING ON SALLY TOURING THE BARS OF THE Atrium Centre. That was nice, wasn't it? Me, a Guardian and a Monitor, going out on a drunk when there was plenty of Guarding and Monitoring to be done. Irresponsible to the nth degree. Sloppy. Well, phooey. The Smythe had given me twenty four hours leave before my Launching and I was damn well going to make the most of them.

"The Atrium Centre". That sounds like quite the pleasure dome, doesn't it? It probably makes you think of the commercial quarter of Tanly on Edge, a place where deals are done and fortunes are made. Or perhaps a shiny new development somewhere in the Archipelago, built of faux marble and artificial chrome. What it actually consisted of was a couple of long dark rooms tunnelled into Sally's bedrock and opening out into an underground circular space a hundred feet or so in diameter which was illuminated during daytime by the light of the Blessèd sun channelled and reflected from the world's surface by a collection of mirrors and lightguides. At night it was lit by tubes, just like the rest of the base.

Apart from its bars the Centre boasted a few shops, a choice of refectories, and a gym, where we Sallians were expected to spend at least one hour in twenty-four keeping our muscles in tone ready for our return to Glory. Normally you were given reasonable advance notice of this and got a chance to build yourself up gradually and without too much pain. Me, I was on the fast track and just come off an intensive six-hour course of drugs and exercise. I needed a drink. A strong one.

I started in the Liquid Lensman, whose main appeal was to fans of straight lines and strong colours. Sharp edges to the tables, then, purple, silver and orange walls and a perfectly dressed barman who greeted me with a wide smile.

'Johnny! S'wonderful to see you! What's your pleasure? Pangalactic gargle —'

'Whiskey, Greg. Make it a treble.'

'Ooh. Ahh. It's serious, is it?'

'I guess. I'm launching tomorrow.'

'Gosh. You'll be needing something extra-special, then.' And Gregory Simmonds, whose day job was in biochemistry, reached under the bar and pulled out a bottle of Glenmorangie. He poured me three thick golden fingers.

'Is that real...?'

'Earth Scotch? No, old fellow, I'm afraid not. But you'll never know the difference. Your health!'

I sipped the spirit slowly. It was sweet-salty-earthy-fiery and infinitely smooth on my palate. 'And one for you, good barperson.'

'Thank you.'

At some stage in the evening I said goodbye to Greg and crossed the atrium to finish off in the Centre's other bar, the Raygun and Helmet. If the Lensman had been a good place to start a drunk, this was a better place to finish it. The ceilings were low and stained a peculiar yellow, the walls were covered with a confused array of pictures – scenes of the Lost Earth, of course, but also of Glory – and the chairs, tables, floor and bar were made of something which may well have been real wood. It was cosy, inviting and not too busy. I switched from shorts to beer in the hope that it would dilute the nature-identical spirit that was swilling about in my insides and, I still don't know how, managed to cop off with Glenys the barmaid ('Hello love!'), who I was sure ran IT services during the daytime.

* * * *

It wasn't the worst hangover I've ever had, but my insides were still churning when I took my place on the launching platform at 07:59 the following morning. I'd been chased out of Glenys's bedroom an hour and a half earlier, held under the shower until I'd had enough, been dosed up with Dramamine against the stresses to come and finally locked into an acceleration suit and ferried out to the launcher. Heather Smythe's voice, coarsened by the phones, sounded in my ears.

'Now Jonathan, just relax and take it easy. Are all your lights green?'

'Yes, Heather.' Of course they were, and she knew it from her telemetry. She was just trying to give me something to do to occupy my last few seconds on Sally.

'Right. I'll turn your suit on.' There was a hum and click and my acceleration suit, which until that point had been like a regular exosuit, only heavier, became rigid. At the same time a membrane expanded inside, wrapping itself snugly around me, limiting my freedom to move and compressing my still unsettled stomach further. I belched vigorously, and that seemed to help a bit.

'Ready?'

'As ready as I'll ever be.' Was my apprehension showing in my voice?

'Just one more thing, then.' There was a hiss, and a concealed hypo shot some CCs into my upper arm. Ah. Perhaps she had detected something. That would be the joy-juice they kept in reserve for the more nervous travellers.

'Here we go then. Hold tight!'

Hold tight to what? I braced myself, pointless though that was. And then like a ghost, with no noise, vibration or harshness, almost gently in fact, a great hand, wearing a soft catcher's mitt, pressed against my back. I was instantly lifted from my feet and projected from the middle of the first launcher ring. The nut-brown landscape of Sally rushed backwards at ever-increasing speed as I shot through the second, then the third, fourth and fifth rings of the launcher at what I estimated to be a steady seven gravities.

I was going too fast to register the presence of the last three rings. Sally fell away rapidly beneath me and I briefly heard the spectral hiss of Sally's attenuated atmosphere rushing past my limbs as I gained height. I say that, but what was actually happening, of course, was that my trajectory was almost a straight line, whereas Sally's ground was curved. My suit rotated slowly as I sped upwards and I caught a few interrupted views of the base before it fell out of sight below the edge of the world.

Higher, higher, until not just the landscape but the whole world became visible. I checked my chrono. Five minutes since my launch and already Sally was a sphere, not a plane. I was on the path to Glory.

Orbit

TO SWIM AMONG THE STARS, UNENCUMBERED BY THE GROSS necessities of matter; that had been my dream when I was a boy. Nothing between my body and the radiations and currents of the cosmos, bathing in the unfiltered light of the Blessèd sun, my course determined by a simple kick of the legs or a reach of the hands. An eternal high-dive into infinite space, a plunge into the limitless depths of the universe...

As my suit and I fell away from the feeble gravity of Sally and entered their transfer orbit to Glory I felt at least a trace of those emotions and sensations that had so bewitched me in my childhood dreams. It seemed as if I were flying free once more, although the light pressure of the suit's ion drive and the occasional burp from the correctional jets rather spoiled the illusion, not to mention the continual hiss and gurgle of the life-systems. But I could twist around and see the rapidly receding dirty football of Sally behind me and, if I lined myself up carefully, possibly even a glimpse of the *Sweetheart* in her low orbit. It was she who was managing my trajectory, not me nor even the suit's brain. Sometime or somewhere between the circle of Sally and the orbit of Glory the *Sweetheart* would hand over control to the 'Down and the mothership would look after me for the final part of my flight. In the meantime, I could do as I liked; insofar as you can do what you like when you're encased in a suit.

The first astronauts discovered it: space, when it's not scaring the whatsits out of you, is kind of boring. The hours pass and nothing changes much. Or, at least, you hope it doesn't. Rapid change and unexpected events are not what you want when you're millions of miles from the nearest help. So, although the view is beautiful and entrancing and the zero gravity of the interplanetary vacuum is liberating, it becomes less entrancing and liberating as the hours pass and turn into days. A certain ennui starts to set in.

There are remedies for this, of course. Some travellers meditate on the One and its Meaning. Some take a dose of forget-it and sleep through the trip. Others turn on the suit's entertainment systems and watch old films or listen to music. And one or two have been known to smuggle a bottle of something nice on board and get out of their heads on that. There are even rumours of special access codes that turn on some normally inaccessible servo-mechanisms for the amusement of the suit's occupant. I know nothing of them, naturally.

The crossing between the orbits of Sally and Glory takes anything between three days and several months if you're following a ballistic trajectory, as I was if you discount the low-g thrust of the suit's ion drive. In this case the alignment of the worlds meant that I was in for a ten-day trip, which is about average. Nobody takes the long, long drop unless they really, really have to. I passed the time with a mixture of drug-assisted sleep, the films of Azio Missanelli, the music of Bernard Herrmann and reading some stories the suit downloaded from the *Sweetheart*'s library. Oh, and I still had most of that bottle of Glen.

The days and nights passed, the suit talked to me from time to time to make sure I was still approximately sane, the main theme from *Taxi Driver* throbbed through my phones. It was a strange kind of semi-existence, and I began to get increasing tired of it as it went along. The suit noticed this, I'm sure, because after the first five days or so of the trip it all became something of a blur. I think I was probably running on a mixture of glucose, vitamins, protein and joy-juice for most of the latter part of my journey. The suit spoke in its thin, breathy voice, telling me the latest news of the worlds, keeping me up to date with the progress of my trip, reassuring me that everything was going to plan, my BMs were satisfactorily regular, we were all right and would I like some oxtail soup now?

'Shut up, suit. Put a sock in it.'

'My only regard is for your well-being, Jonathan. I'm not upset by your negative attitude, you know. I can't be offended.'

'Shame.' I felt like offending someone, although you couldn't call the suit a someone, could you? We were never exactly going to be friends, after all.

The time passed variably and my mood swung between elation and boredom, depending on whether I was relishing my liberty or chafing under the restrictions of the suit's benevolent care. To avoid the slightest possibility of my being blinded by the direct light of the Blessèd sun, the suit kept me facing outwards towards Sally and the parsec-distant stars, so that it was not until I was quite close to Glory that I actually caught sight of my destination. But with only a few hours to go until landfall I was allowed to rotate myself so that I was no longer going arse-backwards into the future. And I saw…

Glory! Not scanned through a scope or a screen, not image-enhanced by clever 'ware, not artificially coloured, clarified or boosted, but the world of Glory herself, seen with the naked eye from a distance of less than ten thousand miles, a gorgeous cerulean orb, streaked with spiral white clouds. The atmosphere blurred the horizon with a fuzzy edge, the view ahead was clear all the way down to the ocean. I imagined I could see the crests of breaking waves, or the swell of Glory's mighty tides as they surged around the world in their endless circumnavigations. I mused; and perhaps floated away from the land, lost in my vision. My birth-world ached in my memory.

* * * *

'Hello, Jonathan.'

A different voice; high, distant and pure, where the suit's had been low and confidential. I recognised it immediately.

"Down? 'Down? Is that you?'

'Welcome to Glory, intrepid space traveller.'

Hmmm. I sat up and paid attention, if you see what I mean. I was talking to the boss. The suit's brain contained a few trillion cells, no more. It was just about bright enough to do its job. The *Sweetheart* was clever, though unimaginative. But the 'Down! She was something else. Nobody had ever discovered the limits to her intelligence. You were supposed to address her with a certain respect, not to say awe. You shouldn't be rude to her, they said. No, no. She was not only supremely intelligent, she was also known for her quirky and occasionally cruel sense of humour. We Monitors knew this all too well.

'It's very nice of you to greet me like this.'

'My pleasure. And look!'

The suit rolled over. I saw space, lots of it, black and sparkly, and the blue arc of Glory's horizon.

'Look at what?'

'Forward a little… Up a bit…'

Ah. It was the 'Down herself, lit on one side by the Blessèd sun, on the other by the blue-green reflection of Glory.

'Cara mia! You're looking good.'

'Thank you.'

'New spars?'

'You noticed!'

'And you've extended your mainmasts again.'

'They give me a certain stature, I think.'

'I'm not sure about that skull and crossbones you're flying, though. Have you turned pirate?'

'Not at all, but I've a friend who's a buccaneer. It's in her honour.'

'You need all the friends you can get, eh?'

'Cheeky sod! Now listen, has the suit told you your approach plan?'

'No.' Good grief. Why the heck hadn't I asked it? Perhaps the doses had been stronger than I thought, or the Glen higher proof.

'Well, you're going straight in.'

Gulp. 'Straight in? What do you mean, straight in? What about the shuttle?'

'No need.'

Silly ship! She was winding me up. Of course there was a shuttlecraft waiting to ferry me down to the surface of Glory. How else was I expected to land? I sighed. Oh well, I might as well play along with her little game.

'Can't I stop with you a while, my love? Play some chess? Catch up on les temps perdus?'

'Sorry, Johnny. Not this time.'

'What a mean old ship you are.'

'Don't say that. We've been such chums.'

The 'Down receded into the distance, above and behind me. I felt a momentary frisson of alarm.

''Down! 'Down! You still there?'

'Yes?'

'All right. Very funny. Hilarious ship. Much applause, well deserved. Now reel me in, won't you?'

'There's no need, Jonathan, just as I said.'

'But... but...' I spluttered. 'I'm falling into Glory! I'll die!'

'There's always that risk.'

'No, what I mean is, if you don't stop me entering the atmosphere at whatever speed —'

'Eighteen thousand, three hundred and forty-two miles per hour.'

' —I'm doing, I'll leave a meteor trail they'll see from Horn to Scrape and my incandescent remains will make the hottest, most vaporous splash you ever did see. I think I'll unlatch my suit now and get it over with.'

'Relax! Don't do it. You'll be fine.'

The ship passed out of sight. My suit rotated itself until I was facing backwards once more and to my ineffable horror I saw the first wispy tendrils of red-blue plasma passing to either side of me and felt the first push of deceleration against my back. I was entering Glory's atmosphere naked and unprotected and the 'Down had completely abandoned me. This was no joke.

Panic enveloped me and squeezed me harder than the suit ever could and I closed my eyes in sheer terror. 'No! No! No!' I screamed at eighteen thousand, three hundred and forty-two miles per hour.

Suit

I SCREAMED AND SCREAMED... AND THEN THERE WAS NO POINT IN screaming any more. Either I was dead, in which case it was all over and done with, or I was alive and the suit was still looking after me. I opened my eyes.

The blackness of space had softened to a navy blue. Above and behind me my ripped-atom ion trail was dissipating into feathery traces, and the terrible pressure of deceleration had become no more than a gentle buffeting.

'Can I see the ground, please?'

'Sorry,' said the suit. 'Our aerodynamic integrity requires the continuance of your current attitude for a further sixty-five seconds.'

Oh, all right. Be like that. So much for the monkey. What about the organ-grinder?

''Down? 'Down?'

No answer. Bah. I'd have stern words with her later. Kick her up the arse. Ship – stern – arse. Funny, eh?

Oh, all right. Have it your own way.

Sixty-six seconds later the suit turned itself over and let me see where I was going. It also allowed me to stretch my arms out to either side and wave them around as if they were wings. Now I was fairly sure that neither the suit nor the ship intended to kill me I was beginning to enjoy myself. My fear had faded, driven away by the sheer exhilaration of soaring through Glory's upper airs, and had been replaced by a mild euphoria.

'Wheee!' I shouted as I turned somersaults and looped the loop. I was losing speed rapidly, if the suit's readout was to be believed.

'Hey, suit, this is fun!'

'I'm glad you're enjoying yourself, Jonathan.'

'I'm glad you're glad.'

We were both on drugs, or so it seemed. What was coming next? 'Where are we landing, suit?'

'Don't worry about that.'

Hmmm. Why not? Let's change the subject. 'I never knew you were equipped for re-entry. Do you have an ablative layer on your outer skin?'

'No. I'm simply very well insulated.'

'So all those impressive flames and stuff were just plasma. Burned air, in other words.'

'Yes, pretty much.'

'They must have seen us over half of Glory.'

'We didn't pass over any inhabited lands.'

'Really?'

'Really. The 'Down made sure of that.'

'Clever old 'Down! Remind me to congratulate her next time we chat.'

'If I can, I will.'

'Thank you. How high are we now, by the way?'

'Twenty-five thousand feet.'

'Fine. So we must be getting pretty close to a land. Wouldn't want to end up in the sea, would we? I don't want to become foy bait, and I don't suppose you do, either.'

'No, that would be most inconvenient.'

'That's one way of putting it.'

'Inconvenient for the foy, I mean.'

I bet.

'So, we're approaching land, are we?'

'No.'

'What? Suit, are you messing with me?'

'Not at all. I have enjoyed your company very much and I look forward to travelling with you again in the future. But for now I must wish you *au reservoir*.'

'Oh what?'

'Cheerio, Jonathan. Happy landings.'

And with no further words the suit opened up its front seam and folded back on itself, ejecting me into the open skies of Glory.

The first thing I noticed was the freshness of the air. Pure and clean, with a slight overtone of salt. I had been breathing canned, recycled and Jonathan-scented air for so long... Then the terror kicked in and I curled myself up into a ball and screamed once more.

I soared across the sky like a loose cannonball, the wind tearing at my face and the one-piece jumpsuit I wore next to my skin. Above me a whooshing roar announced that the suit had lit some kind of heavy-duty propulsion system – a fusion-powered ramjet, say – and was heading back out of Glory's atmosphere at a rapidly increasing speed. Sanctimonious git. I hoped it missed its trajectory and ended up in the Blessèd sun. Bastard.

This screaming was getting to be a bad habit, so I stopped doing it. Although I was crapping myself with fear, I still couldn't quite believe the 'Down or the suit – or anyone else for that matter – actually wanted to kill me. And if they did, why here and now? I could have had an accident anywhere at any time. Why make it so complicated? Why fly me all the way from Sally to Glory just to ditch me in the sea when the suit could have pretended to spring a leak or the launcher could have stuck? So I closed my mouth, opened my eyes and stretched my arms and legs out again like a bird. Actually, I had lost nearly all my forward speed by now, so the bird analogy wasn't all that valid. Stone was nearer to the truth and one that was falling fast at that. I guessed I had no more than a minute or two before I hit the ocean, at which point I would die. The impact would kill me long before any inquisitive foy could find me and eat me up.

Did my personal history flash before my eyes in those last seconds? No, of course it didn't. I felt a little bit sorry for myself – all those classic books unwritten, all those monumental symphonies nobody would hear, those vivid paintings no one would see – but as for the record of my life… Best not gone over again, don't you think? And anyway, I still clung on, as we do even when fate seems to have signed our biography on the dotted line and be preparing to shelve it for the very last time.

And even so, it was with no great sense of surprise that I saw a group of globular shapes coming up at me from below and felt the breath forced from my body by the mono net that caught me no more than a few hundred feet above the surface of the ocean. See! I told you it'd be all right, my smug inner self told me. They wouldn't abandon you like that. They like you far too much!

Shut the plague up, I told it, even as I passed out.

'Wake up, Jonathan.'

I opened my eyes. I was lying on a narrow couch in a dimly-lit room. There was a gentle hum and a slight rushing sound. A face hovered over mine.

'How do you feel?'

I considered. 'Rather bashed around.'

'Let's have a look at you, then. Roll over for me, would you?'

I complied. Presumably I was in a hospital and this person was a doctor. The place certainly smelled like a hospital – that mixture of human odours, antiseptic and masking scent was unmistakeable. Hands poked and prodded my back.

'Sit up, please.' I did, carefully. 'Say ah.'

'Ahh.'

'Look up... down... left... right... Fine. You'll do.'

I stood up. Glory's gravity tugged at me and the floor vibrated and moved between my feet. I grabbed hold of the bed. 'Oops. I'm not too steady. Things seem to be moving around. Are you sure I'm okay, Doctor...?'

'Powell. I'm Doctor Cameron Powell. And the floor's shifting because we're not on land. Welcome aboard the LAV *El Dorado*. Say, why don't we pop down to the bridge? Hold on to me here. That's it. We'll have a chat with the captain. I'm sure he'll answer all your questions much better than I can.'

So I was all at sea, in more senses than one. I wanted answers – good ones, preferably – but was I going to get them?

Wayfarers

I FOLLOWED DOCTOR POWELL DOWN A NARROW PASSAGEWAY, PAST A number of closed and sealed doors. He walked slowly, but even so I found it hard to keep up with him and, as I reached the end of the corridor, my left leg gave way under me and I fell with a heavy crash.

'Providence!' Doctor Powell turned, dropped to his knees and put his arms under mine. I struggled to my feet.

'Sorry, doc,' I said. 'I'm still a teensy bit unstable.'

Doctor Powell smiled ruefully. 'No, no, my fault entirely. I should have known you'd need more time to acclimatise. Would you like to go back to the infirmary and rest a while longer?'

'No, thanks. I've travelled millions of miles to get here. I'm not going to stop now when there're only a few feet left to go. I'm here to see Glory and that's what I'm damn well going to do. Lead on!'

I reached the top of the spiral stairs that led down to the bridge of the *El Dorado* in one piece. Now all I had to do was get down it in the same happy state. Then perhaps they'd give me a drink.

I got to the bottom eventually. Doctor Powell helped me through the little lobby that opened out onto the bridge and guided me to a chair. I sat down heavily and opened my eyes. And there she was. Glory – at last.

We were flying at about five thousand feet, more or less due east, and the Blessèd sun was high in the heavens to our right, or starboard as the airmen say. There must have been a fair breeze at sea level, for the waves – even as seen from this altitude – were foam-topped and glittering silver in the light. The endless, eternal, deadly seas of Glory... Despite my heaviness I got to my feet and staggered to the forward-facing window in front of me. I wanted to immerse myself in this world's blue-green-white splendour. The view wrapped itself around me and I sighed for simple happiness. I had been too long in a suit, or behind vacuum glass. I had breathed too much recycled oxygen. I had seen too much brown dust and sterile desolation. Glory had life in abundance, fresh air and limitless panoramas, and the only brick-red to be seen was in pictures, or the walls of houses. Houses with outdoor gardens leading down to fields of crops – yellow-gold and green, waving in a stream of living air. And always, only a few tens of miles away at the very most, the vast oceans of this world of water.

My breath misted on the glass and obscured the view. I turned and gingerly, reluctantly, holding on to rails and grab-holds, returned to my seat. The view was less spectacular from there, but safer. I would see very little of the world if I broke a leg now and had to spend the next few weeks in plaster. The captain – I recognised him by the four golden braided rings on his sleeve – came up to me and leaned over the side of the chair.

'Welcome back to Glory, Monitor. I am Captain Probert and my ship is the LAV *El Dorado*.'

'Thank you, Captain. I'm very happy to be home. Do you have a moment to spare? There are one or two things I need to know.'

'Certainly, Monitor.'

'When I fell from orbit, and you caught me – what happened? How did you know where I was? Was it a net that stopped my fall? What kept it up?'

'Well, firstly, the 'Down told us where you were.' Captain Probert cupped his left hand in a small gesture – one that I had seen before. 'She knew your trajectory, to within very tight limits.'

'She's a clever old thing, isn't she?'

The captain frowned slightly. 'Yes; she is very holy and very wise.

Anyway, we knew where you were going, so we made a minor course correction.'

'The Down steered me towards you?'

'Of course.'

'And the net?'

'Was held up by our friends the aeroforms.'

'The 'forms?' I gasped. I had never heard of people using Glory's native flying creatures in such a way. In fact, I'd never heard of them working with humans at all. I thought they avoided us as much as they could. Doctor Powell joined the conversation:

'It's mostly down to me, actually. I've got what you might call a special interest in the aeroforms.'

'He'll tell you all about it if you ask.'

'Yes, I will. Later?'

'Surely, Doctor. Meanwhile,' I said to the captain, 'is it okay if I stay here?'

'Yes, of course. Is there anything else I can help you with?'

'No, Captain, I mustn't take you away from your duties. Just one more thing – no, two.'

'Go ahead.'

'The first is – where are we going?'

'And the second?'

'Could a steward bring me a drink?'

The captain laughed. 'Pineapple juice only on the bridge. Board Rules, you know.'

'Oh. All right. Thank you.'

'And as for our destination... It's somewhere special. Somewhere I think you'll find very interesting.'

'You're teasing me! Please, Captain Probert.' I didn't add – because I didn't have to – that I could always ask the 'Down, using a screen, if he didn't tell me where we were going. Screen access was a Monitor's absolute right.

The captain looked at Doctor Powell, who nodded.

'Very well. Our next port of call is Lodge-in-the-Falls. But you're staying with the *El Dorado* until we reach the Island.'

'Where?' I'd never heard of a place called the Island.

'I'll tell you later,' said the doctor. 'It's a long story, and best told when we reach land. I know a drinking hole or two that I think you'll like.'

'It started,' said Doctor Powell, putting down his glass, 'when I woke up one morning on the ship to find I was the only person aboard. I had been cast adrift; me and the *El Dorado*. I know now that I wasn't expected to be on the ship. It was believed that the vessel was completely unmanned and a there was a lot of discussion about me when my... inconvenient existence became apparent. It was a toss-up whether I was going to be allowed to live or die.'

'A discussion? Who was involved?'

'That will become clear, I think, as I go along.'

'So are you saying the *El Dorado* was guided all the time you were with her? Not drifting, as you'd thought?'

'More or less. While I was awake the 'Down let the ship go where she willed. But while I slept, she adjusted the *El Dorado*'s course.'

'Why did she care whether you knew or not? I mean; the 'Down does pretty much as she wants. If she thought she needed to intervene, she would. You know that.'

'Yes, Monitor. Oh, and by the way, you do know about the captain, don't you?'

'I saw him make the Gesture, yes.'

'Good. Then you'll have the good sense to keep any criticisms you may have of the 'Down and her funny ways to yourself; or in the right company, won't you?'

'I have my rights as a Monitor, you know.'

'I know that. You know that. The Board knows that. But the captain's in absolute charge here. He's an airman; and airmen do what they have to do right here and right now to preserve their ships and their crews. They tend to act in their immediate interests first and worry about the long-term consequences later. You might win an appeal against the captain if he decided to brig you; but that'd be in a year's time. You don't really want that to happen, do you?'

'He couldn't do that! The 'Down'd stop him.'

'Only if she knew about it.'

'Ah. All right. So he's a raving Cultist and I'd better humour him. But all I can say is this – if he were in regular communication with the 'Down, like me; if he had Monitor-level experience of the 'Down and her idiosyncrasies he'd be less inclined to regard her as some kind of super-being. She may be bright, she may be powerful; but she has her little foibles, just like you and me. You have to get pretty near to her to discover that.'

I leaned closer to the doctor. 'She may be the Guardian of humanity; but she's not the only one. I'm a Guardian too. Every Monitor is. You're a Guardian. Every doctor is. Every ship's captain is, for all that. We have to work together for Glory's sake, and making a god out of one of us – because that's all she is, really, just one of us – is doing nobody any favours.'

'All the same, Jonathan—'

'All the same, I'll be tactful.'

'Thank you.'

'So go on. The 'Down guided the *El Dorado* without you knowing about it and eventually she hit a land. Was this land the Island you mentioned earlier?'

'Yes; and you'd better keep your voice down when you use that name in public.'

Was there anything I could say or do without causing trouble? I looked up. The bar was nearly deserted and hardly public. Never mind – I wouldn't argue the point. 'I hear you, doctor. Now; another drink?' The doctor nodded and I signalled for two more beers. He took a sip and continued:

'After the ship struck the land and I wasn't killed by the impact the question of what to do with me still remained. The arguments carried on while I did my best to make a home on the land and, even after the *El Dorado* was freed and taken off to be refurbished and repaired, I was still there, scraping along. If it hadn't been for something that happened I might have just faded away – starved to death.'

'That would have been a cruel way to end.'

'But a passive one. I mean, nobody would have killed me, not as such. No gun to my head, no poison in my food, you know? But instead, I had an encounter with an aeroform – a pair of aeroforms, actually – and that changed everything.'

'Look!'

'Look where?'

'Over there.' Cameron Powell took hold of my left arm and wrenched it over to the right. 'There. Where you're pointing. See?'

'Ouch! Yes, all right. You can let go of me now. I can see them.'

Aeroforms. I might have guessed. The good doctor was going to tell me all about his precious aeroforms, as if I cared.

'Doctor, do I really look like some who gives a—'

'Shut up, Jonathan. This is interesting.'

Sure it was.

'Aeroforms! Is that all you wanted me to look at?'

'They are special aeroforms, Jonathan. Unusual. Come; look and learn.'

Doctor Powell took a small instrument from his jacket pocket. It resembled a whistle, made of glass and alloy. He held it up to his mouth and blew – three short notes, intensely sweet.

We were standing at the tip of a steep promontory on the northern coast of the land of Falls, just five miles from Lodge. A mild air was blowing and a cluster of five 'forms was moving with it. I hadn't forgotten the doctor's assertion that aeroforms had held the net that caught me as I fell from orbit, but neither had I given it much credence. There was something about Doctor Cameron Powell that made him difficult for me to trust – or to distinguish between truth and invention in the accounts he gave and the claims he made. The way he looked, or didn't look at you when he spoke. An allusiveness in his speech; nothing was clear or direct or what it seemed at first. The fact that it always seemed to be my turn to buy the drinks. So I'd been charitable and assumed that his apparent untruths were actually metaphors or maybes or perhapses. I mustn't exaggerate this, though. A lot of the time he said what he meant, simply and straightforwardly. But not all the time, and that was the problem. I could never tell when he was kidding me.

I had let him take me up the coast from the shipyard of Lodge-in-the-Falls, where the *El Dorado* was being transfreighted, for this day trip because... because it was something different, a break from the routine of shipboard life. I seemed to have been spending all my time locked into routines while I was on observing duty at Sally's North Pole. It had been irksome to find that the freedom I'd thought

I'd enjoy on Glory was, so far, non-existent. The Board's timetables were far too rigid and inflexible for me in my present state of mind. But I wasn't quite ready yet to adjust to complete self-determination, it seemed. If Doctor Powell hadn't accompanied me on the previous night's excursion into the more extreme entertainments the airman's quarter of Lodge had to offer, I'd probably have woken up in a cell, Monitor and Guardian or not, so when he proposed a trip up the coast I agreed readily enough. It'd keep me out of trouble, if nothing else.

'Nice whistle,' I said. The doctor removed the instrument from his lips. 'Can I have a go?'

'No,' was the curt reply. 'Now watch!'

He pointed to the clutch of aeroforms. I didn't notice what was going on at first, but then it registered. They had been moving with the wind, across my line of sight but now, although the pressure of the air on my face had not altered, they had changed direction and were sailing slowly, but determinedly, towards the doctor and me. He had called them and they had answered.

I had never heard of an aeroform that could propel itself in such a manner. Cameron Powell was right – they were unusual. I stood and watched as the group came closer. Soon they were directly overhead, fifty feet or so above us.

'If you wouldn't mind…' The doctor pointed to the left. 'Twenty yards or so will do.' I walked over the soft, springy grass of the headland. The water was far below us on an ebbing tide and the sound of the waves had been receding steadily while Cameron Powell and I had been looking out to sea.

'Now then. You're going to see something that only a few have ever seen. It won't be pretty, so if you want to go back to Lodge now; well, that's your choice. I'll wait.

'If you stay, you stay. No backing out.'

The doctor was going to continue being mysterious, I could see.

'I'll stay.'

'That's fine. Now wait.' My companion held up his arms. He looked like a priest caught in the act of invocation. Above us the aeroforms began to descend and I caught the sharp reek of venting methane. Slowly, slowly they fell, until they were only twenty feet above ground level.

'I am going to do something I must do. It is an act of obligation and it comes at a cost.'

'Are you asking me for money? How much do you want me to pay?'

'The cost will be mine, not yours. Are you ready?'

'Yes.'

'Don't say I didn't warn you.'

And he showed me the cost. And after that I really did need a drink.

JOY TO THE WORLD

E VERY WORLD THAT ENJOYS THE LIGHT AND WARMTH OF A PARENT sun is divided in two. Of course, there are many divisions in a world, where there is so much space for separateness. There is land, and there is water. There are mountains, and there are ocean depths. There are warm regions, and cold; windy and still. And, if that world is blessed with life, the divisions multiply a hundredfold. There are hunters and hunted, rich and poor, happy and sad. There are the green of woodland, the yellow of cornfields, and the orange-grey of desert; there are land and sea, surface and air, blue ice and green water.

But there is one greater division, and it is one to which the sailing ship *Whistledown* has become well accustomed since she first entered the purlieu of the Blessèd sun and eased herself into orbit around the world of Glory. Every ninety minutes she circles refugee humanity's place of uncertain safety and, if the conditions are right, is seen from a land or from the observation deck of a Board ship, a vivid point of light flying far overhead. She is the guiding star of her children, for so she thinks of the people who live and die on the world below. Did she not give birth to them, after a gestation of many thousands of years in the gravid darkness of interstellar space?

Many of these divisions are invisible on the surface, or at least blurred. Their boundaries are broader when seen from close up. Forests thin out and become prairie. Mountains grow less steep as they fall towards the plain. And the borderland between day and night has many names – twilight, evening, nightfall, sundown. But from a height of one hundred and fifty miles the line of termination becomes clear and sharp and the 'Down passes over it twice every ninety minutes. In less than two hours she experiences dawn and dusk, sunset and sunrise, over and over again, and each event is ended in an eyeblink. The Blessèd sun seems to leap over the horizon or plunge into the darkness behind the world as if time itself had changed its nature and become precipitate, relativistic and quantum.

Time... time has a different meaning on Glory, compared with the Lost Earth. The days are an hour longer and the years only half the length, so that a man of forty-three is just setting out on his career and a woman of one hundred and fifty is enjoying her retirement. Day and night are equal in length, for Glory has stabilised in a perfectly circular orbit around the Blessèd sun and her polar axis points directly up and down. There are no winter or summer, no growing season, no autumn storms or spring greening. Earth crops had to be recompiled by the biotechs of the land of Gold before they would grow properly on Glory, and humanity nearly starved to death before the first wheat harvest was taken in.

Glory lives in an eternal June and the old rhythms of Earthly life have been distorted by the flattening of time. The 'Down sees this and she does what she can to maintain the health of her offspring. She knows that humans need festivals to mark the passing of the years. As the 'Down counts time, it has been two hundred and fifteen thousand, eight hundred and ninety-four million and eight hundred thousand seconds since she sailed through the heliopause of Sol and left the old ruined worlds behind. This number is meaningless to humanity, who merely state that they have lived on Glory for five hundred years or so. By "years" they mean Glorian years, which are marked by the annual celebration of Landing Day, when the whole world downs tools and has a party.

The 'Down thoroughly enjoys Landing Day, for it is as much her celebration as humanity's. It's a splendid chance for her to show off, addressing the peoples of Glory though the big screens her Monitors set up and playing them the music she's composed over the past year. Her shuttlecraft fly aerobatic patterns above the Joyeuse of Horn and make sonic booms over the city of Maybe on Edge. She runs little animated films she has made and comes up with ever more alcoholic cocktail recipes for everyone to get plastered on. Everyone has a foy of a time (except the foys, who are not party animals) and staggers around the following morning in an unrepentant stupor.

This is all very good. This helps maintain humanity's mental well-being. But while it keeps the humans happy, it's not enough for the 'Down, with her long-stored memories of a world now many trillions of miles distant. She remembers another festival, fixed to a different yearly cycle, and because she is more human than she knows (for humans made the tools that built her, and their thoughts are embedded in her DNA), she feels the need to celebrate it.

The preparations take a while. There are laser arrays to get out of storage, fit with battery cells and pass to the tars. While they scurry out along her shrouds, masts and yard-arms and rig them, the 'Down sets the domestics to work on her interior. She no longer fills her galleries with snow following an unfortunate incident when meltwater got into the life-systems and took five weeks to purge, but holo projectors do nearly as good a job of conjuring a winter's day and are far more flexible in use. She likes real trees, though, and has planted a small pine forest on an outer deck, lit by a single lamp-post that oddly lacks an arm.

While her interior and rigging are being fettled, the 'Down calls her comsats back. They are used to this. From time to time each of them returns to its mother for maintenance and refuelling. It is unusual for so many of them to dock at one time, but that is not the kind of thing they tend to worry about – being nothing to do with data bandwidth, signal amplitude or orbital decay – so they moor up at their usual ports and let the tars fuss about them – welding and soldering, painting, polishing and aligning – until they are pristine. They too are fitted with lights.

The ship ticks the fast-fleeting days off on her calendar while, ninety-three million miles from Sol, the Lost Earth spins into Capricorn. Hum and bustle, stress and raised temperatures; but at last everything is ready. The presents have been bought, the food laid in, and there is a pile of sentimental old films set by ready to stream to the Monitors below. She has even hung up a stocking.

The last crystal dawn flashes by and the 'Down sails into another golden day. It's time for the real fun to begin. 'Right then!' says the ship to her comsats. 'Off you go! Now, Dasher! Now, Dancer! Now, Prancer, and Vixen! On, Comet! On, Cupid! On, Donder and Blitzen!' The sats trigger their lasers, fire their thrusters and soar into a new orbit, patterned in formation. Meanwhile the 'Down threads up *It's a Wonderful Life,* draws the curtains and settles down to watch the show while the tars, nestled in a web of ropes and spars, light their multicoloured lamps and beam them to the lands below. The ship gives a happy sigh for the simple pleasure of it all.

* * * *

'Look at that, will you?' says an off-shift Edgeois miner to his ten-year-old son, taking the boy's arm and pointing towards the southern sky.

'All lit up like a bloody Christmas tree!'

But what does he know?

THE FIRST EARTHMAN

S TEP BACK,' YOU SAID. 'GO ON NOW, BACK. BACK, ALL THE WAY. Move.' And you set down the chow bucket and pointed. I shuffled to my feet, still dazed by the light and my sudden waking, and did as I was told, pressing myself hard against the back wall of my cell. Covering my eyes, unable to see you as you turned the key, swung the door open and put the pail on the floor next to the table, I became invisible.

I heard the clang of the closing door and the click of the key in the lock. 'Thank you,' I called to your receding back, but you affected not to hear me. Still, I knew that in fact you did hear me and that you would note in the log that the subject had acquired at least one of the expected social niceties. Perhaps I succeeded in making you understand that I felt grateful for your kindness in bringing me food and providing me with shelter, and that my development was going according to plan.

My breakfast was good to eat. I sat on the floor next to the bucket and consumed its contents in a slow, measured way, chewing each morsel thoroughly. Then I drank; there was water and nothing else, sufficiently refreshing for the climate and my needs. All the time the cameras swivelled and rotated overhead, recording my every action. They watched and noted as I stood by the door, looking out at the courtyard beyond, as I turned away from the outside and used the receptacle you provided, as I curled up by the back wall and dozed in the increasing heat of the Blessèd sun, as I yawned, stretched and woke again. From time to time I drank some more. The sky was clear, cloudless. Only the passage of an occasional ship obstructed the light, and that only briefly.

As I lay, solitary, I had plenty of time to think, and to remember. My memory was not completely reliable; there were gaps in the recent past and further back a kind of barrier beyond which it could not go. I understood that this is the way memory works; that the extreme past disappears from view, as if rounding a corner or falling over a cliff. You told me that this was nothing to worry about. I was not losing my mind. But I still wondered. Especially, I wondered why I could remember nothing before I came to this place.

'Where did I come from?' I asked you once, as casually as I could, trying not to sound as if I were pleading for information. I had suspected for some time that you rather enjoyed the power you had over me and I did not wish to aggravate the situation. Please understand that I was not trying to deprive you of a legitimate pleasure, but I had to fight my corner as best I could, even though I knew that ours could never be an equal relationship.

You made no direct answer. Instead, you asked me if I was happy in my new home. What reply could I give you? I was not unhappy, if by that you meant that I cried myself to sleep every night, but neither did I have very much familiarity with happiness. So I nodded, and you made a note, and my question went unanswered.

It was an hour past midday. You came with a new container of food and while you collected the old one and took stool samples from the bag that lined the receptacle, you talked to me. Like:

'Hello, Monty. Sorry I didn't have much time to talk to you this morning. I've been so busy, you know? It's all down to me. Those lazy bastards up at the Mansion, you know?'

I nodded.

'Do you know what time they get out of bed?'

I shook my head.

'Ten o'clock! And on a lovely bright Hally-morning too! Still lying around in their pits! Idle s—!' You used a common vulgarity.

I looked as shocked as my facial muscles would allow.

'Pardon my French.' You always said that after using one of the stronger verbal weapons in your arsenal. I had no idea what it meant. I hoped you appreciated that I was agreeing with your criticism of the higher-ups, not your mode of expressing it. I did not want there to be any misunderstandings between us.

'So it's all down to me,' you continued. 'Me and you Beasts.' And with a loud rattle you picked up the bucket and the sample bag, shut the door and left. I heard the click of the key in the lock and your footsteps. Then all was quiet again, except for the echoes of the wind in the hills and the sounds of my neighbours shuffling and scratching in their cages.

There came a time when I did not hear the sound of the key. It was in the evening, with Our Moon bright overhead and Sally glowing orange-red to the west of her. The double shadows were sharp against the concrete of the yard outside my window. I know this because I left my place at the back of the cell and crept forward and looked out, expecting to see you return. You did not return, and it struck me that you had seemed a little odd as you doled out my rations and swept out my room. You had not spoken to me. You, who usually liked to pass the time of day with every one of your charges, had been uncharacteristically quiet. I did not know what worries you had – apart from your daily complaint about the unequal distribution of labour here at the Centre – but I supposed they must have been weighing unusually heavily on you that night.

I left my place at the window and went to the door. To my surprise, it was slightly ajar, by no more than a centimetre, but that was enough for me to slip a paw into the gap and slowly, painfully enlarge it. The door was heavy and, although I am no weakling, it was not designed to be opened easily by one such as myself. But it opened nevertheless and soon I was able to wedge my nose into the gap and make enough space for me to slip through and outside.

At first I was badly disoriented. I had been in the yard many times before for exercise and training, but only in your company and only in daylight. It was *terra incognita* to me now. I stepped slowly into the middle of the square and looked around. There were the cells, making up three sides of the square in which I stood. The fourth side was open, except that a wall stretched from one side of it to the other, interrupted by a barred gate half-way along. My cell was on the opposite side of the yard from the gate, so I had seen and heard it open and close many times, admitting you and your colleagues. I crossed over to it. Like my cell door it was unlocked, moving back with a creak of its hinges as I crouched low to the ground and nudged against it. I pushed it open with my nose and passed through, feeling a new excitement squeezing my bowels.

I looked around. Everything was strange. It was hard to make out details because the light dazzled so, but I got a general impression of a wooded country that fell rapidly away into a deep dark valley. A gravel path ran beside the wall and I followed it to the left. Soon it turned uphill to where I could see artificial lights outlining a large block which I knew to be the Mansion. This was the place where I was sometimes taken for testing and evaluation. I turned and looked back. Did I recognise any more of my surroundings? I had been here before, many times, but I had been led on a cord with orders to keep my head down and not to look about me. Sometimes I had been muzzled and blindfolded, but that had been in the early days; those which lay close up against the wall which separated me from my lost memories.

What should I do? I could return to my room, lie down, curl up and go to sleep. I could climb the steep path to the Mansion and ask for help. I could go away from the path, downhill into the shadowed valley, away from the light, into danger. I could simply stay where I was and wait for you to find me. What would be best? What consequences might I face? I did not think that you and your colleagues were cruel people, but neither did I like to defy you. To do that felt wrong, in a deep way, a disturbance in my insides. And yet – this was a rare opportunity. It was change, difference. It was an adventure that was being offered to me and I could not refuse it. My blood was up, my legs moved of their own accord. A rare exhilaration took hold of me and tugged at my spirit. I would fly away and see the world. There were scents and sounds out there that I had never heard or smelled before. I would taste them now.

I turned to the right and went downhill. Soon I fell in with a stream of water – an overflow from further up the peak. I stopped and drank and, feeling that it would guide me, stayed with it as I descended. From time to time there was a lip in the slope and the stream left the ground, fell a few feet and splashed into a pool, foamed and sparkled by the light from the worlds overhead. I wondered if I should take a swim in one of the pools to wash away my scent. Was I being followed? Perhaps not, not yet, but nevertheless it made sense to take precautions. So I changed from one side of the stream to the other as I descended and even waded through it for a few tens of yards. Finally I reached a point where the slope became too steep for me to follow it. I went back upstream for a few feet and then struck out to the left.

By now I was in almost complete darkness. Glory had moved under the worlds so that their light no longer fell directly down upon me but at an angle from the east, where it was more readily obstructed by trees or rocky outcrops. Had it not been for the sharpness of my night-vision, which was working better than I had known it could, I should have been forced to stop in case I tripped and fell helplessly into the unseen void below. I turned aside and followed the line of the hill, trying to keep to the same level and squeezing through the gaps which appeared between the trees and bushes that clad the slope. Soon I entered a wood and the light of the worlds was sliced into shreds by leaves and branches. I was blind.

Again I faced a choice. Go on, and risk the uncertain ground underfoot; its exposed tree-roots, its hidden traps, its sudden drops. Return, and try the other side of the stream, despite the fading light of Our Moon and Sally, or stay put and wait for morning.

Surely that was the worst choice – to do nothing when I had already chosen to act? If I were escaping, and that was surely what it looked like I was doing, then I should keep going and put as many miles as I could between myself and you. But... the initial rush had slowed. I was calmer. It would do me little good to injure myself by risking further flight in this dark forest, suspended over what depths I knew not, full of unfamiliar odours and new-minted sounds – small scratches and pops in the undergrowth, the sharp tang of crushed berries and bruised grass.

I decided, and once the decision was made I had to stick to it. I curled up under a tree, wrapped my tail around its trunk and, my mind set, fell quickly asleep.

The Blessèd sun came and took me by surprise. My room up at the Centre faced south so I didn't usually get the full impact of the morning light. That treat was reserved for my companions in the cages to my left while those on my right had brighter evenings. This light was different. It slanted through the trees, diffused into rays by a low-lying mist. There were no sounds, apart from my breathing.

I stood up and shook myself. Beads of water flew off me in a cloud. My fur had gained a layer of dew as I slept, as had the leaves and branches of the trees and bushes all around, up and down the slope. Now it was light I could see how wise I had been to stop and rest. The hillside was very steep and the fall became sheer as it dropped out of sight into the valley below.

Now I was awake I quickly realised how cold and hungry I was. Thirsty too, though I ran my tongue over the grass and managed to suck up enough dew to dispel my need for the present. The cold would soon pass, I knew. Hunger – that was different. Could I eat the grass? Maybe I could, although you had never given me grass to eat. My rations had consisted of artificial foods in the form of biscuits and porridge, mixed with a little meat. I decided to try the grass and tore a mouthful out of the ground. I chewed it thoroughly. Its taste was sweet and the water it contained refreshed me, but it was hard to swallow and I was not sure that I would be able to digest it, or gain nourishment from it. It stimulated my bowels, however, and I defecated against the tree where I had slept.

And, for now, that was it. I had breakfasted and it was time to start the business of the day. But what would it be? For so long I had had no control over my activities. It had been my part to wait in my room for you to come and tell me what today's routine would be. It might be testing up at the Mansion, it might be exercise in the yard, it might be nothing but lying in my room all day while my neighbours received attention. It had never been my choice. I wondered if it had ever been yours or whether the higher-ups in the Mansion controlled your day as you controlled mine. As in the night before, when I had stood on the path outside the yard, I could do one of three things. I could stay where I was and do nothing, I could return to the compound and look for you, or I could carry on. I hesitated. There was no food here, and little to drink. There was no guarantee that I would find anything to sustain me in the valley (although I considered that the stream I had followed the night before must eventually splash into the valley floor and I would probably find a river or a lake there). If I returned uphill I would receive food, drink, and doubtless a dressing-down. My liberty – such as it was – might be further curtailed, or I might be punished in some way I could not imagine but which would necessarily be unpleasant.

To do nothing seemed unworthy of my impulse of the day before. Further, if I were to be punished anyway how much difference would it make if it were delayed a day or two? True, I would be treated less leniently the more trouble I caused but, short of ceasing me altogether, what could they do? If they had wanted to terminate my existence they could have done so already at any time they chose.

My caged neighbours came and went; and those that went did not always return.

So I carried on. Along the line of the valley side, going down more often than up, as the Blessèd sun rose further and drew the damp from the ground and the air. My own sounds – my breathing, my heartbeat, my paws on the ground, my flanks brushing against the vegetation – were joined by the movement of the trees in a light breeze and the calls of the birds that lived in them. Darkness withdrew from my downhill side – my left – and I grew more adventurous as I proceeded. Nothing could harm me, so long as I was careful and kept a sharp lookout for pits and traps. From time to time I stopped, let my body quieten down, and listened. Listened for sounds from above – of men following my trail, which I could do little to disguise. Listened for their footfalls, their shouts, the racket of their engines or their squawking radios. Listened; but heard only natural sounds. I wondered if I had been missed. Perhaps the idle ones were still in bed. Perhaps you were ill, and my absence not yet noted. I pressed on.

I must have been travelling for at least an hour before I met the creature. Where I had the choice I kept to the trees, skirting around any clearings I found. Although it would have been good to stand in the unobstructed light of the Blessèd sun for a few minutes, I knew that I would be easier to spot if I left the shelter of the trees. See how quickly I learned to behave like a fugitive, hiding in shadows! The vegetation changed in type as I descended, the trees giving way to tall, stiff, segmented stalks which snapped easily in my paws, yielding a soft fibrous interior and an oozing white sap. Each stem made a characteristic cracking sound as it broke. After sucking the moisture from a few I moved on. The stalks obstructed my way more than the trees had done, snagging me as I pushed past them, and my progress became ever slower and more tiring. I wondered if I should take a chance and head straight downhill to get out of this grove of rigid poles, which so resembled the bars across my window at the Centre. I sat back on my haunches and waited for my laboured breathing to subside while I thought.

I fell into a kind of trance, I think. Although I was shielded from the sky, the heat was building up as the Blessèd sun climbed ever higher towards noon. I felt as I sometimes felt when I returned from the laboratories at the Centre – a little drained, needing rest. My earlier keenness had been blunted by fatigue. So I dozed for a few minutes, and I dreamed. Dreamed that I was back in the yard, exercising as I did nearly every day, running to and fro. Across the middle of the yard was a wall, separating me from my cell. 'I've finished,' I told you. 'I'd like to go back to my room now, if I might.'

'Off you go,' you said, pointing.

'But I can't,' I replied. 'There's a wall in the way.'

'No, there isn't.'

'Yes, there is. Look!'

'I see no wall.'

'I do.'

'There is no wall. You are being foolish.'

'Yes, I am. I'm sorry.'

'Go on, then. Back to your cage. Come along.'

'But...'

'There is no wall. Now hurry – run!'

I dug in my back legs and ran. The wall reared up in front of me. I lowered my snout and put on more speed. I would push the wall over. My momentum would blast a hole through it. Cinder blocks would shatter. It would hurt. It would stun me. I did not care. The wall was not real. You had told me that. The ground rolled and crackled under my feet. I was close. Ten feet. Five feet. One foot. Now.

And, as I had so many times before, I woke before the crash could happen. The vertical green bars still surrounded me. Warmth still enveloped me. I had been asleep for only five or ten minutes. Nothing had changed. Except...

Snap.

Snap.

Snap.

I came instantly to full awareness. Somewhere close by, someone or something was cracking the stems, as I had earlier. Was it you? Had you caught up with me while I slept? I had to find out.

I pushed my way through the grove. The sound grew closer, and suddenly I broke out of the thicket and into an open space, covered with short grass. On the far side sat a creature; the first I had seen since leaving the Centre. It was of a similar size to myself, but where my fur was brown and my ears sloped back over my skull, its coat was black and white, with large black patches over its eyes, and small black ears sticking straight up out of the top of its head. It was sitting back against a tree and holding a stalk, which it was crushing in its powerful jaws. It saw me and looked up, unconcerned. It took hold of another stem and broke it.

Snap.

'Hello,' I said. 'How are you?'

There was no reply.

'My name's Montague. What's yours?'

Still nothing. That was discouraging. I was not ready to give up yet, however.

'I'm a wolfbear. What kind of person are you?'

I was curious; I have to admit it. Of course I had seen other creatures at the Centre. They were of many kinds. Some were of simple derivation. They were dogs, or cats or deer or horses. Others were mixed-species, like me. But this one was new. It looked friendly. I would talk to it.

I crossed the glade slowly, doing my best to appear unthreatening. The creature looked up from its chewing as I approached. It seemed unworried by me, which I took as a favourable sign. I did not want to get into any kind of fight – I had little experience of conflict. My teeth and jaws were sharp and powerful, but so, I could tell, were its. I stopped at a safe distance.

'Hello,' I said again. 'My name's Montague.' Still no response. Was my speech hard to make out? You had no trouble understanding what I said, I knew, despite my mouth and throat being non-human.

Louder, then. 'Hello! Can You Hear Me? What Is Your Name?'

The creature looked away and gave a low moan. It did not attempt to reply to me. Was there any point in carrying on trying to communicate with it? I decided to give it one more go. Advancing right up to it I knocked the food from its paw and looked straight into its black-patched eyes. 'WHO ARE YOU?' I bellowed.

'His name's Der-Der and you're frightening him. Stop it.'

The voice – soft and calm, but very determined – came from behind me. I turned. Another of the black and white creatures was standing on the far side of the glade, its eyes as full of anger as this ones were placid. 'What sort of bully are you?'

'I'm not a bully.'

'Then stop behaving like one.'

The newcomer padded over to where I stood. It laid one forepaw on its friend's shoulder and gave it a new stalk with the other. 'There, there,' it said. 'Have some more bamboo. Don't pay any attention. The nasty thing will be going soon. Won't you?' It gave me a hostile look.

'I guess so. But…'

'But what?'

'He—'

'Der-Der.'

'Der-Der… He's the first… person I've met since I left the Centre. I didn't know he couldn't talk.'

'You still shouted at him.'

'I'm sorry.'

'Don't tell me, tell him.'

I turned, abashed. 'I'm sorry I upset you, Der-Der. I didn't mean to. It was very ignorant and stupid of me and I apologise.'

'That's better. You can get on your way now. Go on, push off!'

'Please…'

'What?'

'You see, I only left the Centre last night. I don't know what to do. I don't know where to go. I don't know anything. Can you help me?'

A sharp look. 'Are they following you?'

'The humans? I don't know. I don't think so.'

'So you've been Released?'

'The gate was open. I walked out.'

'Hmmm. I see. You do look pretty helpless. Have you eaten today?'

'Not much. Some grass.'

'Anything to drink?'

'Water from the grass.'

The creature regarded me for a minute. 'Right. Well, settle down here, in the shade. I'm hungry. Have some bamboo if you like. Your name's Montague, right?'

'Yes.'

'And you're a wolf/bear hybrid.'

'Yes.'

'Okay. Now pay attention. I'm Marian; and Der-Der and I are pandas. Giant pandas, in fact. We're stronger and quicker and fiercer than we look, so don't mess with us. You may think you're pretty tough, but you've never lived wild, have you?'

'No.'

'Do you remember anything before you came to the Centre?'

'No.'

'Right. Let me fill you in. Do you know what this place is?'

I thought. 'The hill? Sorry, I've not been told.'

Marian tilted her head to one side. She seemed amused. What's the name of the world?' she asked.

'Glory.' You had taught me that. I pointed upwards. 'The Blessèd sun shines down on us by day and the worlds light the way by night.'

'What are they called?'

'The worlds? There's Hally, and Sally, and Our Moon.'

Marian nodded. 'You're doing better than I thought you would. So, just to finish off, where are we now? I mean, what land are we on?'

'I don't know. What's a "land"?'

The panda waved her left paw, being careful not to startle Der-Der. 'It's all this, all around. This hill, these woods, this soil, the rocks underneath them. Everything that we can walk on, everything that goes down to the sea.'

'The sea?' I replied, puzzled. 'I don't know what you mean. What's "the sea"?'

'You don't know about the sea?' Marian snuffled her laughter.

'Well, I can't tell you. Describe the sea to someone who's never seen it for themselves? I don't think so! You'll have to find out yourself.'

'But how? Where should I go? I don't know how to find the sea. I'm all astray.'

'I suppose I'm going to have to help you.'

'I would owe you a great debt of gratitude.'

Marian snorted. 'That, and one Token, will buy you a cup of coffee in Phyle.' I shook my head, confused. I had absolutely no idea what she was talking about and she knew it. She also knew I would never admit to my ignorance, and she knew I knew that, as did I.

For a moment I envied Der-Der his simplicity.

'Der-Der, darling, listen to me carefully. I'm going to have to go away for a few days; I'm going with Montague to help him find his way to safety. He's rather lost, you see.

'You must stay here and look after yourself. You can do that, can't you? Look, there's plenty of bamboo for you to eat. If it gets cold you can bed down in the moss in the forest.

'Is that all right, love?'

Der-Der lifted his head to Marian's face. I saw no exchange, and nobody spoke – nothing that I could hear – but an understanding must have passed between them.

'I'll be back soon. Before you know it, I promise.'

The pandas embraced; black fur on white, white fur on black. Seeing their intimacy, I was briefly swamped by a feeling of terrible loss. Their loss, for their parting, but also mine, for I had never known such closeness myself – not on this side of the wall. I was desolated by my sorrow and turned away from the pair, trying to grant them the privacy they deserved. They held one another for several long minutes. I stood at the edge of the grove, staring south while the Blessèd sun poked through the trees to my right.

Presently Marian rejoined me and, turning, blew Der-Der one last kiss. She looked at me with regret haunting her eyes. 'Come on then, Monty.'

We headed directly downhill. The panda led the way and I followed, picking my way carefully.

'You'll have to go faster than that.'

'Yes, sorry. I'm not used to this. It feels like my rear end wants to run past my front paws, if you see what I mean.'

'It's just the same for me.' That was true – Marian's powerful-looking hindquarters were built for pushing, just as mine were. Going downhill felt all wrong. 'You have to take short steps and let your back legs drag a little. Watch me and you'll be all right.'

So I watched her and I did my best and slowly we descended the slope. The stream I had crossed on the night of my escape had cut a gully into the side of the hill and our path drifted across towards it as time passed until we found ourselves climbing down into it and scrambling over the boulders the water's grinding had exposed. I worried that we were exposed too. There was no cover apart from the occasional tree growing slantwise out of the side of the rift the rushing water had etched out of the land, and the Blessèd sun shone more and more directly into our eyes as it approached its highest point. Not only were the heat and glare becoming uncomfortable, but the feeling that we were being watched – examined as you examine me under the lasers in the Mansion's laboratories – was gradually overpowering me. But there was water – as much as we could drink – and as much shade as we needed, bearing in mind that progress was what mattered most, not comfort.

At no time did I wonder how it was I knew about the movement of the Blessèd sun through the heavens or the way running water eroded the landscape. Nor did it surprise me when I realised that I knew – as I had *always* known – that I was treading the soil, drinking the water and eating the plant life of the land of Gold.

All that day we scrambled down the stream-path that led from the heights of Gold. It was less than twenty-five hours since I had left my home in the compound but I was beginning to realise, if not yet fully understand, the implications of my freedom. Nobody would bring me food and water any more, nobody would check my pulse and temperature, nobody would clean out my room. I was in charge of myself now. All the same, I was still very far from complete independence. Without Marian's guidance I would by now be wandering aimlessly in the woods. I would have been retaken and be once more in your custody if it had not been for her help.

I thought more about the subject of independence as I followed the panda's shuffling frame down the hillside, through clean air and vivid patches of mottled shade. I was no longer part of an institution – the Regeneration Facility, I remembered it was called – and I had absented myself from your research programme, but I was still no more self-motivated than I had been before. In that respect I had merely exchanged one boss for another.

But the open air – so devil-may-care in its intimacy with my skin and fur, scented with pollen and the perfume of flowers and something else I couldn't identify – made the blood surge through my veins and lifted my emotions to the point where nothing could worry me; not even the shadow of my imprisonment. I would have sung, had my throat been equipped for singing.

The heat of the Blessèd sun became intolerable around midday and Marian and I took shelter under a grove of ash trees and lay there panting with our tongues hanging out.

We didn't talk much. I was, I must confess, somewhat in awe of Marian. She was so in control; of me, of the situation, of Der-Der. I wondered about him as we lay among the fly-buzzing undergrowth and waited for the temperature to fall to the point where we could continue our journey. What was he? Outwardly, he and Marian were identical except for their gender. They were giant pandas, with black sticking-up ears, patches around their eyes and an air of amiable composure. I almost said idiocy, but that was certainly not true of Marian whose eyes glowed with shrewd intelligence. Der-Der was different; he was little more than an animal, or so it seemed. Why was Marian looking after him? What advantage was she gaining from their lop-sided relationship? There was so much I still didn't understand. The heat and my tiredness made it hard to think coherently.

After an hour or so it became possible to move on once more. Gradually the slope became less steep and the stream grew broader, shallower and less deeply dug into the hillside. Walking became easier too, and we made greater speed, hindered only by the vegetation which grew ever thicker and more green. The grass sparkled, the Blessèd sun arced over the heavens to our left and we forged our way downwards and onwards, wading through the tributaries which joined the main stream every mile or so and keeping out of sight of the buildings which were becoming increasingly frequent as we went on.

That night, as we lay comfortably couched under the worlds and the stars, our stomachs comfortably full of fruit and nuts from a nearby orchard, I felt an urge come upon me that I had never experienced before or else had forgotten. Marian was dozing next to me, sharing our mutual warmth, so it was a simple matter of instinct to reach over to her, extend my claws, and scratch her deeply behind the ears.

Her reaction was so fast it took me completely unawares. She swung her right forepaw around like a club and stuck me squarely across the muzzle, jerking my head back and nearly wrenching it from my shoulders. I fell hard against a tree. It felt as if I had been lifted bodily and thrown into the air.

'Try that again, you *animal*, and I'll rip your guts out!' The panda put her forepaws on my shoulders and pushed me hard against the ground, crushing me under the weight of her body. I looked up at her with dazed eyes.

'Don't you... I mean, I thought perhaps...'

'Shut. Up.'

'But listen... I'm part bear. I'm sure we'd be good together. You know, compatible.'

Marian glared down at me. 'Get this, pooch. Listen up, doggie. Understand. You lay another paw on me and I will kill you. I'm not interested. End of.'

'You mean it's Der-Der. I'm not Der-Der and it's him you want.'

The panda ignored me.

'Is it because he...?' I stopped talking just in time. Marian raised her paws and turned her head so that I could not see her face. I wriggled out from underneath her, gasping for breath. She spoke into the night.

'You know nothing. Nothing about me, nothing about Der-Der, nothing about this land, nothing about the world or the stars or the Blessèd sun. You are ignorant. I knew that when I took you on. You are not the first of your kind that I have met. But I did not think you were stupid as well as ignorant.'

'I'm not stupid.'

'No? Then prove it. Look around you. Pay attention to what you see and hear. Keep them in mind. Try to comprehend them, if you can. Work things out in your head.'

'I am remembering things. I'm sure I know more now than I did when I left the compound. But you're right. There's still a lot I don't understand.'

'Then concentrate some more. Make an effort. Do you think I'm on this trip for the good of my health? Or because I *like* you? Now, I'm going for a walk. I want to be left alone. You stay here, little puppy-dog and don't try to follow me. And if you ever try another stunt like that...'

'Yes, Marian. I'm sorry. I won't.'

'Then perhaps you've learned something after all. Maybe there's hope for you yet.'

The panda shuffled off towards a nearby copse, leaving me alone and unable to sleep. Thoughts spun around in my head; of humiliation and shame, of course, but also... questions. Who was I? Why was I here? What was I doing? What would become of me?

There were no answers – none that came close to satisfying me or giving me peace. On and on they churned, and even as I tried to calm myself and tell myself there was no point in fretting – that in the end I would find out all I needed to know – I could get no rest beyond a few minutes of dream-haunted sleep.

The Blessèd sun rose and I rose with it. Marian had returned at some point during the night and lay gently snoring a few yards away.

It was the beginning of the last day.

The slope had come to an end. It had run out of steam, as it were, and become a flat grassy plain, interrupted by woods and cultivated land. Marian and I followed a staggered course, working our way around the perimeters of the forests and farms. We spoke little; and what we did say was direct and to the point. It was clear that the panda saw me as a burden, her guardianship of me a duty to be done. But there were so many questions in my mind...

It was still a puzzle, why she had left her mate to help me. There seemed to be no reason why she should have agreed to take me on. She didn't particularly like me and she had left her beloved Der-Der all by himself in helpless isolation thousands of feet up the peak from which we had descended. She would have a long and wearisome climb when she returned to him. I could think of no justification for her apparent altruism.

And there was another question. Where were we going? There would surely be a time when Marian would announce that we had arrived at our destination and that her task was complete. But I had no conception of where this destination might be, or what I would do once I reached it.

In the meantime we followed the Blessèd sun southwards, ever southwards, and I continued to drink in the beauty of the greater world. For it *was* beautiful – far more lovely than I had dreamed it could be when I was living under your wardenship in the compound. My heart was lifted by the sheer physical exuberance of our surroundings; the air was richer and more full of life than it had been further up the mountain, the sky brighter and more blue. The ground was soft under my paws, not rocky or hard, and despite the way it slowed me down and blocked my forward vision, I loved the tall grass with its cool scented pollen drifting in the gentle breeze. Because of this obstructing grass, I had to follow Marian's lead and accept on trust that she knew where she was taking me. We were still tracking the river, but keeping a fair distance from its bank because the ground became increasingly marshy as you approached it. The river was slowing down and spreading out, like a man approaching his middle years.

From time to time a cloud crossed the sky in front of the Blessèd sun and robbed the air of its radiance, but these interruptions were short and, in the brief respite they gave us from the heat, welcome. Marian must have been suffering dreadfully from the lack of shelter. Her fun was thick and shaggy and better suited to the cooler airs of the mist-drenched slopes far above us, while mine was short and bristly. There was more of wolf than bear about me, that much was obvious. Wolf and bear – yes, but what else?

Every fifteen minutes or so Marian stopped and held a forepaw up for silence while she listened carefully. What she was listening for I could not say and I could hardly ask her; not while she needed me to be quiet. I supposed she was trying to detect the sounds of men out looking for us. There were man-made sounds all around us already, of course. The farms we skirted were being worked by machinery – some manned, some robotic – but those sounds did not seem to worry her. Each time the Blessèd sun was dimmed she looked upwards in alarm, expecting, no doubt, to see an aircraft overhead, but there were none, merely wisps of cirro-cumulus. She must have heard something else, concealed in the soughing of the grass, because she never looked satisfied but continued our hike with a sad shake of her head, giving off an increasing sense of unease that I could not help picking up myself.

So our journey continued, in a jumble of intense pleasure and nervous uncertainty.

You would have been impressed by the way I adapted myself. I worked out – eventually – that I would make much better progress across the water-meadows adjoining the river if I raised myself up onto my hind legs. With less effort than I expected I became upright. Suddenly my eye-level was above the tops of the grass-stems and I could see for miles rather than a foot or two. 'Marian, look!' I cried out. 'Can you do this?'

'No. And stop showing off. Who's in charge here?'

'You are. But I'm not showing off, I'm finding our way. You tell me where we're going and I'll lead us there.'

The panda put a paw up to her ear. Then she lifted herself up, trying to copy me, I suppose. For a few seconds she teetered there, but fell back to earth with a heavy thump.

'Damn. All right, Montague Mutt, I suppose we'll have to do what you suggest. Tell me what you can see.'

I looked around. 'The river's about a hundred yards to the left of us. There's grass to the front of us and to the right. Then some stumpy hills and then nothing.'

'Nothing?'

'That's right. The hills are blocking the view. Wait a mo.' I turned around, nearly falling over. Behind us the mountain rose, up and up and up, rocky and forested and steep. I might have caught a glimpse of the Mansion and the compound but it was hard to tell through the haze. It was quiet; no sign of men at all, except for a hint of smoke behind the trees to our right.

'So, where now?'

'We'll keep on following the river. You can get down now if you like.'

I was feeling somewhat unstable, so I fell forward onto my front paws, shook my head and waited for Marian to start again. We kept on with our former track, except that now whenever we stopped I rose up and took a look around. Every time the view was the same, except that the hills in front of us grew a little nearer each time and, once or twice I thought I saw a disturbance in the savannah behind us – an irregular oscillation of grass stems – but when I looked again it had stopped. A pocket of swirling breeze; that was all it was. Nothing human.

Eventually, after an afternoon made up of quarter-hour walks and two-minute observations we reached the first rise of the hills. At the same time the character of the soil changed, becoming loose and granular, and the grass turned stiffer and sparser. The river to our left was now flowing through an impassable swamp, busy with flies and marsh-reeds, and there was a new, sharper smell in the air, carried by a light wind blowing straight in our faces. We climbed the two-hundred-foot incline of the hill, relieved to give our powerful rear legs a chance to work as they were intended. And at the top... everything was different.

The hill – it was a sand dune, of course – fell away steeply and turned into a beach. But not a beach as I had once known them, with lazy waves lapping across rippled sands or boisterous rollers charging over shingle and rocks. This beach went forward four hundred yards and then simply ceased; dropping away into abrupt, final nothingness. The sea – the sea! – itself only became visible an uncountable number of miles in the distance. From my left came the far-off sound of falling water. I turned and looked. The river was suffering the same fate as the beach, cast into oblivion. It had carved a horseshoe shape into the land as it fell so that I could see the foaming glitter of its fall, a mile or more away. Flying spray cast a rainbow over the near side, refracted through the mists that hung over all, blurring the sky.

These things were strange and extraordinary, but I hardly noticed them. There was something resting on the shore that was much more mysterious. A giant butterfly made of white metal, standing high on stork-like legs linked to saucer-shaped pads, stood on the sand. Four ovoid pods, open at their narrow ends, were fixed to the upper surface of each wing and at the front, where a real insect's head would have been, flashed windows of transparent crystal. A fin rose from the tail end of its body and on its side was painted the number 2. I looked and marvelled and tried to find some place in my memory where such a sight might once have been cached. Tried, and failed, despite a nagging insistence that meaning – vital meaning – must be linked to it. The wall of memory still stood.

But even this alien craft was not the strangest sight on this strange shore. For somebody had set out a table and two chairs in the shelter of one of the butterfly's wings and in one of the chairs was sitting... I don't have to say, do I? You raised your arm and waved to me.

'Monty! You made it! Well done! Terrific – come on down and join us!'

I looked at Marian. 'Did you know about this?'

'What do you think?'

What did I think, indeed? It was bloody obvious what I thought. 'You've betrayed me, then.'

'I've brought you where you need to be. Monty, don't you realise what's been happening? Look around you. What do you see? What is this place called? You know, don't you?'

The words came unbidden to my mind. *The Hanging Coasts of Gold*. One of the natural wonders of Glory, to be compared with the ice-caverns of the Floating Pole, or the Spine and Shore of Edge or the Ringlands of the Archipelago of Grain. The tide was out now. When it came in, the rising sea would swallow up the waterfall and wash gently across the treacherous sands of the suspended beach.

'Yes,' I said with a sigh of resignation. 'I know.'

'Then let's go.'

I followed the panda as she made her ungainly way down the scarp side of the dune, not looking back. It was only a short walk across the beach, but difficult for me as my undersized paws sank deep into the loose-packed sand. They were wolf-paws, not designed to support the weight of my bear-body. At least, not in this gravity... Marian reached you first and I caught up with her a minute later. By the time I reached the shade of the butterfly-wing, you and she were deep in an intense conversation.

'Wait,' you told me, and to Marian you said, 'No, that's not possible.'

'But you promised,' said the panda, and for the first time her voice lacked the confidence and certainty that had coloured her speech with me. 'Please...'

'You know what can and what cannot be done,' you replied.

'But I have fulfilled my part of our bargain. I have brought him to you and see! He is nearly ready.'

'You have done well, I agree.'

'Excuse me,' I said, 'but would someone tell me what the hell's going on?'

'Wait.'

The Blessèd sun was not far from setting now. It was low in the sky to our left, casting lengthening shadows across the strand. I looked up at the orange-lit nose of the vessel, twenty feet above us. There it was, its name, the letters star-burned but still clear, the single word *Show*. Of course; what else would it be?

So much was becoming clear to me now, so quickly. 'No,' I said. 'I have waited long enough.'

'So have I,' said Marian.

'Then wait no longer. Look behind you...' You pointed back towards the dunes. I didn't see at first, what you were pointing at, but Marian did. With a soft, yearning cry she turned and ran – faster than I would have believed possible – to where her faithful Der-Der stood, with his head tilted to one side and a joyful smile on his face.

With a soft whinny of delight, Marian skidded to a halt at the foot of the dunes where Der-Der waited for her. The pandas embraced as I had seen them do when they parted, but this time with joy instead of sorrow. They clung to one another, white on black, black on white and, I am sure, spoke of their mutual love. I watched, half awestruck, half jealous. They had something I had not, and it was wonderful.

'Sad, isn't it?' you said.

'Sad?' What in the world could you mean?

'Yes, sad. They're so ill-matched. We can't possibly let them breed, and as for full incorporation...' Your voice tailed off. 'It's out of the question. Completely impossible.'

I looked at you. 'Sorry?'

'You don't understand yet? But you will, Monty, you will. I can see you're nearly as advanced as Marian has suggested. Only a little further and you'll truly be one of us. As much as you ever can be, of course.'

You still spoke in mysteries, but I reflected that I had learned a great deal in the two days and nights since I had left the compound. No doubt there was still more that I had yet to discover. You reached down and put a hand on the bristly fur behind my ears. 'Not long now.'

The two pandas padded slowly across the beach towards us. You advanced to meet them. 'See!' cried Marian. 'You cannot deny us now.'

Your reply was too soft for me to hear. Marian's was not. 'How dare you! How dare you call him a failure!'

'But he is,' you said. 'Look at him. Look with open eyes and you will see it.'

'I tell you again; I have done as you asked. I have brought him,' she meant me, 'to you. I have trained him. I have uplifted him, as you required. He is close – very close. You can finish what I have started.

'And now, Doctor Ilse Hight, I want my payment. I deserve it. It is my right.'

You sighed. 'I cannot give you what you ask. Look at Der-Der. *Really* look at him. Do you see any hope? Don't you think that, if he could be saved, he would have recovered by now? How long did it take with Montague? Two days? And how long have you and Der-Der known each other?'

'Thousands of years, of course. Why do you ask?'

'And here, on Gold?'

Marian's reply was muffled by the fur that puffed out around Der-Der's neck. You heard her all the same.

'Two years. Longer than that. You have been trying to bring him back for over two years now and you have failed. Let go, Marian. Let go.'

'I will not!' The panda left her mate and approached you. 'I will make you!' She came closer still and reared up on her hind legs, as I had shown her on the grassy plain behind the dunes. 'Take us to the Mansion now. Reincorporate us! Or I will kill you.' Her claws slid out, lethally sharp.

Dismayed, I withdrew behind the table.

You reached to your belt and drew out a shining metal thing.

'Step back!' you said. 'Or I swear I will shoot you.' You pointed to the sky. A vivid lance of fire flew from your hand, crackling and scalding the air as it passed.

Marian fell onto her forepaws.

'Coward!' she spat. You lowered the weapon so that it was pointing directly at her face.

'I have told you to go. Now go! And take the empty cripple with you. There is no hope for him, and if you carry on in this manner you too will be condemned.'

'What is happening?' I asked in an unsteady voice.

'Silence!'

And now memory becomes deceptive and unreliable once more and I cannot easily piece together the correct sequence of events in my mind. I know that Marian turned. I recall that your hand twitched threateningly. I saw how her shoulders slumped. I do not remember if she said anything. And I was not Der-Der, so I do not know what he saw and I cannot begin to imagine how he interpreted it. Except for this; that he saw his mate treated cruelly and menaced with a deadly weapon. And I know that he was brave and loyal and strong. And so his ruined mind saw a threat to the one he loved the most in all the world, and so he reacted in the only way he could.

With a wild cry Der-Der lowered his head and charged straight at you. His right forepaw reached out to rip your face. And so, I suppose, in your turn you did the only thing you could. You pulled the trigger of your weapon and its sharp beam raged forth and ripped Der-Der's head from his body in one short stroke, so fast he had no time to scream. The dying panda crashed into the *Show's* forward landing strut, shaking the whole craft. His head rolled a short distance from the table and spilled its contents onto the virgin sands. The stench of cooked flesh and burned hair was abominable, and I retched black bile, bitter and burning in my throat. I had never seen anything so terrible and the horror it engendered in me was like a monster, a physical thing, looming up in front of me and blinding me with fear.

I looked up, blinking back the darkness that had invaded my sight. You stood, dazed, by the table, a few feet from me. The muzzle of your gun glowed a dim orange. Ten yards away, Marian was frozen in shock and unable to move. I vomited again as Der-Der's body twitched and his contracting lungs groaned and sighed. Blood pumped onto the ground, the flow dwindling even as I watched. We did nothing, any of us, for many, many heartbeats. Then Marian shook her shoulders and slowly walked towards us. You raised the gun again.

'Do not be afraid,' she said, almost inaudibly. 'I will not harm you. There is no need to murder me as well.' She lowered her face to Der-Der's and nuzzled it for a few moments. She may have said goodbye to him. And then with a shake of her head she turned and faced south towards the invisible sea. The Blessèd sun was now only a finger's width above the hills and the panda's shadow streamed across the ground to her right. She walked away from us.

'Wait!' you called out. 'Wait! Come back! We must talk.' But I could tell that we had come to a place outside speech and so, I think, could you, for you fell silent. Marian broke first into a trot and then a full run. She sped away from us as quickly as she had run to greet Der-Der only ten minutes before. And when she reached the end of the shore she did not stop, or hesitate, or turn and look back, but with a great heave of her powerful back legs she threw herself into the air and leapt over the edge of the land and soared headlong into the gulf beyond and plummeted to the unseen ocean, many hundreds of feet below. The rays of the Blessèd sun caught her in her flight, dyeing her coat in patches of funeral scarlet and black. And then, soundlessly, she was gone and all that remained of her were footprints embossed in the blood-red sands of that final hanging shore.

I am not exactly imprisoned, but neither am I free. I cannot leave the new land to which I have been transported. I cannot even leave the building – for my own safety, you tell me. 'But,' I say, 'I'm fully restored now. Completely human. Look!' and I point – but with paws, not hands, and words still come slowly from my mouth. Slowly and malformed, for I am still outwardly a wolfbear and my throat and vocal cords are not well shaped for the production of human speech.

I am still not properly adapted to live with humans. I cannot work the knobs and switches you use to turn the lights on and off, nor can I adjust the electric heating. I cannot prepare food, and anyway my tastes are confused. My mind yearns for the cooked meals I remember from before my change, but my belly growls for raw meat and my jaws long to rend and chew.

You come to my room – although it is still better called a cell or a cage – and bring me my food. Sometimes it is a fresh-killed haunch of meat, sometimes chocolate cake or apricot jelly. You serve me bread and cheese or fruit and raw vegetables and make notes of my appetites and choices. Every meal is a test. Am I Monty the wolfbear, or Lieutenant Montague Parker, shuttlecraft pilot? What is my true nature; human or bestial?

I do not know how to pass the tests you set me. How can I establish my full humanity with you? I have surely not failed yet, or you would have ended me, as you ended Der-Der.

'Listen', I say. 'If I were still an animal I would have killed you when you beamed Der-Der. I would have seen an enemy who murdered a friend who was my equal. I would not have been capable of the deeper analysis. I would not have understood that you acted in what you saw as self-defence. If it were not for my humanity I would have launched myself at you with my claws unsheathed and I would have torn out your throat. You might have been able to kill me before I killed you or you might not.'

'Is it not significant,' you reply, 'that I allowed you to stand so close to me? Did I not trust you then, as I do now?'

It is true. We are separated by no more than three feet of open space and you appear to carry no weapons.

'But,' I say, 'you slaughtered Der-Der as though he were a beast. That wasn't right. He was more than that, wasn't he? Marian knew it and if she were here now she would say so. She would tell us all about him.'

'She is not here,' you say, rubbing your eyes. You look tired. At this moment I can easily believe that you regret the pandas' deaths as much as I do. I wonder – have you got into trouble over her loss? Have you been disciplined by your superiors? Has this failure been noted in your personnel record, has your pay been docked, have you been demoted? Or are your skills so indispensable that you cannot be held to account for this disaster even though you surely could have averted it? Would the work of the Institute on Gold come to an end without you? I cannot tell. Although the wall of memory is no more – or so I believe – there are places beyond it where I have never been and of which I can have no recollection. Biotechnology was never my specialisation, at least as far as I remember, or am permitted to remember.

You look down and turn to leave, even though our interview has only just begun. I hear your voice, almost inaudible:

'It was the most terrible thing I have ever seen. I cannot understand it – oh, but I can, I do.'

I weep then, human tears falling from canine eyes.

And one day a new person comes to see me.

'Hello, Monty,' he says, and extends his right hand. I take it in my paw and we shake, as humans do. He tells me that his name does not matter.

'What brings you here?' I ask, half expecting to be told that this does not matter either.

'My sister told me about you.'

'Your sister?' Briefly I wonder if he means you.

'Yes,' he replies and looks away for a moment. 'She spent some time here, a year or two ago.'

'Ah,' I say, to fill the gap.

'But never mind all that. I'm here now because there are changes coming. Big changes, affecting the whole world, and ones that I think you could be an important part of. Follow me.'

The man attaches a lead to my collar and takes me from my room to a new building, like a large metal shed. Keys rattle, gates clang and buzz and we enter a laboratory, one that I have not seen before. It is filled with a curious structure, made of webbing, plastic and metal. At the heart of this structure is a harness. I catch its purpose immediately and allow the newcomer to help me into it. Another man is standing at a control panel. 'Hi, Emmy, hello Monty,' he says. 'My name's Jonathan. I'm here to operate this rig.'

'I see,' I say, and perhaps I do.

'Does this seem familiar to you?' he asks. I nod.

'Good. Then let's see what happens when I activate it.' He turns to a screen and launches a program that puts me through a new set of exercises, completely different from those that you impose on me. They are new, as I say, but also old. I recognise them, for they come from a place behind the old wall of memory. And even though my muscles and limbs are also new and different, my body remembers its old reflexes. I recall the feel of the controls under my paws, as I recall the feel of my sometime lovers' skin under the human hands I once possessed. I hang suspended in a mesh of mono, facing a bank of pedals and levers.

A voice, not human but high and oddly inflected, issues from a speaker. A microphone catches my responses.

'One hundred and fifty-three magnetic.'

'Check.'

'Two hundred and ten knots.'

'Check.'

'Five hundred feet.'

'Check.'

'Flaps down.'

'Check.'

'Okay, Monty. Flare out. You have the con.'

I pull on the stick and the Fleury generators in the floor push and pull against Glory's gravity, giving me the sensation of vertical acceleration. I bank slightly to starboard. It's time to make my approach.

'O'Hare Tower, this is STS-1004 *Aaron*. Do you copy?'

'We copy, *Aaron*. Welcome home.'

I have performed those same exercises many times now. Before, in the control web in the laboratory on the Island, now in corespace on board the sailing ship *Sweetheart*. These exercises are risk-free. There is no death lying in wait for my mistakes, no lives depend on my skill. In that sense, at least, I am not in danger. But in another… I still fear what personal consequences may result from failure. I am surely not the only edition of myself in the *Sweetheart*'s core and I would be easy to replace if I did not perform nominally, as they term it.

The landscapes over which I seem to fly are becoming increasingly familiar to me. I am being trained by a process of repetition, doing the same exercise over and over again until its patterns have been imprinted on my brain to the point where my instinctive reactions and these new, overlaid responses are indistinguishable.

Time means very little to me now. I understand that coretime is flexible, so that real seconds may feel like years, while decades may be allowed to flit by in subjective minutes. The ship talks to me from time to time, using your voice.

It is likely that were I to attempt this mission in realtime I would go insane. Perhaps this is what happened to me on the voyage from Earth to Glory. Alternatively, maybe I spoiled in transit and my persona had to be reconstructed synapse by synapse from backups and co-data. I do not know, as that information is not considered necessary for the successful completion of my mission.

And my mission is of supreme importance. Once a human pilot, then a refugee, then a disentangled skein of neurons in a hybrid host, now a fractal structure deep in virtual space, one day, I have been promised, I will be rebodied into human form to pilot the shuttlecraft *Cressida* to a safe landing on humanity's home world.

This much is clear: I shall be the first man on Earth. But I shall not be alone, for I carry two companions with me still, burned indelibly into my memory. I can never leave them behind, because they were there at the moment I regained my humanity. I believe they were its cause. Marian and Der-Der sit next to me in the control cabin, fixed in time, loving and doomed, truly human, forever embracing by the dunes of the last hanging shore of Gold.

THE EVENTIDE

I AM NOT GOOD AT KEEPING A DIARY; AN EMBARRASSING CONFESSION for a man in my walk of life, who is often required to account for his actions, their justifications and their consequences. It is something I have to remind myself to do and although I have never been accused of neglecting my clerking duties, I have always regarded them as irksome necessities, to be dealt with as quickly as possible. Many of my colleagues, I know, enjoy keeping meticulous journals, but I am not like them. Because of this deficiency of mine, what follows is not exactly a journal and it is most certainly nothing remotely as formal as a daily log. It is simply my telling of some events that once happened to me. I have chosen to set them down, more or less in order, as if I were living through them again. I find that to re-read what I have written is a comfort; a way of living once more the experiences they describe. It brings them back vividly to me; more vividly, I fear, than they can ever do for you who read this, and have not my advantage of pre-knowledge.

The smallest detail, and my memory is triggered (as yours can never be) and I find myself standing once more upon the land of Peirie, feeling the wind on my chest and the sea-air in my lungs and the warmth of the Blessèd sun upon my face. It is to receive both a benediction and a curse, for those happy times can never come back to me with their original freshness intact, and when I return to them it is as one who can no longer be surprised and delighted by their novelty. Such it is to grow daily older.

So here you have it; my non-journal with its everlasting nostalgic value to me, but which may strike you as being no more than a bald listing of happenstances. My previous attempts at describing certain passages in my life's journey have done no better. That, I am afraid, cannot be helped. Had I but the smallest fraction of the literary abilities of the least of the writers of Earth, perhaps this narrative would cast the same spell on you as it does on me. Who can say? But for now, if you will, please read on:

Every morning I leave my home of concrete, sticks and leaves and walk down to the lagoon to check the nets. Their contents determine the shape of my day. If they have caught some fish, then my time will be occupied with gutting, skinning and filleting them and laying them out to dry in the rays of the Blessèd sun. If they have not, then I will harvest seaweed and boil it or climb the path over the pass and search the Outer Ring for shellfish.

None of these tasks are sufficient to engage me for the full twenty-five hours of every day. Were I a castaway once more I should be spending most of my time struggling to survive, but I am not. I am here by choice, and before I came to this place I took every precaution for my personal comfort and safety. My diet may be restricted, but I have an adequate cache of supplements – vitamins and minerals – to keep myself free from diseases of deficiency. The wind blows constantly; and it can get very hot during the day and equally cold at night, but my shelter is well-built and free from draughts and my bed is soft and warm. I enjoy fresh water, light and air; simple and pure. I am safe in my isolation. This is my home. It is the place that is mine and mine alone.

I have, you might say, the ideal life – or, at least, one edition of it – and should be considered lucky. And yes, I am fortunate; as fortunate as anyone could reasonably expect to be. I am comfortable and well-fed, and I have chosen to be where I am today. The same could be said of all the present inhabitants of Glory, of course. We have all chosen to be here. There were alternatives, which we rejected; each of us for his or her own reasons. A few were squeamish, others feared the long dark, still more could see nothing for themselves in the future they were offered. But most of us – and in that number I count myself – are here because we could not conceive of any alternative. Our world of Glory is too beautiful for us to turn our backs on her. We love her too much.

I have told you how I gather my food and how I prepare it for storage. You may be surprised that I go through these archaic procedures. What's wrong with using a freezer? Why all this sun-drying and boiling? My reply is that I am doing my best to get by without the kind of technology that relies on the continued existence of electrical power, and when you smile and point to the pocket laser I use to ignite my dried-kelp fire and the solar array that charges my house's batteries, I simply point out that the laser's battery will probably outlive the both of us and that if it came to it I could illuminate my home with fish-oil lamps. (I have a pico and a factor, of course, but I have not used them since I came here. They are strictly for use *in extremis*.) More to the point, though, is the absence of wood on the Ring. Even if trees did grow here I should soon deplete their stock if I used them for fuel; whether in one year or ten would make little difference. Or, perhaps, all the difference there is. Who can tell? Oh, but that is a foolish question. It aggravates the truth we all know, as a needle removing a wood-splinter tears at the flesh that surrounds it, but it can make no difference to it, because it is an uncertain truth. This is something that we who chose the way we did know full well, and have always known. We had to pay for our places here, and that knowledge is the coin we used. None of us can tell.

Enough of existential matters! Let us return to everyday practicalities. Today, it turns out, is a day without fish. This is not my fault. There was no mistake in the deployment of my nets. They were fastened correctly to the rocky outcrops to either side of the lagoon, their floats were properly attached with the appropriate knots and I rowed out and set them at the right time of the day, just as the Blessèd sun was setting. If fishing were a predictable art I would now be hauling in a fine catch of trout, salmon and bream, but it is not. I shrug, and hang the nets on the jetty's posts ready to put out this evening. There is no crisis, nothing to worry about. I have two weeks' worth of dried fish stored in my hut. I will not starve. Instead, I shall take a walk and visit the northern side of the Ring, but I shall not, as I may have intimated in the third sentence of this account, look for shellfish or seaweed. No; the weather is fine and I shall enjoy looking at the open sea for an hour or two. So I leave my boat moored up at the landing stage, return to the hut, take up my scrip and fill it with a few pieces of flaked salmon and some oven-baked laverbread from the store-cupboard, and a one-litre bottle of water from my solar still. As I leave, I turn and wave towards the Peak – this is a behavioural tic I have developed, to signal to people whom I know exist but who are as invisible to me as I am to them – and start the climb up to the pass.

It is a fine thing; to walk a path and to know for a certainty that it has been worn by my feet and my feet only. It is, to be sure, rather a stretch to call it a path. It is merely the route I use to cross from one side of the Ring to the other. But, all the same, it is mine. Every grain of dust that has been tramped down, every pebble that has been moved aside, every patch of lichen that my hands have slipped on and, annoyed by its slipperiness in the wet, cut away, speaks of my presence alone. Glory is a broad and spacious world, but her lands are small and largely well-trod. Her wild places are precious.

I sometimes wonder if I have violated the purity of this world by making my little path. We know our history, we Glorians, and we know what our ancestors did to the Earth that we once called Lost; the plunder and the despoliation. But we also know that the Earth, having once spurned us for our vile treatment of her, has offered us the chance of forgiveness. It is in the belief that I am treating her as gently as I can that I ask Glory to forgive me too, as I displace her stones and tread down her soil.

The path clings to the side of the hill, as every path through a mountain pass must if it is not to become impossibly steep. It rises steadily, keeping the rock to its right and the open air to its left. I speak of a mountain pass but that is an exaggeration. I should hardly be able to take this route twice in one day if to do so were to set out on a major expedition. The nearest true mountain is Leaven Peak, twenty-five miles behind me across the Inner Sea, although the Greater and Lesser Fang, jutting skywards four miles to my left, present, I am told, an interesting challenge to rock-climbers. Thus my feat of alpinism is in reality no more than a gentle ascent of five hundred feet or so, followed by a descent whose fall varies between five hundred and a thousand feet, according to the tides. I know by the almanac and the positions of the Blessèd sun and the worlds of Hally and Our Moon that the tide is in, and that consequently I shall go down about as far on the other side of the pass as I have gone up on this.

After half an hour's easy uphill walking I reach the saddle of the pass. Before me lies the open sea, behind are the Inner Sea and the Peak, to either side green-encrusted rock rises another thousand feet into the blue-white sky. The Blessèd sun is nearing his zenith and in times past I would have checked my watch and looked to one or the other side of him, seeking the fast-moving bright star that was the 'Down. Perhaps I would have waved to her, and it is quite possible that she would have seen me, if not directly then through her many groundside eyes. But not today and not for many days past, too many for me to count. Today's sky is clear, apart from a thin layer of high cirrus cloud. There are no birds, no aeroforms.

I must take care as I follow the vestigial trail back down to sea level. Not for fear of slipping and falling, though that would be bad enough, but for the sake of my right knee which, if I jar it, will give me several wakeful nights of pain and discomfort. Were I to fall and fracture a tibia... no, that would not be fatal, even though I would be stranded all alone on the deserted Outer Ring. I have friends in high places, you might say, and they would, I know, come to my aid. All the same, I am careful how I tread; my footsteps follow one another, left-right, left-right and precisely placed, as I clamber down to the cove.

The tide is on the cusp as I meet the waterline. Here, where the water stops rising, the waves have worn a narrow beach, sandwiched between the arid hillside above and the flooded rocks below. I find a sheltered spot, dig a shallow hole in the sand and lower myself into it. The sand moulds itself around me as I wriggle down, making the most comfortable form-fitting chair you could imagine. I eat my lunch and lie back, waiting for the sea to retreat over wet granite and reveal the shellfish – safe from me today as this is not a harvesting expedition – that live there. And, lulled by the waves' murmuring and the gentle airs and the warmth reflected by the cliffs to either side of me, I doze off and don't wake until the water has receded two hundred feet or more and the Blessèd sun has vanished behind the cliffs to my right. The sky is darkening to purple and the stars are coming out. Perhaps, if I look carefully, I will see Sol, in the constellation of the Cat, but it may be that humanity's home star is hiding behind the dust-brown world of Sally, now rising in the west.

It is time I went home, before it becomes so dark that I lose my way, or trip and fall into some dusky abyss of stone and scrub. I stand and gather up my belongings and turn to go. But… something catches my eye, something out at sea. I make a telescope of my right hand and peer through it. I traverse the visible arc, back and forth, and I see them. Lights. There are lights out there, clearly visible now that the horizon has fallen with the tide and the Blessèd sun has set. Three lights, one green, one white and one red, many miles distant, I know not how far. I shake my head. What can they mean? I look again, but a tendril of mist passes between them and me, and I can no longer make them out. I could stay and wait for them to reappear, but I dare not. My return home will be perilous enough as it is and I must leave this instant. Tomorrow, I tell myself. Tomorrow. I will return to my little beach, equipped with double rations of food and water, a coat and a blanket, and wait for the lights to reappear. In the interim, all I can do is find safety and construct hypotheses in my mind to account for what I have seen. For I am a man of science, as I am sure you will appreciate. It is fortunate that I have slept this afternoon, as I do not think I will sleep well tonight. My mind will be too busy for sleep.

* * * *

I say I am a man of science, which is not the same as saying I am a scientist. But in my profession I make hypotheses– or guesses if you prefer – on the basis of my observations and test them against reality. I use my guesses as the basis of experiments and I let the results of those experiments refine my ideas and guide me in my future actions. I should add that, although a scientist likes it when the results of an experiments correspond with his guesses, a true scientist likes it even more when they do not. And so it turns out; my prediction that I shall sleep badly tonight while my mind tries to construct meaning around the lights I have seen turns out to be wrong in detail, if not in overall effect. For, after a difficult climb back up to the saddle of the pass, guided only by ruddy Sally-light, and a dangerous scramble down the other side, I reach my hut only to find that its door will not open. It is obstructed by the body of a person lying prone across the threshold.

To say that I am surprised would be no exaggeration. I am utterly astonished. My home is visited rarely. Sometimes the keeper of the northern sea-lock knocks on my door to let me know that an unusually high tide is expected to flush the Inner Sea and that I should keep my eyes open in case the water rises far enough to flood me out. I like to return his calls from time to time to make sure that he is keeping well. Apart from these occasional encounters I see few of my fellow humans and so I am briefly taken aback by this night-time apparition. I stand still for a moment, nonplussed. Then my professional training takes over and I bend down and shake the person's shoulder. Surely he or she has not crawled to my doorstep and died there? But no; after a few vigorous shakes the person groans and turns over. I see that it is a woman, so dark-skinned that it is hard to make out her features in the dim light. 'Come,' I say, 'let me help you up.' I slide my arms under her shoulders and lift and with some straining – for she is heavily built – I pull her to her feet. She leans against the wall while I open the door and I have to support her as we enter my home. Switching on the light, I notice immediately that she has a problem with her right ankle – a torn Achilles tendon, perhaps. I will have to examine her more closely in a moment, but for now I help her onto the bed and fetch a glass of water from the cistern. 'Drink this,' I say. 'Slowly, now. You're bound to be a little dehydrated.'

'Thank you.' Her voice is weak but steady.

She drinks the water, and when she is feeling better I help her to sit up on the edge of the bed while I look at her leg. There is considerable swelling around the ankle, which may confirm my initial diagnosis. 'Did you slip and fall? Bang it against something?' I ask.

'No, I twisted it. There was a hole in the rock... my foot got caught.'

'I see. Well, I'll bind it up for now and we'll have another look in the morning. You can sleep here.'

'Isn't this your bed?'

'I shall be perfectly comfortable in the armchair.'

The woman bows from the waist, slightly awkwardly. 'Thank you. You're very kind. Mister...?'

'Doctor.' I extend my right hand. 'Doctor Cameron Powell.'

The woman laughs. 'You're a medical doctor? I collapsed outside a doctor's house?'

'Yes. This must be your lucky day.'

'I think it must. I'm Martha.'

'Martha...?'

'Martha McLuskie.' We shake hands.

'Pleased to meet you, Martha McLuskie.'

After I have bound Martha's ankle and helped her into bed I retreat to my compact living-room, wrap myself in a spare blanket and try to compose myself for sleep. This is – as my hypothesis predicted – slow to come. Two extraordinary things have happened today. Two.

And... there is a McLuskie sleeping in my bed. There's a name, eh? There's a name!

I rise the following morning to find that there are, of course, no fish waiting for me to harvest from the lagoon. How could there be when I left the nets drying on the jetty the day before? I don't know why I even bothered to go and look. It must be something to do with my sleepless night. Still, it is pleasant to rise from my chair and go down to the shore, feeling my limbs straightening themselves as I walk. The air is fresh but hazy and all I can see of Leaven Peak is its summit peering out above the mist. Typical enough for this time of day, but the Blessèd sun will soon burn away the vapour and the view will clear. Unless, and I must check my almanac again, this is a Hally-day when the giant inner world will transit the Blessèd sun and moderate the force of its rays. I say check the almanac, but it has become strangely inaccurate over the past year or two. Nothing to be alarmed at, a difference of a few degrees of space or minutes of time, no more, but strange all the same. (Of course, I know what this minor loss of precision may portend, but I prefer not to think too hard about it, as do we all.) What to do for now? I could drop the nets into my boat and row out into the lagoon and set them, but perhaps I should leave that for later. Meanwhile I will check them for rips and mend them as necessary. Before that, however, I must attend to my patient.

Back home, I dip into my precious store of coffee and make a jug for us both. Just the one ship is left on the Bright-Leaven run now, and it only makes the crossing once every few months. Fresh coffee has become a rare luxury; likewise sugar from Edge, and milk from the meadows of the western Peak. This coffee is harsh, bitter and black, but that's the way I like it. I hope Martha McLuskie likes it too.

Whether she does or not she thanks me as I help her to sit up in bed and hand her my best coffee mug. She smiles to see its inscription.

'You flew on the *El Dorado*?'

'I was ship's doctor for more than ten years.'

'That was one of my son's ships.'

'I might have met him, then.'

'Yes, you might.'

'What did he do?'

'He was a flight engineer.'

'I don't remember a McLuskie on board the *E-D*.'

'He served under a different name.'

'Oh. I see. Has he…?' I look upwards.

'Yes.' Martha turns away for a moment. I have seen it often, that turning away.

'Okay,' I say. 'I'll bring you something to eat in a minute.'

While she drinks the coffee I attend to my toilette. I have no desire to look like a wild man, so I shave with a ceramic blade and take my customary swim, towelling myself down with a sheet of everlasting tufted mono. I put on clean clothes and a pair of sandals. When I return the mug is standing on my bedside table, half-finished, and Martha is fast asleep once more. Good, I think, and I don't mind the wasted coffee one bit. It is pleasant to have company – albeit company that fidgets and snores – and I shall enjoy it for now, while it is fresh and new. No doubt we will tire of one another sooner or later.

While Martha sleeps I busy myself around the house. Now I have a guest it behoves me to sort it out a bit. I am not untidy – no airman, even a proxy airman such as myself, can afford to be untidy. There is no room on board ship for untidiness. But nevertheless there are surfaces I have not dusted for a week or two and my few pieces of furniture are not best arranged to allow an invalid to pass. Around midday Martha wakes again, and I give her a bowl of light gruel and some water. Now would be a good time to conduct a proper examination.

It is customary in the medical profession to describe a patient's age in Earth years, not Glorian. The reason for this is that our literature (and especially the pharmacopoeia) is based on the time-scales of the home world. It would be an appalling mistake, for example, to prescribe a drug in quantities suitable for an adult of twenty-four to a child whose age in Earth terms was only twelve and this practice helps prevent such accidents from occurring. Hence, when I do the clerking for my new patient I describe her thus: A woman of Afro-Caribbean heritage in her late fifties or early sixties, well-nourished and in good general health. Evidence in her hands and spine of a hard working life, but basically vigorous and sound. No signs of fracture in her ankle, but some local trauma and internal bruising. I prescribe two days' bed rest.

'You mean I must stay stuck indoors for two whole days?'

'Not necessarily indoors. I could improvise something for you outside. Use a cushion or two. But I don't want you putting any weight on that foot. If the pain and swelling have gone down after two days we'll know it's only a sprain. If they haven't, I'll put in a call to Porth Leaven and they can send a skiff across and look after you there.'

'You have a phone?'

'Yes, all doctors do, even now. No screen, though.'

No, all the screens across Glory are blank; their Monitors departed or forced to find new occupations. The 'Down graciously left us a few sats to support the phone system.

'I keep it in a cupboard with a notice pinned to the door: ONLY FOR USE IN CASE OF DIRE EMERGENCY. I don't think this counts as a dire emergency, do you?'

'But...' Martha's voice falls away. 'No, I don't suppose it does.'

Martha McLuskie lies quietly in bed while I leave the hut to row out beyond the lagoon and fish with rod and line for a couple of hours. It is important for her recovery that, if at all possible, she should have fresh food to eat. I catch a few whiting and a brace of sardines. They will do well enough. But when I return I find that, against all my instructions, my patient has got out of bed and is sitting on the ground with her back to an outside wall. 'I told you to stay put,' I say.

'I get stuffy indoors.'

'Doctor's orders.'

'Pah! Your job is to make me better, not give me orders.'

My bedside manner has never been widely praised, but I manage to maintain my composure. 'I have caught us some supper,' I say. I show her my catch.

'Do you have a knife?'

'Yes.'

'A sharp one?

'Yes.'

'Then give it to me. And those fish.'

I lay the fish by her side and fetch a chopping board and a molecular knife from the kitchen. 'There.'

'Thank you.' She looks closely at the knife. 'This is a good blade. Do you perform surgery with it, Doctor?'

'No. I am a general practitioner.'

'A good one?'

'Very good. I'm the best GP on the Ring of Leaven.'

Martha grins widely. 'You're the only GP on the Ring of Leaven!'

I bow.

Martha balances the chopping board on her knees and in a flashing succession of knife-flicks she fillets the fish, removing their skin, insides and bones in a few deft movements.

'There!'

'Thank you. I'm surprised you've still got all your fingers and thumbs.'

'I've done this kind of work before.'

'So I see.'

An appalling thing has happened today. Something so dreadful that, did I not feel obliged to write the truth – the whole truth – in this account, I should omit it. But no, record it I must. It was this morning; three days after I found Martha McLuskie lying on my front doorstep. She was lying on the bed and I was examining her ankle, which I am now quite confident is not broken, and massaging it gently, when, looking up, I caught sight of her face. It was perfectly relaxed and her lips were drawn back in a slight smile. And suddenly, from out of nowhere, I registered the whole of her; her breasts, her belly and her thighs and the place between them, though she was fully dressed and I was attending to my doctor's work. I felt, as if they were real, the weight of her breasts in my hands, the pressure of her rounded belly against mine, the parting of her soft thighs and my sweet, welcome entry into her. I looked away, certain that I wore a satyr's face.

'Okay, Martha,' I said. 'Lie back and rest.' She sighed, and I heard the groans and whimpers of passion in her throat.

I left the room as soon as I could, hoping that Martha's eyes were closed and my physical response not visible to her. What should I do? To return to the bedroom and seduce her was quite unthinkable. To relieve myself outside; no, that would be a mean and dirty act.

Doctors are taught how to deal with inappropriate sexual reactions to, and from, their patients. One withdraws and requests a colleague to take over the case. Excuses are made. It happens to everyone sooner or later and, although there may be smiles and a little joshing between fellow medics, we have an understanding that such a matter, properly nipped in the bud, does no lasting damage. We acknowledge one another's humanity. But this was different. I had no nearby colleague, as Martha had so rightly observed, nobody to step in, nobody to save me from guilt and shame.

Guilt and shame – I understand them. And so I expiated my sin as I have learned to do. I walked to the end of the jetty, took off my clothes and laid them carefully on the boards, lifted my arms in a gesture of supplication and called for my saviours to come to me.

And they came, and they wrapped me in flame, and they burned, yet again, the guilt and shame from me, and left me purified by pain.

It is now five days since we met and my patient is raring to go. Go where? She hasn't told me yet but it has, without my quite understanding how or why, been agreed that I will go along with her for at least part of the way. Perhaps I needed little persuasion.

My life here is, as I have suggested, safe and pleasant, but it does not offer much variety or mental stimulation. I had thought I had had enough of travel and adventuring, but now I know better. I have been living like a hermit for too long.

While she was recovering from her twisted ankle, I retraced Martha's steps as she described them to me and rescued the pack she lost when she fell. It looked as if she were following the path from the northern sea-lock along the inner side of the Ring. That would, on the face of it, make sense. The Outer Ring is steeper and more dangerous than the Inner. It was just bad luck that Martha hurt herself when she did, though neither she nor I can explain why she did not turn back to the sea-lock, where the lockkeeper could have helped her. 'I knew I had to keep moving,' she said, and left it at that. People often act irrationally when in pain, despite the self-preserving powers of instinct.

It is fortunate that Martha has a change of clothes. I dread to think what would have happened if I had had to wash her intimate apparel. Instead, I let her go down to the water to scrub and dry her things. My wounds have healed now and I can move freely.

So here we are, standing outside my hut at midday, shod for a hike and carrying packs full of food, water, spare clothing and lightweight woven-mono blankets. My whistle is tucked safely away in an inside pocket.

'Okay, Doc?' says Martha.

'Okay. Oh, by the way…'

'Yes?'

'There's just one thing. Which way are we going?'

'That way!' Martha points uphill.

'Over the pass?'

'Yes.'

My pass, I should have said, but it's become evident to me that Martha must have had her route already mapped before she set out on her expedition.

As it is my pass I lead the way. The Inner Sea drops quickly away behind us. I can't help looking back and seeing my home merge into its surroundings and the lower parts of Leaven Peak become clearer. I give its people my customary wave. The air grows fresher as we climb and when we reach the col it swirls around Martha and me and dries the sweat from our skin. We take a mouthful of water from our flasks.

'How are you?' I ask. 'Leg all right?'

'Yes, it's fine.'

That's good. I should have followed her uphill, the better to observe her fitness, but I feared my reactions to the sight of her body moving in such close proximity to mine. Damn. I thought I'd left all that behind me on the jetty.

'Right,' I say once we are rested and ready to move on, 'you lead off. Follow the path down. I'll tell you if you stray off the line. And take care!'

'Yes, Doc.'

It is two hours after the meridian when we reach sea level. I timed our departure so that, as before, our arrival would correspond with the high tide. Had I been wondering what we would do once we entered my secret cove, my question would have been answered several minutes before we got there. I smile. To my no great surprise, there is more to all this than I had first thought. Before, there was only a middle-aged woman with a famous surname who had crawled to my front door suffering from a suspected broken ankle. Then, there was evidence that she had been walking with some purpose in mind. Now, it is clear that she is not the only agent involved here (my own involvement is, after all, completely accidental).

For, rocking gently and securely moored to a stake driven into the ground is a small boat, with her mainsail furled around her boom and the name *Albatross* written in faded gold lettering on her bows. Martha smiles to see her, but I catch that it is not a smile of unalloyed joy. Pain and distress are mingled with it.

'Doc,' she says, 'this is the place I was trying to get to. I can carry on by myself from here on. Thank you for all your help. I couldn't have made it this far by myself.' She extends her right hand. I take it, ready to shake and say farewell, but she pulls me to herself, wraps both arms around me, and gives me a gargantuan hug.

'You berk!' she laughs, and I laugh too. I feel her body quivering with mirth. 'What is the matter with you?' I splutter in response. We rock back and forth, stricken with a serious case of the giggles. I revel in our closeness. After a while we separate and I help Martha to get into the boat. I throw her pack after her and untie the mooring rope. We are at the full flood of the tide now. She must set sail immediately, or wait another day. I suspect this boat has been waiting here for several days while Martha has been delayed.

'You know where you're going?'

'Yes.'

'I'll cast off, then.'

'Thank you.'

I let go of the rope and Martha pulls it on board. She takes a paddle from under the thwarts and uses it to turn *Albatross* around until she faces out to sea. I stand and watch as she unfurls the mainsail and hauls it up the mast. The wind catches the canvas, forcing the boat to heel over hard to port. Martha quickly catches the tiller and straightens *Albatross* out. I wave. 'Goodbye!'

Martha calls back, 'Goodbye.'

I watch as they leave and I turn away; and then I turn back. 'Wait! Please wait! For Providence's sake, wait!'

My clothes have been draped across the foredeck to dry. If Martha notices the fast-fading stripes on my back, arms and chest she is tactful and says nothing about them. Meanwhile, I consider the situation I have so impulsively thrown myself into. I am at sea – the open sea – in a sailing boat of no more than twelve feet in length, steered by a McLuskie. We are perhaps five miles from shore, but the Outer Ring has receded shockingly quickly behind us. *Albatross* is sailing at a steady four or five knots, bouncing across the wave tops and driven by a steady breeze on the starboard beam. It is, in other words, a great day for sailing.

I wonder how Martha knows which heading to set. Our course appears to be more or less due north, but it isn't obvious where we're making for. However, one thing has now become extremely clear to me. The night I met Martha I saw lights out at sea where there should have been no lights. I put them to the back of my mind while I looked after my patient, but the appearance of *Albatross* and our setting out to sea imply that there must be a connection. Something is out there, something waiting expectantly, and Martha was trying to reach it when she had her fall.

This comforts me. We are not sailing aimlessly into the void. There is a destination. But then it strikes me that, had she not been hurt, Martha would have been at *Albatross*'s helm three days ago, maybe four. What if this destination is no longer where she expects to find it? What if it no longer exists? And there is another thing. How long can we endure out here before we have to return to Leaven? Martha brought eight days' supply of food and drink with her, but now there are two of us. If the winds stay in the east or move to the west then we will be able to sail back to the south as quickly as we are presently heading northwards. But if the winds should fail or change direction…?

I do not regret the impulse that led me to jump onto *Albatross*, even though I fell short of her and took a soaking, and anyway my clothes will be dry enough to put back on before it gets too dark and cold. But I have put my life at the hazard, and I know that if I do have to call for help it will come to me, but not necessarily to Martha. I am not sure how I could live with the disgrace if I were borne away to safety while she was left behind to drown or die of thirst.

'Martha,' I say later. 'I think we should talk.'

'Yes, Doc?'

'First thing is, we've got enough food and water for two day's outward sailing. After that, we'll have to turn back. Are two days going to be long enough?'

'I think so.'

'You think so? You don't know for sure?'

'No, I don't. Now, do I get to ask you a question? Is it my turn?'

I nod. 'Feel free.' *Albatross* is making good headway, as Martha sits in the stern with her hand on the tiller and an eye on the burgee flag at the masthead. The waves splash rhythmically under the bow and our wake twinkles in a phosphorescent stream stretching back to the south. Nothing is left of the Blessèd sun but a fast-fading red glow in the east and the navigation beacon at the top of Leaven Peak drills a yellow-white beam straight into the sky, lighting up a few wisps of low cloud. It is our sole fixed point, out here on the darkling ocean. I am fully clothed once more. It will be cold later.

'Where are you from?'

'You mean, where was I born?'

'Yes.'

'I'm Hornese.'

'"Hard to please", eh?'

'Of course.' I am used to this slur on my birthplace. Everyone from Horn is assumed to be posh, to coin an old Earth word. 'My turn now. You're from Leaven?'

'That's right. "Close to heaven", as they say.' How could I possibly argue with that?

Martha's turn again. 'Have you always lived by yourself?'

'Since I left home, yes.'

'Never with anyone special?'

'That's two questions, but… no, not really. I'm a difficult person to live with. Pernickety, someone once said. Pedantic. Awkward. Uncommunicative. Inflexible. Formal. Emotionally constipated. A bit odd.'

'You don't seem all that bad to me.'

'That's different. I'm a doctor and you're my patient.'

Martha doesn't speak for a moment or two. I'm not sure why. Did she see my lustful face after all? Is she disgusted by my hypocrisy? I break the difficult silence with a difficult question.

'Now for me. Forgive me, but I must ask this: You had two children. A girl and a boy. Your husband was killed by a foy and your daughter was lost at sea. Your son took ship with the 'Down.'

'Is that a question? The answer is yes, yes, yes, yes and yes.' So, she is not a distant relative of the famous Annie and Emmy McLuskie. She is, as I had suspected, their mother. Enough probing; I think I had better bring the conversation round to more immediate matters.

'Does it bother you that we are miles away from land and that a foy might come at any time and kill the both of us?'

'No, it does not.'

'And your confidence is based on the fact that we found this boat waiting ready for us? And that you expected to find it?'

'Waiting for me. Yes. That was nine questions. Now, you answer one. Three days ago, when I was still laid up in bed, you came back to the hut with fresh blood seeping through your shirt and a look on your face that frightened me half to death. You moved stiffly all the next day and you seemed to be in pain. Did you slip and cut yourself on the rocks?'

'No, I did not.'

'Are you going to tell me what happened?'

'No.'

'Why not?'

'It's private.'

'I see. Then, Doctor Powell, can we agree to keep private things private?'

'And not ask awkward questions?'

'Pah! You started it.'

'I did not.'

'Oh Providence! Forget it. I'm sorry we began all this. Let's sleep now. It's been a long day.'

'All right.'

And Martha McLuskie takes down the sail and puts out the sea-anchor, and we lie in the bottom of the boat and wrap ourselves snugly in our blankets, with our feet facing the bows and our bodies safely separated by *Albatross*'s mast and centreboard case. Overhead our running lights trace red, white and green figures of eight, while the worlds and stars rock back and forth, to and fro, back and forth, to and fro, wishing us good night and what dreams may come.

It strikes me the following morning, as I rise carefully and creakily from the bottom of the boat, that I have done a very stupid thing. Not in jumping on board *Albatross*, nor in upsetting Martha the night before, but in leaving my phone behind. It is still in the hut, on a shelf in the cupboard with the silly warning notice on its door. Obviously I should have brought it with me. If Martha had fallen again as we climbed the pass I could have used it to call the Peak and someone would have come to rescue us. Obviously. Or, more to the point, we could have used it out here to fetch assistance if we were blown so far out to sea that we couldn't get back to land before our food and water ran out. But I have got out of the habit of carrying my phone and I never expected to be making an impromptu sea-voyage.

We share out our breakfast, but don't say much to one another. We're both feeling a little bruised. I ask Martha if I can help her with the boat in any way and she politely declines my offer. She was expecting to make this trip alone, I suppose, and had prepared herself to do so. I am not good at striking up friendships (or rescuing them) and have little small talk, so I keep my peace and hope my reticence is not mistaken for sulkiness or anger.

The day passes slowly. We continue on our northerly course, the wind continues to blow steadily from the east, and Martha and I sit quietly, she in the stern and me on the starboard gunwale, balancing the craft and keeping her mast upright and her wake straight. We each look away while the other slips into the water to wash and see to nature's needs. The Blessèd sun slowly crosses the sky from port to starboard, interrupted now and then by scattered patches of low cloud and the iridescent patches of colour that are low-flying aeroforms, feeding on patches of algae. At midday we take careful sips from our water flasks and eat a few pieces of fish. If only I had thought to bring a rod and line! From time to time we exchange places and I take a spell at the tiller. Martha tries not to let herself get too exasperated by my wobbly wake and flapping mainsail. I look astern every now and then. There is no sign of land behind us now – the Peak has sunk below the horizon and we are surrounded by featureless green sea and blue-white sky. They meet at a fuzzy line, distant and vague. This is a nameless ocean we cross, as are all of Glory's deeps.

I remember how the sea and sky looked from the observation deck of the Board ship *El Dorado*. Different they were, and yet the same. Below us, the same blue-green watery plain interrupted only by the occasional shadow of a voyaging foy and the darker green of the weed-patches we called sargassos. Above us, the huge seven-hundred-metre bulk of the ship's Ray tanks, keeping us safely aloft, and beyond that, the 'Down in her ninety-minute orbit. We would once have called that orbit eternal, but nothing is eternal. Not the 'Down, not the *El Dorado* and not humanity. We shall all die, and our species will die with us. Not so the foys: *Foialensis Gloriana Magnor*, once refugee humanity's greatest threat, then the subject of an uneasy standoff and still, despite our technological superiority, the true rulers of Glory. They have lived through many Great Tides in the past and they will doubtless survive the next one too.

The Board ships were very safe, despite being mere bubbles of alloy and mono and exposed to Glory's winds and storms. Even the LAV *El Dorado*, on which I was once cast away, was repaired and flew again; and that after a crash that should have torn her to shreds. I am not sure that brave little *Albatross*, be she ever so solidly built, could stand up to such abuse. I look to the sky again. Help would come if I called, but would it come soon enough to save Martha and me?

The day drags on, silent expect for the creaking of the boat's planks, the thrumming of the wind in her sheets and lines, and the occasional functional words exchanged between Martha and myself. Like all such days, however drawn-out the individual minutes and hours may be, it eventually comes to an end; the Blessèd sun sets and we heave-to once more. This is it then. This is the end of our journey. Tomorrow we will have to turn back to Leaven. I have carefully rationed our food and water and we have consumed exactly half our stock, despite the day's heat and the desiccating effect of the wind. I was ever a good manager of resources. We will make it safely home, Providence willing. As I watch and wait the sky darkens with equatorial rapidity and once more Martha and I settle into the bottom of the boat to sleep.

I wake later, shaken from my rest by a dream in which a woman who is partly Martha and partly other women I have known including, most shamefully, my mother, comes to me naked, and with an invitation in her eyes that I cannot mistake. The sky sways overhead and I catch sight, as I have sometimes done before, of a spangled lance of vivid green, like a frozen meteor trail. I recognise it – it is the trace left by one of the 'Down's boost lasers, illuminating a thin reef of interstellar dust just as the Peak's sounding beacon lit up Glory's clouds the day before. One end of this perfectly straight line rests on the world of Sally, the other points directly to the unseen 'Down. Martha is muttering in her sleep and I think of rousing her to point it out, but I am not sure she wants to be reminded of the son who has gone and whom she will never see again. For surely he, like all the 'Down's passengers, has been laced into a fractal, to be re-bodied by the biotechs of Gold when the ship attains the orbit of Earth.

'Martha,' I say the following morning, 'I think you know what we have to do now.'

'Do I? Tell me, Doc, what do we have to do now?'

'We have to turn around. Do a one-eighty. Head south. We can't go any further north.'

Martha shakes her head. 'No.'

'No?'

'No. We carry on.'

'But...'

'I know what you're going to say. We'll run out of food and water. I don't care.'

'But we will run out. We have to turn for home now.'

'I say we do not have to turn around. We have enough to get to where we're going.'

'Where's that?' I stand up in the boat and grab hold of the mast. I point to every quarter of the compass. 'Look! There's nothing there. Just empty sea. Have you any idea how lucky we've been? There haven't been any storms. The sea has been calm. No foys have come to devour us.'

'We still have two days' supplies.'

'Yes.'

'And it will take us two days to get home.'

'Yes.'

'And during those two days, as you say, we'll be at risk of being killed in a storm or gobbled up by a marauding foy.'

'Yes.'

'Well, doc, you're right. To sail for two days is a big risk. But I say that our destination is no more than a day's sailing from here. Half a day, maybe. Where is your risk now, Doctor Powell? You want us to sail for two days; I say we have less than a day to go. I make that less than half the risk of being swamped by a wave or eaten by a foy. What do you have to say to that? Whose choice is safer now?'

'You're mad! There's nothing out here! Nothing at all.'

'And I say there is. Do you think I'd have come this far if I hadn't believed that?'

'You may believe it, but why should I?' The boat rocks violently as I gesticulate in my frustration. Why won't Martha listen to sense?

'Sit down, Doc. And listen. I don't mind your being here, even though you're so pedantic, awkward, uncommunicative, inflexible, formal and emotionally constipated, not to mention odd. But I'm on a mission and I know what I'm doing. And, Doc; it seems to me that you have two choices. You can stay here with me and help me. Or you can swim home.'

'I could take the helm myself.'

'You wish! You can't sail – not at all – and you've no idea how to handle a boat. I don't count that silly little coracle-thing you use for fishing. And anyway, how are you going to take the helm from me?'

Martha must weigh twenty kilos more than I do. I shrug.

'All right. You win. I may as well die here as anywhere else.' I have never been much good at persuasion, so I abandon my mutinous thoughts and take my place on the starboard gunwale. We resume our northerly course, and from here on Martha and I start to get along a little better.

'Nobody's going to die,' says Martha.

When the foys appear, it is as tiny shapes humped on the horizon. I point them out to Martha.

'That's fine,' she says, and I shrug again. What is one more piece of lunacy now? We plough on, although the wind is tending to veer to the north-east and we are forced to tack to continue on the course that Martha has determined. The foys come no closer, so that is something, I suppose. Not much, though, as the wind continues to gust and blow against us. I sit next to Martha, tuck my toes under *Albatross*'s footstraps and lean out to prevent her capsizing in the contrary gusts. The sky is clouding over rapidly. A storm has come upon us.

'Keep on?' I shout to Martha, even though I know it is a stupid question. She nods. We have no choice now. With the wind spinning around us all directions are equally unsafe. The priority now is survival. I am sure I learn more about sailing in the next hour than in the whole of my previous life. *Albatross* is thrown from wave to wave, she ships water repeatedly as her gunwales dip into the water and I have to dive under the wildly swinging boom as we lurch from the port to the starboard tack and back again. Martha and I take turns with the bailer, even though there are buoyancy tanks under the seats and, in theory, we cannot founder. We are both soaked through. This is it, I think. This is the finish. We cannot survive this heavy weather much longer and it could go on for hours on end; possibly days. I should not be surprised. Nobody ever said Glory's oceans were guaranteed to be completely safe, her winds always constant or her skies forever cloudless. I could ruminate further about my life and this its imminent close, and perhaps take the time to mourn my own death – but there is no time. No time that is my own. Time belongs to the whipping spray and the gusting wind and the heaving seas, and all our mindfulness and strength have been taken over by the raw necessities of survival. And anyway, if I were to say goodbye; who would I say goodbye to? Nobody; and that is a blessing. Nobody to mourn me, but myself, and so it is to myself that I send my hasty farewells.

And then, just as I have convinced myself that this is where my adventure ends, the wind settles in the south and the skies clear. Martha lets the mainsail out to port and I fly the jib to starboard. We sit side by side on the transom as *Albatross* flies gull-winged northwards. Martha keeps a careful eye on the masthead flag as we go. Should the wind veer just a little to east or west we would be in danger of jibing and would almost certainly go over. 'Only a squall,' I say. 'Nothing to get het up about.'

'Nothing at all,' says Martha, and we laugh. I take our stores of food and water from the foredeck locker and divide them into four equal parts. We each eat and drink our quarter-share while *Albatross* skips eagerly across the sea. It is freckled with foam now, this ocean, and we must be doing eight or nine knots. I grin broadly; my fear has been replaced by exhilaration and I cannot help rejoicing in the freedom of our passage. I remove my wet shirt, hang it on the port halyard and let the sun and air dry it. Martha keeps hers on. I count myself fortunate that we are both facing forwards and I am not distracted by the sight of her wet clothes clinging to her body.

It is a couple of hours later that I first notice the green patches floating on the surface of the water. At first I suppose them to be outcrops of algae such as the aeroforms draw up with their streamers, but when one of them bumps solidly against our bows I take a closer look. They are something I've never seen before. Imagine a clump of weed, sticking out of the water in a marsh. It is a metre or two in size, grassy stems stick up out of it, waterfowl may build their nests on it. Now take that fixed piece of land and set it adrift scores of miles out to sea and, while you're at it, add a peculiar smell – half fish, half ammonia, with faecal overtones. Then let me add that this smell is instantly recognisable to all of us; that of the decaying corpse of a stranded foy.

And this is what I see, a tiny floating land, stinking of foy. As we carry on northwards, many more of these verdant patches of land appear, some as small as the one that bumped against our boat, others ten yards or so across – it is hard to tell from our water-level viewpoint. Martha smiles to see them. 'Not far to go now, Doc,' she says, and this time I believe her. The tiny lands grow more and more frequent and ever closer together, so that we find ourselves sailing in the midst of a sea of green, and I hum an ancient song brought down to us from the days of Earth, about a man who sailed to sea and lived in a yellow submarine. Reaction is setting in after the stress of the storm (the medical man within me knows the names of the chemicals that are coursing through my brain) and I find myself feeling dreamy and detached and a little silly, almost as if I had taken strong drink or chewed *gree*. Perhaps I cannot manage too much strangeness, not when it comes piled up upon itself as it has these past few days. I sit with my back resting against *Albatross*'s mast and let my consciousness drift. Is this the place that my life has been leading all these years? Here, rocking gently in an equatorial ocean, with the Blessèd sun full upon me and this woman sitting confidently at the helm of our tiny craft? I cannot yet say. Only Providence knows, and she is economical with her insights, I find. All the same, it is clear that we are entering a new world.

The breeze continues to drive us northwards and soon we are taking in sail and crawling gingerly through an emerald and turquoise maze, changing course again and again to avoid the bobbing tufts of land, and it seems to me that we shall shortly find ourselves running aground, although the sea is countless fathoms deep beneath our keel.

Both of us have fallen silent. We have run out of words to describe the otherworldliness all around us. But, when I turn and look at Martha's face, I see a look of vivid expectation in her eyes. We are nearing the end of our voyage, although we are still many miles out at sea, and she is, I can tell, waiting with joy for a greater joy to come. And so we go onward, and soon the water channels narrow to the point where we can go no further, and we leap ashore (only it is not ashore – the land bobs and sways under our feet, just as *Albatross* dips and curtsies as we disembark from her) and moor the boat the best we can, seeing that there are no rocks or trees to tie her painter to.

'This way!' says Martha and points to the north. It is mid-afternoon and the Blessèd sun shines bright and clear above us. I retrieve our belongings and our supplies from *Albatross* and say goodbye for now and call on Providence's watchful eye to take care of her. We shoulder our things and walk across the spongy turf, watching our feet and springing across the metre-wide gaps between the little lands, although they grow smaller and less frequent as we go on. The stench of foy gradually recedes, probably because we are getting used to it, except for one brief spell when it intensifies and a fifty-foot wide hump runs across the surface of the land, reminding us that we are separated from the water by no more than a foot or two of matted vegetation.

'That was a foy, wasn't it? Passing underneath us.'

Martha nods. Neither of us need to ask what would happen if a foy were to sound from directly below. The answer is obvious. First the spines, then the head, then the hundred-foot long neck, lastly the massive body. Utter destruction and fear. And death. This little world would be torn apart and our bodies thrown into the waves, to be picked off at leisure.

We walk for a few hundred yards, no more, but slowly, as it is hard to walk quickly when you never know if your foot is going to land prematurely on a piece of land rising with a wave, or drop an unexpected six inches when it falls away. We fall over frequently, only to land on soft, resilient clover and sea-grass and rise once more, laughing as if one or the other of us had just told the most marvellously funny joke.

We walk and bounce and trip and tumble onwards and it is Martha who first sees the house – dark-green-walled against a blue-green background – and she raises her right arm and waves. 'Kris! Corrie!' she shouts. 'We're here!' A figure emerges from inside and waves back.

Kris and Corrie are the only residents of this seaborne land. 'What do you call it?' I ask Corrie, and Kris answers for the pair of them.

'Home, usually,' she says, 'but its proper name is Peirie.'

'Peirie?'

'Oh, it's something we dreamed up. Don't worry about it, Doc. Just our little joke.'

I decide not to worry about it. We have more important matters to see to. I say that Kris and Corrie are the sole residents of Peirie, but that will clearly not be the case for much longer, as Corrie is massively pregnant. 'Let me look you over,' I say. Martha nods her approval and I check Corrie as best I can with nothing but my medical knowledge and my hands – I left my diagnostic instruments at home – and find that she is no more than a few days from full term and that both she and the baby are healthy. 'You're doing nicely,' I say and all three women beam, though I suspect they knew that perfectly well already.

We doze away the rest of the afternoon. Later we have a light supper of fish and herbs and then it is time for bed. Martha and I are weary after this full and busy day.

Kris and Corrie have, despite Martha's and my protests, given up their bedroom to us and moved onto a couch in the other half of the house. Martha abandons the argument before I do. She knows strong, determined and immovable women when she sees them. The result is that Martha and I have to share a bed; something I find intensely embarrassing and uncomfortable. That first night I withdraw from the room and try to creep from the house and lie down outside, but Corrie is awake and shoos me back indoors. I return to bed. Martha and I sleep back to back and I try as hard as I can to ignore the closeness and physicality of her presence. Completely without success, of course, and I lie wakefully reciting the Periodic Table and as much as I can remember of the contents of my home on the distant Ring, while still fearing that I will spill my seed and stain Kris and Corrie's clean sheets.

The next morning Corrie rests and Martha stays with her. This is Corrie's first pregnancy – at sixty-eight Glorian years old she is an elderly primigravida, as the unflattering medical description has it – and no doubt Martha is entertaining her with tales of her own childbearing experiences. I hope she does not frighten the poor woman. I have already told her that I can see no reason why everything should not go completely straightforwardly.

'Leave them to it,' says Kris. 'I'll give you the tour.'

And she does. We leave the house, which Kris explains was grown rather than built, and look at the windmill-pump that raises water from the sea below us, and the solar panels that power the purifier and the desalination cell, and the storage tanks which hold the drinking water that is the final product of the process. 'A thousand litres a day if we need them!' boasts Kris, regulating a vernier gauge with a small screwdriver.

'So Martha and I won't strain your resources. We won't be a problem.'

'A problem! No, far from it.'

'But you were only expecting her, not me.'

'Oh, we knew you were coming a couple of days ago.'

'You did? How?'

Kris laughs; a gurgle deep in her throat. 'Come on, Doc! Isn't it obvious?'

'Yes, I suppose so.' *Is it?*

'Never mind that, Doc. Come and look at the bog!'

'The bog? You mean the land is leaking?'

'No, you silly man! It's our composting toilet!'

I suppose I should be glad that we are not fouling the sea with human waste. Otherwise, I expect it would drive away the fish that swim beneath us and the aeroforms that hover over our heads, darting off from time to time to feed along Peirie's coastline. Instead, it fertilises Kris and Corrie's vegetable patch and small orchard.

'How long have you two been here?' I ask, picking a tomato and popping it into my mouth.

'Fifteen years.'

I look around me. Fifteen years. That means they've been here since before the 'Down's departure. It also implies something else.

'You're Golden, aren't you?'

'Yes.'

'Ah.' That explains a lot. It explains why the low-tech, low-energy biological systems on Peirie work so well. A suspicious thought strikes me. 'You're not hiding a picofusor anywhere, are you?'

'Certainly not! We don't need one.'

I am impressed. Kris and Corrie's little ecosystem has been stable for more than a decade, without the help of an external power source. That means that, although it seems to have little resilience – what happens if the water-pump fails or a virus gets into the crops? – it must actually be much tougher than it looks.

We continue with the tour. I am shown the fishing-hole and the intelligent fishing-rods that catch sea-bass, trout, salmon and cod all by themselves. There's a pond next to it where the live fish are stored, like a large keep-net. Struck by a sudden thought, I ask after *Albatross* and am told not to worry about her. She will be fine where she is.

'So,' I say, 'you're happy to live here, just the two of you, and drift wherever the currents may take you.'

'We're certainly very happy. As for drifting, well… You'll see, Doc. You'll see.'

We have circled the land and returned to the house. We sit with our backs to the wall, drinking the sour-sweet juice of miniature apples from precious aluminium cups and keeping out of the direct rays of the noontide Blessèd sun. I hear Corrie's and Martha's voices murmuring inside.

'Just one thing,' I say.

'Yes?'

'Exactly how long has Corrie been pregnant?'

'Sixteen years,' says Kris. 'You're not as stupid as you look, are you, Doc?'

Altogether, I spent about three weeks on Peirie. That time, as I remember it now, was mostly occupied in doing next to nothing. No, that's not quite right, I was busy most of the time, but it was a low-level, unruffled form of busyness. There was nothing frantic about it. If you were to draw a graph, such as a scientist might make, of time against activity level, it would resemble a broad plain, interspersed with occasional bumps. It is those bumps that come most readily to the mind now, and that I can commit most easily to the page. They make, I am sure, for a disjointed narrative; but that gives a false impression. It is my telling of this story that is disjointed, not my experience of the events that comprise it. For that I am sorry, and I beg you to excuse the stop-start nature of my literary ramblings.

It is a great pleasure to eat freshly cooked food once more. Kris and Corrie have had all day to work up a welcoming feast and that evening they do us proud. Ray-wings baked with herbs in a methane-fired oven, steamed sweet potatoes and runner beans, with fruit to follow. And then…

'Real coffee?' I say in amazement. 'From Bright?'

'The best,' Kris says. 'But not from Bright.'

It certainly tastes like coffee grown on Bright but, let's not forget: Kris and Corrie are Golden. They could have synthesised the coffee beans in a private lab. I'm sure I've not seen everything there is to see on Peirie. Only; why would they go to so much trouble just to tease me? All the women here seem to be making fun of me in one way or another. I decide to ask another question:

'You guys all know each other, don't you? I mean, you knew each other's names before we got here. Nobody seemed surprised.'

'We weren't surprised, but we had been worried. You were late.'

'And you weren't surprised because… you… oh, Providence. Kris, you said it was obvious. You've got phones, haven't you? Unofficial phones.'

'Bingo!' says Martha, and she grins. 'Pirate phones!'

'And when I heard you talking in your sleep, on *Albatross*, you were…'

'...talking on the phone. That's right.'

'So why didn't you tell me, you silly woman! I was worried.'

'Because,' says Martha, 'I didn't trust you. Not then.'

'And now?'

'We'll see. And don't you call me "silly woman" again. Ever.'

I should be bored, but I'm not. Perhaps if I had come here directly from my job in the Air Service, with its strictly regulated hours, its clear lines of command, its duties and its checklists, I would now be feeling the gaps in the days that would once have been filled with work. But I have been living a solitary life for a number of years and, truth be told, have fallen out of the habit of observing schedules and talking to people; of living with them and sharing their labours and needs. So it is with some uncertainty and a readiness to be rejected that I go up to Kris and ask her if there might be something useful I can do, especially now that Corrie has decided that she is ready to let her pregnancy resume its progress all the way to delivery rather than hold it in abeyance any longer. 'That's because we're here, isn't it?'

'Yes, Doc,' says Kris, and I know that she is telling me at least some of the truth. I am sure that it was Martha's arrival, not mine, that made Corrie finally decide it was time for her to give birth.

At any rate, Kris graciously agrees to let me supervise the catching of the fish; once I convinced her (and Martha has backed me up) that I had been successfully supporting myself by fishing while I was living on the Ring. It continually catches me by surprise when I consider that that time – which is less than a week ago – already seems to be a long-gone part of my personal history; an earlier life that I have left far behind.

So while Corrie prepares herself for the arrival of her child and the house seeds itself a nursery annex of fast-growing bamboo, I sit and doze by the fishing lines, watching for tell-tale twitches of the rods and reeling them in manually if the servo motors delay by more than a few seconds. That is; if I am awake at the time. The tension of the days Martha and I spent on board *Albatross* has taken its toll on my energy levels – far more than I had expected – and I am prone to half-hour snoozes. I must be getting old.

And when I wake I marvel yet again at the strangeness of this place; where the land rides upon an ancient deep; where the grass ripples and sways, and hills become valleys and rise to become hills once more, as we drink in the rays of the Blessèd sun and swim through Glory's endless rolling seas.

It is on the seventh day that the fear I first experienced immediately after our landing on Peirie and then forgot in the newness of everything I found here is brought forcibly back to me. I am sheltering in the lee of the house, watching the roof knit itself together over the new nursery, as the wind has risen and the Blessèd sun is obscured by clouds. It has become, by equatorial standards, cold, and I can feel rain in the air. I have deserted my post by the fishing-hole – a court-martial offence on board ship – and taken cover. If the weather gets any worse I plan to go indoors and chat with Corrie and Martha. Perhaps they will let me help them with preparing lunch. Meanwhile, Kris is somewhere on the north side – or should that be coast? – of Peirie, attending to something or other. Nobody seems to feel the need to keep me up to date with what is going on. I should resent this, but no. I am on holiday, and I refuse to count the days until my vacation ends.

I sit back, supporting my head with my hands, and watch the constant motion of the landscape. I have got used to the way this land flexes with the waves, but when a hill suddenly rears up in front of me – a hill of at least eighty feet in height, so high it makes me wonder that the land has the strength not to tear along its summit – it startles me. The hill moves under the land, making the house sway violently from side to side. I hear the crash of falling pots and pans from within and I call out, 'Martha! Corrie! Are you all right?'

Martha's head appears at the door. 'We're okay. Go and find Kris!'

'Right you are.' That sounds much calmer than I feel.

I run as fast as I can to the north, following the moving hill, which seems to have slowed down. In fact I outrun it, and find myself climbing its near slope, even though I could go around it if I wanted. I am panicking as I run, and I pant with exertion and fear. This is the wrong way! I should be going in the opposite direction to this small mountain whose origin has become horribly clear to me. I slip and fall back several times as the incline steepens towards its summit and every slip and every fall deepens my panic and my fear. A deadly familiar reek fills my lungs. Scrambling to the top, and expecting at any moment to be cast back down the slope, I catch sight of Kris, who is standing not far from where the edges of the land of Peirie begin to fray into a lacework pattern of smaller, semi-joined lands. They are the older cousins of the clumps of grass Martha and I encountered when we first came to this place.

It takes me a minute to recover my wind but as soon as I can breathe normally I shout, 'Kris! Kris! Hey! Get away from there!' I wave frantically down towards her. 'You'll be killed!'

Kris cups her hands and shouts back. 'It's all right! Come on down!'

'Are you sure?'

'Sure I'm sure.'

I must be insane. I start to descend Kris's side of the hill, but it moves away from me again, so that even while I walk forwards I am actually retreating back down the side of the slope that I originally climbed. Kris disappears from view, hidden once more by the summit. I plod onwards nevertheless. Down, down, and by the time I am standing next to Kris, breathing heavily and holding my side, the hill has completely disappeared.

This is not necessarily a good thing.

For before us, rising slowly from the water – first the spines, then the dripping, mottled grey-green head, then the hundred-foot long neck and finally the gigantic dorsal-finned back – is what may be the largest foy I have ever seen, and certainly the closest. It opens its yards-wide mouth to take in a hurricane of air and as it breathes out again it is as if every rotting dustbin outside every gutting-shed in all the lands of Glory has been dumped outside our front door. I nearly faint from it. As it is, I take hold of Kris's shoulder to steady myself. I wonder if I should say goodbye to her, for surely this is our death that is regarding us with its slow-spiralling eyes, their protective membranes fully withdrawn, and displaying its rows of teeth – each as long as a grown man is tall and as sharp as a scalpel. I have to exercise all my self-control to avoid soiling myself in my terror.

The foy shakes its head from side to side and small grassy patches fall from it; the remains of the pieces of Peirie's fringe that the creature tore as it surfaced. I am mesmerised by this sight – I watch as each tiny island of green tumbles into the ocean. 'Should we run for it?' I ask.

'No fear!' says Kris. 'That's the last thing we should do.' She puts her hands on her hips and looks the foy straight in the eye.

'Lucy!'

The foy dips its head.

'What the hell do you think you're playing at?'

Kris stands silently for a few seconds.

'Well, I should hope you're sorry, shaking us up like that. And you're late!'

Another pause.

'Okay, I'll let you off this time. You'll just have to work a bit harder to make up for it. There's a lot of catching up to do.'

Another silence.

'Then you'd better get going right away, hadn't you? No time to lose. Get a wiggle on!'

The foy looks – can this be possible in a one-hundred-metre long sea-monster? – apologetic. It turns away and dives slowly and carefully, raising hardly a wrinkle in the surface of the sea.

'Sex!' says Kris. 'Why does it always have to come down to sex?' She gives me an exasperated grin. 'Come on then, Doc. Back to the house. There's bound to be some tidying up to do and it'll go off in a strop and stop growing the nursery if we're not nice to it. It's done that before. Oh, and Doc?'

'Yes?'

'Do close your mouth, there's a good chap. You look like a particularly foolish species of guppy.'

I am sitting next to Martha on one side of the dining table. Kris and Corrie face us on the other; Kris dark, stubby and intense, Corrie blonde, willowy and easy-going. The house is in a festive mood and its walls have sprouted flowers – peonies in here, geraniums in the kitchen, and buttercups and daisies in the nursery. The women have spent most of the afternoon weaving split ends of new-grown willow to make a baby's cot. I have been learning how to stuff a mattress. The thought strikes me that this work would have more easily done by feeding organic material into the factor (yes, Kris eventually admitted that Peirie had one), programming it, and letting it get on with the assembly by itself, but I can also see that everyone is enjoying making the baby's necessities by hand. After all, although I have a factor and a picofusor in my home on the Ring, I can manage perfectly well without them.

While we work, we chat. 'It's all foy-shit, basically,' Corrie says, apropos of nothing in particular. Our conversations have been like this all day – unfocused, jumping from one topic to another without warning.

'How do you mean? What's foy-shit?'

'Everything,' Corrie says. 'Everything you can see.' She waves her arm.

'Everything?'

'Just about. Look, it works like this. Foys eat stuff. Fish, krill, algae, you name it. Lots of it. They're right at the top of the food chain. And after they eat stuff, they dispose of it.'

I nod. 'It's a natural biological process.'

'Depending on how their innards are working and what they've been eating, the excrement either sinks to the bottom of the sea, or rises to the surface and floats there. That's what you can smell when the wind is blowing from the sea to the land.'

I nod again. 'And that's why properties in the Midlands of Edge cost so much. One of the reasons, anyway. No foy-stink.'

'So, there you are. With all that super-fertile foy-crap floating around, it's a given that vegetation is going to grow on it. There're just so many seeds drifting in the air, and circulating in the upper layers of the sea.'

'And that's what the little islands we found on our way here were,' says Martha. 'Foy-shit, with grass growing on top. And the grass came from…?'

'From us of course. Us Golden. We made it. I mean – you did want to have nice lawns on Glory, didn't you? Play cricket, bowls? Take afternoon tea?'

I walk like a sailor – swivel-hipped, up and down, left and right – across a constantly undulating meadow of matted grass and seaweed, from which I have been assured all remnants of foy dung have long been absorbed and denatured, to the east end of Peirie. Kris accompanies me. 'It's time you were properly introduced,' she says.

How she can imagine that staring at the gargantuan rear end of a foy can in any way constitute being "introduced" to it escapes me.

'Lucy!' Kris bellows. The foy turns its head to look at us. 'Here's someone I want you to meet.'

Kris speaks more softly to me. 'Just say hello and tell her your name. I'll listen to what she says and relay it back to you. You'll have to speak up.'

I cup my hands. 'Hello! I am Doctor Cameron Alexander Powell of the Land of Horn. It is a great pleasure to meet you.'

Kris tilts her head to one side and listens to an answer only she can hear. 'She's never heard of anyone called "Doctor" before. Tell her what a doctor is,' she says.

'I make people well when they get an infection or injure themselves. I heal them. At least, I try. "Doctor" is the word that describes what I do. It's my title, not my name.'

More silent foy-speak.

'Then welcome, Humanhealer Krisfriend Cameron Alexander Powell of the Occupied Land of Horn. I am Braveplunge Smartfins

Humanspeaker Krisfriend Corriefriend Lucina of the Great Western Chasm. It is a pleasure to meet you too.'

The foy bows and I bow back.

'Great stuff,' says Kris. 'Well done, Doc. Oh, and while I've got you here—'

'Yes?'

'You may as well know we're keeping our eyes on you.'

'What do you mean?'

'Martha. She looks strong—'

'She is strong.'

'But she's been by herself for a long time now. Just remember that.'

I have no wish to hurt Martha or defy Kris, so I bow my head in acknowledgement.

'I will.'

'You better had.'

We stand and watch as Lucy turns her gaze to the east, the direction in which she is towing our little land of Peirie. Infinite volumes of water throb and swirl beneath us.

'It made no difference in the end, you and Martha being late,' Kris says as we return to the house. 'That daft creature was later still.'

'You mentioned sex?'

'That's right. She was chasing tail, somewhere a couple of thousand nautical miles to the south-west of Falls. Some guy she met.'

'Oh, right. I understand. Some things never change. But... how can you hear her, when I can't? Telepathy?'

'No. She just uses different frequencies to speak. Ones we can't hear without assistance. I've got a transponder implanted behind my right ear that makes them audible to me.'

'And she speaks human languages, not Foyish?'

'Oh she speaks that too. Thirty distinct dialects of it. But the foys are better at understanding our speech than we are at talking theirs, probably because we can't physically speak it. Or even pronounce it.'

I suppose that pretty much explains everything, except why this enormously powerful sea-creature has agreed to harness herself to twelve plaited lengths of seaweed and tow us and our land to a destination that only she and the human women know.

Ah! Silly doctor! That would be it! It's just one more example of something that women understand and men are completely clueless about. Right. That makes perfect sense.

I wonder if Lucy is pregnant too?

Impressions of my idyll on Peirie come back to me now, one by one, as I sit alone on my jetty and attempt to write them down in their proper order. Some of them make little self-contained episodes, like Lucy's first appearance, while others are like glimpses of a landscape caught through the windows of a train, such as you might use to travel from Scarp to Shore, on Edge. They are snapshots of a scene that is both constant and changing and whose changes are but steps whose leaps only appear sudden because of the gaps in my perception of them.

And so it is that the memory that comes back to me most frequently is like a movement caught in a strobe light, a moment stored on silicon. It is night – a night of worlds with Sally-light rust-red on one side of the sky and Our Moon's mercury glow brightening the horizon on the other. The weather is warm, and neither Martha nor I can sleep in the closeness of indoors.

Separately we have left the house, each carrying a blanket against the morning dew, but together we have snuggled under the blankets and laid ourselves down on Peirie's resilient, ever-moving mattress of sea-grass.

We lie spoon-fashion; Martha behind me with her arms folded over my chest, me in front. I feel her body pressed warmly against mine and desire comes, but it is no longer shameful to me; and as we speak it fades again and I am free of its curse. We talk – Martha of her life in the village of Parrolindon on the south coast of Leaven Peak. Of day-trips by tram to Porth Leaven to go shopping, or watch the Board ships come sailing in from Falls and Horn and Scrape and Edge. Of her son Emmy's delight in the ships, and his study of their workings and how clearly Martha and her husband Alastair saw the boy's future.

'He was always quiet, that one,' says Martha. 'Always with his head in a book, or up at the Monitor's house looking at tech stuff on the screens. He loved to read; anything would do. Data books, old Earth poetry, story books. It was no surprise when he joined the Air Service.'

'And Annie?'

'Yes, Annie. Oh, I never understood her. She was so wild; so sure in her ways. She would never listen. She always did exactly what she wanted. Alastair doted on her. Of course he left her his boat, when he…'

'When he died,' I say, unhelpfully.

'Yes, when he died. When a foy killed him. While he was trying to rescue one of his crew.'

I change the subject and tell her about growing up on Horn; of that land's rigid caste system, of its strict hierarchy of knowledge and power. 'It would have been completely different had I been born on Edge,' I say. 'Anyone can do anything they like there. But a doctor – that was what my parents insisted I should become. They didn't have the money to raise me into the service of the Board of Trade, and I wasn't clever enough to enter the School of Horn as an academic. I wanted practical work, so a doctor I became.'

'To become a doctor is to join an honourable profession.'

'It is; but in the end we are no more than the handmaids of the Golden. They tell us what to do and how to do it. They know how we humans work. They made us, after all.'

'They made the first landers. But I was born in the normal way, and so were you. Weren't you?'

'Yes, I was. Martha…'

'Yes?'

'I am glad you are here with me.'

'Thank you.'

'But I'm not going to make any assumptions. Love has never come easily to me. I don't trust it.'

'Let's not talk about love, Doc.'

'No, let's not. We have a deal?'

'We have a deal.'

We lie still and watch the worlds spin against the stars. We have no need to talk about the all-enveloping mystery we call love.

Another scene – this one is particularly hard to forget…

'Right!' says Corrie one morning after breakfast. 'I've had enough of wallowing around like a great fat foy. Let's have this baby!'

'What, now?' I say.

'Yes, right now. Kris!'

'Lover?'

'Get the water boiling! Bring me hot towels and a cup of tea! I'm ready to pop!'

'Is there anything I can do to help?' I say.

'Keep out of the way?' says Kris. I must look rather offended because she adds, 'Sorry, Doc. Didn't mean to be rude. If you'd like to observe and lend a hand if we need you to get involved, I'm sure it would put our minds at rest.'

This is scant consolation, but I smile as graciously as I can and take up a position in the corner of the bedroom next to Martha, while Corrie lies on the bed and draws up her clothes. Kris stands at the end with a basin in her outstretched hands.

I know from my professional reading that human childbirth on Earth was a long drawn-out and painful process that could take more than a day from the breaking of the waters to the delivery of the child. Things are much better on Glory since the Golden made certain minor changes to our anatomical details, but what happens next takes even me by surprise. There is a splash and the basin fills with fluid. That's Corrie's waters breaking. Then Kris puts her head down and says, 'Off you go, girl! – one, two, four, eight, ten, fifteen, twenty centimetres! Okay, my dear, we're all set and fully dilated. Everything's the right way round. Now, if you could just give a quick shove and...'

And smoothly, freely, with no pain or distress, the child slips out of Corrie's womb, down the birth canal and lands safely in Kris's arms.

'Bingo!' she says, and taps the baby between the shoulder blades. It – he, it's a boy-child – responds with a healthy yell.

'Scissors please, Doc,' Kris says. I turn and Martha, who seems to be rather better prepared than me, hands over a brand-new pair of scissors, still warm from the factor.

'If you'd like to do the honours...?' Finally catching up and understanding what is required of me, I snip the baby's umbilicus and tie it off.

'Ready for part two?' asks Corrie.

'Sure, go ahead.' Kris holds out the basin and Corrie delivers the placenta. I find myself wildly wondering if we will be eating it later, stewed with onions and carrots and served with home-grown noodles and runner beans. Meanwhile, the boy starts to wail and doesn't stop until Corrie puts him to her breast. He sucks vigorously, while Corrie closes her eyes. Kris lies next to her on the bed and helps her to hold the child.

I look at Martha, and she nods. We leave the room as quietly as we can. I check my watch. Eleven minutes have passed.

'Bloody Golden, eh?' I say, and laugh. 'Too damn right,' Martha replies and we both burst out in a fit of hysterical giggles. We shake with our shared hilarity and hug each other tightly lest we fall over and end up rolling on the floor, laughing.

It is two days later. After one of my regular stints watching the fishing lines I wander over to the east side of Peirie to say hello to Lucy. In what must be an astonishing feat of patience and endurance she has been towing us steadily for eleven or twelve days – they have become blurred – with no more than an hour's break twice a day to dive and moisten her back, which would otherwise grow dry and in danger of cracking under the continuous rays of the Blessèd sun – and hunt for food. If only I could talk to her and hear her replies! Silhouetted against the sky, a clutch of aeroforms keeps station above us. Kris and Martha have both remarked on them. 'It's unusual for the same flight to stay with us for so long at a time,' says Kris, walking up from behind, her cushioned footsteps unheard beneath Lucy's breathing and the sloosh-slosh of water propelled by her fins and tail.

Abruptly aware of the passage of time, I turn to Kris and ask, 'Are we there yet?'

She smiles. 'Nearly, Doc, nearly. Less than a day to go. Enjoy it while it lasts.'

'Why, are there bad times coming?' Although, as this has been such a good time, any change may seem to be bad.

'Not bad times. New times, different times.'

'How's the baby? Is it your turn to feed him?' Both Kris and Corrie have started lactating together. The boy is putting on weight rapidly.

I call him "the boy" because he has no name as yet. When I ask when his naming ceremony will take place, all anyone will say is "soon" and "there's no hurry". That is fair enough. The boy is healthy and he is growing well. He is in no danger of dying nameless.

Kris grins. 'Are you trying to get rid of me?'

'No, stay. There's so much I'd like to talk to Lucy about. You couldn't arrange an implant for me, could you? At the moment it's like talking through an interpreter, or listening to half a phone conversation.'

'We'll see, Doc.'

'It'd be nice if…'

'Shush a moment, Doc.' Kris has her hand cupped over her ear. 'Yes, Lucy?'

'What is it?'

'Doc, run back and tell the others! It's Land Ho! Lucy's spotted land! We've arrived! You beauty!'

Lucy turns her head towards us and smiles broadly, as only she can.

* * * *

It comes again to me now, as it occasionally came to me then, that my time on Peirie was one of almost completely unblemished happiness. It is not often that we humans get to experience such times and simultaneously know that we are experiencing them. They were the good old days, but they were the blissful present too. Such awareness is rare, I have found.

The conventional response to such a statement is that all good things must end, and you may be expecting me to go on to describe how this Golden Age was transmuted, by some malign alchemy, into base metal. That would conform to a familiar narrative, would it not? But the truth is that, although there were many changes to our lives as Peirie's voyage reached its end, they were not bad changes, just different. And revelatory, and with the sense that life – the new life of refugee humanity on Glory – still lived in a spirit of optimism, despite the departure of the *Sweetheart* and the 'Down and the loss of so many of the gifts they had given us.

I say that I was happy. I will not say that I deserved such happiness, nor that it would last.

Lucy unhitches herself from the towing-lines when we are still half a mile from our destination. I stand on Peirie's eastern fringes and watch as the foy ducks her head and dives, leaving the water quaking behind her. Three rowing-boats set out from the opposite shore, and people on each craft catch hold of the lines and bring them to land, where they tie them to stakes. We have docked, it seems. Kris, Corrie and Martha, who is holding the baby, stand by and watch. Then, 'Come on, chaps!' says Kris, and we tramp round to the south of Peirie and find *Albatross*, still safely moored and only a little full of water from the overnight rains.

'Bailer's in the forrard locker,' says Martha. 'Remember? Hop in,

Doc, there's a good chap.'

I follow instructions, find the bailer and scoop up several pints of water and throw them overboard. Then everyone else gets in. Martha hands the baby to Kris and takes her customary place by the tiller. The rest of us sit where we can. I raise the mainsail and take hold of the jib sheets and we cast off and set a southerly course, steering to the east as soon as we are clear of Peirie's bobbing outliers of matted grass. The strait between our land and the new land opens up to the north, but we pass it by and continue eastwards, only making deviations to the south when we need to. The sea is mild, the wind blows moderately from our stern, and we humans sit and watch as the new land slips past on the port side.

It is clearly not a land of the kind I am familiar with. The lands of Glory are nearly all partially-submerged mountains, with the human-habitable areas being those parts that stand above the water, including the rise and fall of the tides. Only Edge is notably different, and it is a tilted table-land with no obvious peaks, apart from the area around the skiing resort of Knot and the ridge that runs down from Maybe and Shore to the southerly beach and the spires of Stilt Town.

This land is flat – as flat as Peirie – but many times larger. From our position only a foot or two above the waterline it is impossible to see far into it, but we catch sight of fields and woods and the occasional house, standing next to the waterline and as green as Kris and Corrie's home on Peirie. It immediately becomes as plain to me as it must be to you that this land is like Peirie – it is a mass of vegetation floating on top of the ocean, but clearly much larger and, I guess, thicker. To support full-scale trees, the bed of the land must be several metres deep. I surmise – and it turns out that I am right – that the wave-motion which makes of Peirie's surface a semi-solid sea is absent here and that only the very longest and deepest rollers have any effect on the way the ground rises and falls. From time to time the view is obstructed by rows of hedges, acting as breakwaters against the waves. Surely only a land that does not yield to the motion of the waves as Peirie does would need this kind of protection.

It is impossible to tell how large this land is. If we were circumnavigating any of the fixed lands of Glory we would see promontories and bays – the first standing proud of the waterline, the second receding into the hazy distance. But here distances are hard to estimate, and it is only when we approach what looks like the mouth of a river and Martha steers us to starboard and we head in a northerly direction that I realise that this land does indeed have some kind of geography. We sail up a channel that is perhaps fifty yards wide for a quarter of an hour. I look around us. Next to me is Martha, sitting in the stern, with her lips set tight together and her eyes fierce with anticipation. Opposite me sit Kris and Corrie, arm in arm and holding the baby between them. We have spoken very little up to this point – only to pass on practical matters, such as moving to keep *Albatross* level, or to soothe or change the child. But now a deeper hush falls upon us, broken only by the soft lapping of water against the hull or the quick flap of a slack sheet. We are waiting for something to happen.

And it does, but I quickly sense that it is not the something which the women are looking forward to, just another waypoint on our journey. The channel opens up into a wide lake, or bay, much bigger than my little inlet on the Ring of Leaven. On the far side of it is an actual town, with wooden buildings of up to three stories high, with streets running back from the shoreline, with shops and houses, with jetties sticking out into the water, and – I can scarcely believe it

– a sandy beach. As we go onward and the waves turn from rollers to breakers I realise that there is no longer an uncountable number of fathoms of water beneath our boat's keel, but only a yard or two. We could, if we wanted, jump over the side and wade no more than chest-deep in the water – warmer now that it is not circulating down to the lower depths – until we reached the shore.

We tie up at the nearest jetty and climb up onto it. A deputation is waiting, and Kris formally introduces each of us to its leader. He is a man of a hundred and fifty years or more, and he is grave in his speech and careful in his movements and dignified in his bearing. After learning all of our names (except, of course, for the child's) he tells us that his name is John Houlder and that he is the mayor of the town of Newton-on-Sea on the land of Hope.

'Not,' he adds with a twinkle, 'that anybody calls it that. They call it—'

Martha interrupts him. I am amazed by her rudeness. 'Is she here?'

John Houlder is not offended. 'Not at the moment, Martha McLuskie,' he says. 'She told me she was tired of waiting for you slowcoaches and landlubbers, as she put it. She'll be back in,' he looks up at the Blessèd sun, 'an hour or two. Until then, we have prepared accommodations for you. Please, follow me.'

And we do, to a suite of rooms on the first floor of a waterfront house. Martha and I are, once more, given a shared room. We make a quick exploration of its facilities, and then we stand by the window, arm in arm, and look out across the bay. Were it not for the lack of rocks, cliffs and distant peaks I could believe myself to be back home on the inside of the Ring of Leaven.

'Can you guess who I'm waiting for?' she says.

I believe I can, but that guess is so wild and so ridiculous that I dare not voice it. Instead, I say, 'No, I cannot. But I can see how much this matters to you.'

'It does,' she says. 'It matters a great deal. Doc, will you hold me as you have before? Can we lie next to one another as we have before? And will you help me to pass this last hour in peace? For I fear that, left to myself, I may eat myself up or burn myself out.'

'Yes,' I reply. 'We will lie together as we have before. But then… then we will go out and see if the town of Newton-on-Sea on the land of Hope has such a place as a café that serves a decent cup of tea. I'm parched!'

We are both fast asleep when there comes a loud and determined knocking on the door. Kris comes in without waiting for a response and sees us together. 'Get up, sleepyheads!' she chuckles. 'Come on! Move yourselves! They're coming!'

Who's coming? I'm tempted to ask, but decide to wait and see. Martha jumps up and digs her elbow into my side; accidentally, I am sure.

'Doc? Will you come?'

'Of course.'

Why does Martha look so strange? This is surely the end of a long journey for her. She should be bright and expectant. Her expression should not be so uncertain and full of doubt. And she must know that she does not need to ask me to come with her. Of course I will come with her. I take her hand and together we follow Kris down the stairs. Martha grips my hand tightly. Her trust – it is almost childlike – triggers a rare surge of empathy in me.

A small crowd of people has gathered on the waterfront; Corrie and the baby and John Houlder among them. They are all staring intently towards the channel which we sailed up no more than an hour or so before. I shade my eyes with my hand and... I see it. It is a foy's head, less than twenty feet above the water level, coming slowly towards us. There is something odd about it – but I am not an expert on foy species and anatomy. No doubt some foys have differently shaped heads from others. I realise, as must you, that the reason so little of its neck is showing is that the bulk of the creature is well below the waterline. It would not fit in the channel otherwise. The people around us wave as the foy approaches, and were the whole set of circumstances I find myself in not already so strange, I would marvel to see humans greeting the coming of such a huge and dangerous creature. The foy does not acknowledge our welcome but swims steadily on until it has completely entered the lagoon. It surfaces, and seawater washes across the jetty while waves break on the beach. The foy – and I had thought Lucy was big, but she is a minnow compared to this one – raises its head to its full height and looks around.

And then part of its head comes off. I blink. What in the name of Providence is happening? Something moves between its head-spines. I blink and look again. Is this a foy-calf, huddling next to its sire or dam? But no. Definitely not. With a cry of 'Wheeeee!' a figure leaps from the foy's head into clear air, performs two double somersaults and hits the water like a plummeting arrow. It disappears from view for a few seconds, then regains the surface and skims across the waves at incredible speed, only to dive at the last minute and emerge once more, flying through the air and landing in the middle of our little pack of people. Two of us catch her. They look as if they have handled this situation before.

'Hey, Mum! You got here at last. What the hell kept you?'

Martha is silent for a moment. I am standing close to her and so I feel her body shake with emotion, and I see her tears fall; though I cannot tell whether she is shedding tears of joy or of sorrow.

'Mum? Mum? Talk to me. Please, say something.'

Martha's mouth works strangely. She has become incapable of speech. Then, with a terrible effort:

'Annie, Annie... Oh, Annie!'

'Mum, are you all right?'

So this is the famous Annie McLuskie. She who was lost, and believed dead along with the crew of her ship, the *Guiding Star*. Annie, the last ship's captain of Glory, who led what was hoped to be humanity's return to the oceans, who faced down a foy on the open sea, who ultimately led her crew to disaster. I find myself wondering about her story, as Kris, Corrie and I wait outside the room where Annie and her mother are speaking privately and, I hope, gladly, together. Clearly, something radical has been done to her.

'Did your lot have anything to do with this?' I ask Kris. 'You Golden, have you been up to your old tricks?' For rumours have long been rife about the experimentation and bioengineering that take place on the land of Gold. Nasty rumours as a rule; of the creation of monsters and mutants, and of painful operations carried out for their own sake; and over these tales hang older, darker stories of the latter days of Earth.

Kris is neither defensive nor aggressive. 'Yes, the Golden saved Annie, at the 'Down's request. She had been very badly injured and was considered likely to die without our intervention.'

'Did Annie choose to be modified in that way? Or did you just think it would be fun to give her a tail instead of legs, and gills as well as lungs?'

'Her legs had been burned away in an explosion.'

'That doesn't answer the question. You could have created prosthetic legs for her, or regenerated the flesh and bone. She could have walked again. Instead, you've turned her into a freak. She can't walk. She has to use a wheelchair on land, or be carried like a baby. How does that help her? And look at what you've done to the rest of her! It makes me feel ill. And how can she ever have children? Look at her!'

'She can have children, if she wants.'

'Only with your help.'

'Yes. With our help,' says Corrie.

It is a moment before I catch her meaning.

I am honoured to be invited to the child's naming ceremony. It is held in the council chamber of Newton-on-Sea's Town Hall which, on this happy day, is brightly decorated with streamers, bunting and home-grown roses, red, yellow and white. Actually, none of Hope's five hundred and seventy-six inhabitants call this place Newton-on-Sea except formally and on legal documents. It's Annietown in day-to-day parlance. I stand next to Martha, Annie, Kris and Corrie on one side of the council table. John Houlder stands on the other side. Resting between us is a silver bowl, full of freshly-drawn seawater.

'Who names this child?' asks the Mayor.

'I do,' says Kris.

'I do,' says Corrie.

'I do,' says Martha.

'I do,' says Annie.

'Who wards this child?'

'I do.'

'I do.'

'I do.'

'I do.'

'And so do we all,' we respond.

Corrie hands the baby to John Houlder.

'You are Coriander; she who bore the child?'

'I am.'

'You shall give him his first name. Then you, Christina, then you, Martha, then you, Annalisa. Are you ready to name him?'

'We are'

'And are you all in concord regarding his names?'

'We are.'

'Then, by your courtesy —'

Kris: 'He is Alastair,'

Corrie: 'Michael,'

Martha: 'Cameron,'

Annie: 'McLuskie,'

Robert: 'Of Newton-on-Sea on the land of Hope.' He bathes Alastair in the waters of Glory. Everyone applauds. My eyes are quite blinded with tears.

It is a week later and our extended family is gathered together in the big downstairs room of Annie's house. It is an unusual room in a number of ways. It is of necessity on the ground floor, as a pool of water is set in the middle of it, and it has a channel that allows Annie to swim to and from the beach without assistance. A picture window on one side opens out onto the bay beyond and we can see Annie's foy waiting out there. He dives from time to time, as Lucy did, to keep his skin from drying out. I have been introduced to him – his complete name is Deepdiver Farswimmer Brightwater Icecracker 'Downspeaker Anniefriend Gloryguardian Thrarn of the

Gulf of Basrum. At least, I think that is all of it. He may have a few more names that I have forgotten. He is an old and wise foy; so old that I believe – although I cannot be sure – that he has already lived through at least one Great Tide. I find myself wondering whether he still speaks to the 'Down and, if so, how.

At the other end of the age scale is Alastair, who sits on Martha's lap except when Kris or Corrie nurses him or he joins Annie in the water. We take it in turn to admire his deep blue eyes, perfect light-brown skin and the beginnings of a head of dark curly hair; and all the women are besotted with him. We eat as we ate on Peirie; fish, sea- and land-vegetables, followed by fresh fruit, and we talk about nothing in particular, or whatever interests two or more of us. The conversation flows organically around the table. Annie has told me much of her story; of her upbringing on Leaven Peak and her father's death, of her first meeting with Deepdiver, of the aftermath of the *Guiding Star*'s destruction, of the involvement of the 'Down, of the work of the Golden. She talks little of her brother Emmy – like her mother she is in mourning for him. He is dead to them; his sleep will take him thousands of years into the future and when he wakes the tale of humanity on Glory may have ended long before.

'This is the way it is to be for we who have stayed behind, isn't it?' I say. 'Leaving the fixed, solid lands behind us and taking refuge on the seas. How many of these floating lands are there?'

'Hope is the biggest,' says Annie, flicking her tail. 'Truth is growing well, and Perseverance has just begun. Its first two lands started to join together last year.'

'Like Peirie accumulated from smaller pieces. Will Peirie become part of Hope?'

'Maybe. Maybe not. It's up to Kris and Corrie. And Mum, of course.'

'And is everything working out as you planned it? Was this always your big idea?'

'Not quite. Not quite like this. See, I had a dream when I was a girl. It was about what I would do when I grew up. I was going to be a ship's captain: Cap'n McLuskie, the Terror Of The Seas. My ship would be called the *Sea Hawk*, and she was *huge*. She had three-hundred-foot tall masts, hundreds of yards of ropes and lines, and acres and acres of sails. There were ten thousand passengers and crew on board and she sailed all around Glory, calling in at every port in every land. When the Great Tide came she was going to be lifted clean over it. Everybody on Glory would know my name and the name of my ship. We would go wherever we liked.

'That was just a dream, though, and I was only a kid then. I'm a grown-up now and this is the real world. My beautiful *Sea Hawk* will never be built. But look! We've got something just as good. Better, actually. No captains or commanders, petty officers or ordinary seamen. No watches or duties, orders or punishments. Just people, living happy and free. And foys, too,' she adds, looking fondly into Deepdiver's wide green eyes.

'The old enmity is over?' I ask. 'Our crimes are forgotten and they have forgiven us at last?'

'The foys do not forget, ever, but I believe that we are forgiven. Deep tells me so, and he is a truthful creature and a leader among his kind.'

'And when the Great Tide comes, we will all be saved? Everyone on the seaborne lands?'

'Yes. I promise it.'

I like to walk with Martha, hand in hand through the streets of Annietown, talking. It seems to me now, as I write, that the weather is always kind and the seas are always calm and the Blessèd sun shines brightly, but not oppressively, down on us. Sometimes we go down to the beach and bathe. At others we join in with the work of the people of Hope, and I look at minor injuries and ailments and treat them as best I can, while Martha runs workshops on the preparation of fish. All this time, and despite the smiles and welcomes we receive everywhere we go, I feel ill at ease. I cannot get comfortable with this life, partly because it is a way of living that I have not experienced before. From my upbringing on Horn, though my medical training and my joining the Air Service, I have lived in closed circles, with my position clearly defined by profession and rank. Nobody has a profession or rank here, apart from the mayor, and everything is open.

Oh! But that were all! In time I am sure I could adjust to this new existence, which must reflect humanity's first years on Glory. This second chance, this new opportunity to become true Glorians, not mere colonising Earthmen. But it is not all. I have said that I do not believe I deserve happiness, and that is true. It would be a terrible thing if the cancer of guilt that festers inside me were to escape its isolation and infect the innocence of the people of Hope. Or worse, Martha.

No. I must not allow that to happen. I must leave. Only... not quite yet.

When we are not busy, we are free to stroll through the woods or walk along the shoreline. We sometimes sit with our feet dangling in the sea and look across the narrow strait to Peirie, riding next to Hope but not yet joined to it. Aeroforms catch the light of the Blessèd sun and refract it into new colours – reds and oranges and purples. They are a relief to the eye, after the everlasting blue-green-grey of the sea and sky and this wide, exposed, flat land of Hope.

I wonder what the future holds for Peirie. Annie has told me that it is possible that, when the Great Tide comes, the large habitats will have to be allowed to break apart before the steep waters tear them to pieces and that intentional weaknesses have been grown in Hope's structure to permit this to happen. Smaller places like Peirie may be kept separate as a form of insurance.

I ask Martha about her uncertainty when she greeted Annie.

'I couldn't help it, Doc,' she says. 'My daughter; she was my little girl. She was whole. She was perfect. She was beautiful – so beautiful. It was my joy simply to look at her. She wasn't... modified. Altered. Crippled. She'll always be a cripple to me. It's a horrible thing to say.' The words come out slowly, one by one. I try to comfort her.

'It's a natural feeling. I get it too. It can be overcome.'

'But you must have had to deal with injured men all the time. You must have got used to it when you were with the Air Service. There were accidents, weren't there? Serious ones?'

'Yes. Some of the men were very badly hurt. Some died, despite my efforts. Others were maimed for life.'

'Maimed.' Martha pauses and looks at the ground for a moment. 'Yes. That's how I see Annie. She's maimed.'

'But she's happy. She's got the life she wanted.'

'I know that. I know that perfectly well. But in here,' Martha thumps her chest,' I don't know it. I don't believe it. They took my little girl away and they gave her back to me damaged. My lovely brave girl. You must see that.'

'I do.' The Blessèd sun looks down on us. The aeroforms hover and wait.

I am nearly at the end of this clumsy, ill-fitting narrative. It must seem to you, the reader, that I am telling a love story; that Martha and I, enjoying being together and having learned to trust one another, eventually consummate that trust in an act of physical love. And that I overcome my doubts and we live happily ever after and that, if you are reading this in some postdiluvian sanctuary, we survive the realignment of Glory's orbit and the all-engulfing tides that follow and live to continue our story and that of refugee humanity in peace and contentment.

But that is not how this story ends.

It ends after a restless night in our chaste bed. I am the restless one, and I have done my best not to disturb Martha. But somewhere between the setting of Our Moon and the rising of Hally I come to a conclusion. It is painful – so painful that I can hardly bear it – but it is the only course I can take. It will involve great suffering, but it will be a physical agony, not a mental one. It will heal.

I rise early, go down to the kitchen, and brew coffee and make toast. I take cups and plates up to our room, balanced on a tray along with a pitcher of tomato juice, and we sit up in bed and eat our breakfast.

'Martha,' I say, as casually as I can, 'I think I would like to pop over to Peirie with you today. I'd like to see how it's getting on.'

'Kris was there last week,' says Martha. 'Everything's fine.'

'Just the same, I'd like to see the old place again. I miss it, in an odd sort of way.'

'All right, Doc. We can go. Are you okay? You look a little funny.'

'I'm okay.'

Martha tidies our room and makes the bed while I do the washing-up. Then we walk out onto the promenade, waving to and greeting the other early-rising inhabitants of Annietown, step onto the jetty and find *Albatross*, neatly moored up where Kris left her, bouncing on a light swell with her halyards rattling against the mast and ready for us to make sail and cast off. Martha insists on sailing the boat down the channel for me, despite my protests. She doesn't trust me to make even so simple a voyage as this by myself.

We speak little as we navigate to the open sea and retrace our route around the south of Hope to Peirie. Martha lets me take the helm and mainsheet once we are sufficiently far off land that she can correct any errors I make. I find myself enjoying the sensations of being once more in command of a small boat. I have learned that you steer a boat with your whole body, not just the tiller, and that the slightest tightening or slackening of the mainsheet can have a drastic effect on *Albatross*'s progress through the water. I wonder if I should change my mind – nobody would know – but then I glance at Martha and know that I must not. She catches me looking at her and gives me a smile in return. I feel like a traitor.

Martha takes over once more as we near Peirie. 'Next time, Doc,' she says. 'When you've had a little more practice.' She flicks the tiller over and *Albatross* lines up tidily against a grassy bank. I jump ashore, Martha tosses me a mooring pin and I stamp it into the yielding turf and tie the painter to it with a tolerably good clove-hitch. I look up at the sky. Yes. Everything is ready.

Feeling more wretched with every step I take, I follow Martha into the house. It is fully-grown now and its rooms are ready for Kris and Corrie, Martha and me, and baby Alastair to live in. I go into the kitchen and fetch a sisal bag from a cupboard. It is one I have used in the past for gathering crops. Then, while Martha is distracted by some weeds that have rooted behind the sofa, I slip out of the house as quietly as I can.

I take up my position on the southern shoreline. I take out my whistle and blow three notes. I lift my arms to the sky. I am seen, and recognised.

But I am also seen by Martha, who has not been fooled by my attempt to escape unobserved.

'Doc? What's going on? What's that bag for?'

There is no kind way to tell her. 'Martha, I'm leaving. That bag is for my clothes.'

'Leaving? Leaving where? Leaving who? Where are you going?'

'I am going home.'

'Home? But… this is your home now, isn't it?'

'No. It is not my home. It can never be my home.'

Martha takes hold of my arm. 'But…' Her face is frozen in a mask of dismay and incomprehension.

'Martha, you must leave me now. Go on, walk away. Get back on board *Albatross* and sail her back to Hope and don't ever think of me again. I cannot see you anymore. I must leave. Now.' I shake her hand off me.

'What are you talking about?'

'Didn't you hear me? I told you to go. Go back to Hope and Kris and Corrie and Annie and Alastair. Go away and don't come back.'

'Go? What do you mean, go?'

'I mean go. It's the best thing you can do. You must not stay here with me, and I cannot stay with you.'

'I still don't understand.'

'Must I spell it out? Don't you get it? I am wrong for you. You must escape me now, before you get hurt. You must have no more to do with me. You cannot. If you stay here now you will see something that you will wish you hadn't. You will see the horrible truth about me. I do not think you will be able to endure it.'

Martha does not move. She crosses her arms across her chest and stands firm. She does not turn away.

'You must think very little of me, Doc. You must think I'm fat and ugly and boring and dull and uneducated. It's odd – to begin with I thought you didn't like women, but I know that's not true. I've felt it when you lie next to me. Doc, why won't you make love to me? Am I ugly? Am I dirty? Do you find me disgusting? Do I smell like an old woman?'

'You are none of those things. You are a strong, beautiful human being. It has been a privilege to know you. You could never bore me; you've seen too much of real life for that. But I cannot love you. I cannot love anyone. It is I who am dirty. I am stained through to my soul by a terrible crime. I will carry its guilt with me until I die.'

'I don't know what you're talking about.'

'You're better off that way.'

'Don't you dare speak to me like that! I am not stupid! I am not a child! I am a grown woman! I have given birth. I have loved a man – a good man – who loved me back; and who died. I have lived as a widow. I have worked hard to support my children, and I have lost them as well. What do you think you can tell me, or show me, or do to me that will make you abandon you here, all on your own? What do you take me for?'

'I have already told you what I think of you. You are a truly adult human being. But you would gain nothing by hearing the whole truth about me, nor by witnessing the penance I must do for the crimes I have committed. I am not a moral example from which you can learn. I am deeply immoral.'

'I don't believe it.'

'That – forgive me – is because you know me less well than you think you do. And there is another thing. There is something I must not ask of you. Do you know what it is?'

Martha looks at me strangely and shakes her head. 'I think I do. I could never leave my daughter and grandson behind. Not now that I have seen them together. I cannot return to the Ring with you.'

I nod. 'Thank you,' I say. My last hope is gone, I see.

'We need a doctor on Hope.'

'You have the Golden. You don't need me. And I have no right to call myself a doctor. I carry a moral disease. Hope is new and fresh and clean – I am old and stale and dirty to my core. If you stay with me you will become like me. I couldn't bear that.'

She shakes her head and tries again. 'Will you abandon a child who bears your name?'

'Is that why you named him after me? To blackmail me?'

'No, and don't be such a bastard! I did it to honour him.'

'You made a mistake. I am not honourable.'

'This is not the Doc I know talking.'

'That is what I have been trying to tell you. You do not know me. Now! Go away now! I do not want you to see me as you will see me if you stay.'

'I will not go away.'

I stare at the ground.

'Then I'm wasting my breath. I give up. Stay, if you must.'

'Doc, please! Let us not part in bitterness.'

'No. I'm sorry.'

I remove my clothes and tuck them into the bag. Naked, I stand with my arms outstretched, as a man might stand who was waiting to be crucified. I lift my head to the skies and the faithful aeroforms come. They take up their positions directly overhead and unroll their streamers. I close my eyes and wait.

The first streamer bites into my skin like the lash of a terrible whip and I cry out. It encircles me from shoulder to ankle, looping around me and stinging ever more fiercely where it comes into contact with my naked flesh. A second strike; and a third, and a fourth and my body jerks and twists and writhes in pain. Every streamer is covered with a myriad of minute sucker-teeth which puncture my skin and torment every nerve ending I have. The blood flows freely from my lacerations and scatters itself in carmine spots upon the ground. I howl and scream uncontrollably. I am mindless and delirious in my agony. Martha watches, and through half-closed eyes I see that she is crying helplessly. She does not turn away from me.

'Doc,' she cries. 'Make it stop!'

'I cannot,' I gasp. 'I must not.'

And slowly, by the grace of the aeroforms, the web of fire in which the streamers have captured me begins to cool a little. The streamers' tiny teeth are still gripping and tearing my flesh, but a natural anaesthetic secreted by cells under their dermal layer is combining with my body's endorphins to give me some relief. After a few minutes – too few, by the aeroforms' cruel mercy – the pain has become manageable and I can speak normally again.

'This is what you did back on the Ring, isn't it?' says Martha. 'When you had all that blood on your shirt.'

'Yes.'

'But why?'

'For the mortification of the flesh. For the assuaging of guilt. As an act of penance.'

'Penance? Penance for what?'

'I once did a terrible thing.' And I tell Martha about the time I was cast away on a hidden land after the wreck of the runaway Board ship *El Dorado*. Of how I watched my stocks of food grow lower and lower and came to dread the starvation that I knew must come when they finally ran out. Of how I made a spear and set out to slaughter aeroforms for food, not knowing then that they were sentient creatures (but that was no excuse. I should have seen it). Of how my attempt to kill an aeroform went horribly wrong, of the comrade that tried to save it, and how terrible was the death that took them both; the fire, the torment and the needless suffering. And the screams. Especially, the screams.

'It was like humanity and the foys all over again, only this time it wasn't history. It was happening right in front of me. It was personal. It was I who had murdered two gentle, helpless, trusting, beautiful creatures, not someone in a book or a show on a screen.

'And I was I who had to try to make things right.'

'By letting them torture you? Do they like to hurt you?'

'No, I don't think they do. But I must show my contrition to them. Just saying I'm sorry isn't good enough. I'm a doctor. I'm supposed to preserve life, not destroy it.'

'So the aeroforms are intelligent. We should have known.'

'It's a group intelligence. They're not individuals like you or me or the foys. But Martha, do you see now why I have to go?'

'Not really. But I don't see any way I can stop you. Oh! You men! Why do we let you break our hearts?'

'We don't mean to.'

'But all the same, you do.'

'I'm sorry. If there was any other way…'

'There is! Come back and let me help you. I'd do anything—'

'You know why I can't do that. Now go! And lead a good life. For me. Oh, and could you do me one last favour?'

'Yes, Doc.'

For one giddy moment I waver. This woman has just said she would do anything for me. Nobody has ever said that to me before. And yes; I could ask the aeroforms to release me, and I could let

Martha take me to Hope – or we could stay on Peirie until I have healed – and we could live together. Yes, that is what we could do – what we should do. It would be a new life for us both. The temptation is so strong it takes me by the throat and shakes me. It is only by the merest sliver that I refuse to yield to it.

'If you could tie the handles of the bag around my ankle? Don't worry about the aeroforms. They will not hurt you.'

'Okay, Doc.' Martha does as I ask.

'And stand back. Goodbye, Martha.'

'Goodbye, Doc. Oh, what will you do without me?'

And with a rush of air I am borne skywards. Martha's face lifts towards me as I ascend, and I see them for the last time; the smile and the tears.

I sit on my jetty and write, and my last words have been of Martha. I cannot bring myself to write any more of her for now. The memories are too bright, too joyful, and too full of pain. I close my book, tie a length of cord around it, and put it to one side.

In the hut the pico bubbles away to itself and creates energy from sea-water, and the factor makes any small articles I may need – clothing, cutlery, plates, reels, knives, buttons, fish-hooks; you name it. I keep my phone switched on and fully charged, ready for dire emergencies. All three devices were parting gifts from the 'Down and none of them are fully trusted. Who knows when or why they might stop working? But, in the meantime, I may as well take advantage of them.

The Inner Sea is very lovely today. The rocky summit of the Peak rises clear above the haze, clouds lope across the sky, pale green waves break on the shore and run up and down the beach. The water glints and flickers in the light of the Blessèd sun. This is my home, and I am content to live in it. The ground is firm and unmoving and the arms of the bay beyond the lagoon enclose me in their sheltering embrace and keep me safe. Soon, I shall go out in my little boat – while remembering the feel of *Albatross*'s tiller as it leapt under my hand – and check my nets. If they are torn, I will ask the factor to weave me new ones. I will gather what fish they have caught and take them home and cook them for my supper. My life is safe and simple and pure in its isolation.

Some days I climb to the summit of the pass and look out over the ocean with the binoculars the factor has made for me. I know that I am very unlikely ever to see one of the floating lands. It would be too dangerous for them to approach the Ring because of the risk of running aground and breaking up. But still I look, and sometimes I stay after dark and fancy I spy navigation lights far out to sea; green, white and red. I wave, though I know I am unseen. When I return home I make a point of looking down as I cross the threshold and I never forget to check my phone for missed calls.

One day, it may be, I will feel an unfamiliar compression in the air and look up and see the birds take wing and flee the land, and the fish desert the shores and leave my nets empty. They live closer to the world than we humans. Perhaps they read the future better than us. A minute, or an hour or a day later – who can say? – the ground will lurch beneath my feet, and the Blessèd sun and the worlds and the stars will skid across the sky and the world of Glory will tremble to its core. The pinnacles of the Joyeuse on Horn, the houses of the wealthy on Edge, my little hut on the Ring; all will totter and fall in dust and ruin. The pent-up oceans will rush over the sea-bed like milk in a tilted bowl and the long-awaited Great Tide will be here at last. When that day comes – and it may not be for a thousand years, or it may arrive tomorrow – humanity will, finally, be ready for it.

The free-floating lands will ride safely upon the rising waters, and the mountain-tops of Gold and Leaven Peak will look down on them and smile.

And I – I will see the waves crest the far wall of the Ring and surge across the Inner Sea and crash against the Peak in a cloud of glittering spray and I will not fear them, for I believe my friends the aeroforms will come to save me, and I will stand naked before them and raise my arms to them, and they will encircle me in cleansing fire and lift me up to heaven.

And on that day, with my life surrendered to them in final payment of my debt, I will accept their forgiveness and be at peace.

A GLORIAN CHRONOLOGY

c. 2140 CE	Birth of Montague Parker.
c. 2180 CE	The Ochre Plague.
c. 2200 CE	The *Sweetheart* leaves the orbit of Sol.
c. 2230 CE	The *Whistledown* leaves the orbit of Sol.
c. 7000 CE	The *Sweetheart* and the *Whistledown* approach the orbit of the Blessèd sun.
c. 1200 BL	Birth of Deepdiver Thrarn of the Gulf of Basrum.
c. 800 BL	A Great Tide. Glory's orbit is realigned and her poles flipped.
221 BL	The *Sweetheart* enters the orbit of the Blessèd sun.
220 BL–150 BL	The *Sweetheart*'s bots and crew build braking lasers on the worlds of Amen and Salvation.
150 BL–20 BL	The *Whistledown* decelerates into orbit around the Blessèd sun
Year 0	The *Whistledown* enters orbit around Glory. The First Landers descend to Horn in the shuttlecraft *Ready*.
0 AL–50 AL	The Golden bootstrap life on the lands of Glory. The Hungry Years.
50 AL–215 AL	The lands are settled. Rise to prominence of Edge as a trading nation.
209 AL	The 'Down and the Council of Edge negotiate an agreement with the foys, giving humanity limited access to the oceans. The Board of Trade is established on Horn.
217 AL	The Great Betrayal. Edgeois forces fire on and kill foys, who retaliate by sinking their ships and banishing humanity from Glory's oceans. The

Board becomes the prime facilitator of inter-land trade, which is conducted by the ships of the Air Service. Nation states are abolished and henceforward Glory is administered by the Board and the 'Down.

256 AL | The tale of Jack, Imogen and Ursula.

364 AL | Events of *Johanna and the Gleaners*.

420 AL | Imogen's Garden is planted.

480 AL | Birth of Cameron Powell.

490 AL | Birth of Martha Hitchin.

492 AL | Birth of Alastair McLuskie.

530 AL | Alastair and Martha are married.

532 AL | Birth of Roy Awdry.

533 AL | Birth of Annalisa "Annie" McLuskie.

534 AL | The runaway LAV *El Dorado* is wrecked.

537 AL | Birth of Michael Emmanuel "Emmy" McLuskie.

557 AL | Death of Alastair McLuskie.

560 AL | Martha gives *Mustard* to Annie. Annie enters the Landing Day Regatta Beginners' Handicap, but is beaten by Roy Awdry.

561 AL | Annie renames *Mustard* to *Albatross*. Annie and Roy race to the Ring. Meeting with Deepdiver. Annie is given the freedom of the seas.

573 AL | Emmy begins his studies in aeronautical engineering at the School on Horn.

576 AL | Annie and Roy build the *Guiding Star*. Destruction of the *Guiding Star* by the 'Down. Death of Roy Awdry. A critically injured Annie is taken to Gold. Emmy begins his training for the Air Service.

580 AL	Emmy is dismissed from the Air Service and lives rough in Lodge-in-the-Falls.
581 AL	Annie and Emmy meet for the last time on Leaven. Annie's farewell to the land.
591 AL	Foundation of the Seaborne Land of Hope.
593 AL	Emmy attempts to destroy the 'Down. The Return begins.
597 AL	Montague Parker is restored by the Golden.
599 AL	The *Sweetheart* leaves the orbit of Sally carrying Montague Parker.
602 AL	The *Whistledown* leaves the orbit of Glory carrying Emmy McLuskie.
608 AL	Cameron Powell meets Martha McLuskie on the Ring of Leaven. Birth of Alastair Michael Cameron McLuskie.
649 AL	Cameron Powell returns to Hope. Death of Martha McLuskie.
651 AL	Death of Cameron Powell.
709 AL	A Great Tide. The Seaborne Land of Trust founders and is lost.
718 AL	Death of Annie McLuskie, First Citizen of Glory.

N.B: Dates prior to the Landing are reckoned in Earth years. Post-Landing dates are Glorian.

About the Author

Peter Kendell lives in a small town in the south-east of England. He co-edited and contributed to two anthologies – THE LAST POST and THE FAMILY WAY – and is the author of THE BOY AND OTHER STORIES and THE BOOKS OF GLORY, all published by Chalk Path Books.

About the Artist

Jenna Vincent is a printmaker, fine artist and illustrator living in Sydney, Australia. She studied Printmedia and Drawing at the Australian National University and finds the fantasy in the ordinary. She has produced illustrations for commercial organisations, small press publications and local arts initiatives and her work has been shown in galleries across Australia. In her spare time she paints birds.